On Ice

STELLA STEVENSON

THE ARCTIC
BOOK ONE

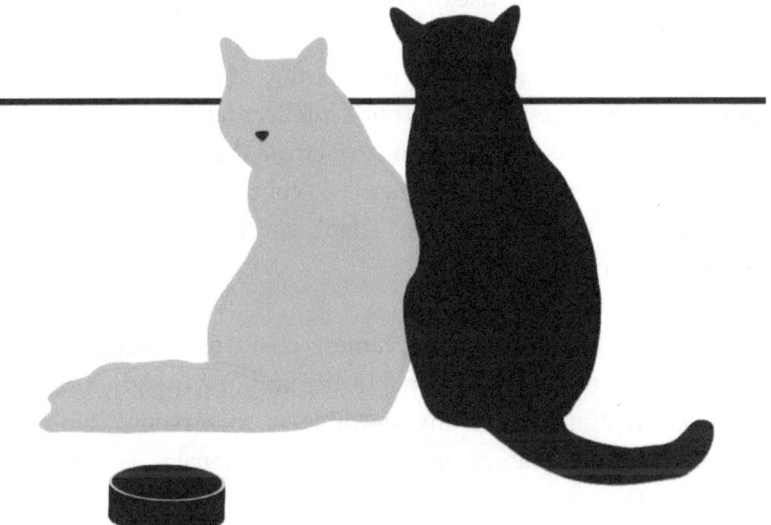

COPYRIGHT © 2023 by Stella Stevenson

All rights reserved.
Cover art by Stella Stevenson

E-book ISBN: 979-8-9868421-6-5
Print ISBN: 979-8-9868421-7-2

No part of this book may be reproduced in any form or by any electronic or mechanical means, including information storage and retrieval systems, without written permission from the author, except for the use of brief quotations in a book review.

The scanning, uploading, and distribution of this book without permission is a theft of the author's intellectual property. If you would like permission to use material from the book (other than review purposes), please contact Stella at stellaleestevenson@gmail.com. Thank you for your support of the author's rights.

This is a work of fiction. Names, characters, places, and incidents are either the product of the author's imagination or are used fictitiously, and any resemblance to persons, living or dead, business establishments, events, or locales is entirely coincidental.

Normally I'd say that this book is for anyone struggling with grief, fear, or hopelessness in situations beyond their control. You are not alone and your big feelings are valid no matter how terrifying...

And this book is for you...

But it's also for my dad.

I'd give almost anything for one more hug.

AUTHOR'S NOTE
includes possible spoilers

When I first started writing this book in the Fall of 2022, it was a way for me to wrestle with my own father's cancer diagnosis from 2016. At the time that I drafted this story, my father had undergone multiple surgeries, several rounds of chemo, and was living cancer-free. I spent years trying to ignore the fear and the pain from that period of my life. This was my way of exploring and releasing my own deep-held fears while also exploring the way that cancer and illness deeply impacts family and relationships.

In March of 2023 my father passed away unexpectedly. It was a freak accident and our family was left reeling. Unsure about what came next. Revisiting this book, preparing it for publication was suddenly a different experience. It was painful and horrible and torturous going back through some of the memories that fueled Quinn's journey with her father, but at the same time it was important.

For anyone dealing with the diagnosis of a loved-one, I hope this book helps you feel a little less alone. While there are two characters who have experience with cancer, one on-page and the other in the past, the ending is happy for all involved. This book is about love, grief, hope, trust, and fear.

Possible triggers include **cancer (no death)**, **childhood cancer (past, no death)**, **amputation (past)**, **depression**, **grief**, & **anxiety**. There is on-page discussion of medical procedures and treatments. This book also has **profanity** and **sexually explicit scenes.** It is meant for readers 18+

If any of these topics are triggering for you, please pick a different title. Your mental health and well-being are more important than a book. If you have additional questions about any of the triggers, or just need someone to talk to, feel free to email me at stellaleestevenson@gmail.com or contact me via Instagram @stellastevensonwrites.

Please see my website **www.authorstellastevenson.com** for a full list of content warnings.

"It's all wrong. By rights we shouldn't even be here. But we are. It's like in the great stories.... The ones that really mattered. Full of darkness, and danger, they were. And sometimes you didn't want to know the end, because how could the end be happy? How could the world go back to the way it was when so much bad had happened? But in the end, it's only a passing thing, this shadow. Even darkness must pass. A new day will come. And when the sun shines, it'll shine out the clearer."

Samwise Gamgee

1
QUINN

Sometimes, doing the right thing sucks.

I turn the volume up on my ear buds, but I still can't drown out the cacophony of noise that pulses inside the walls of The Stand. The crowd is about a hundred people thick and every one of them is wearing a baby blue jersey with the familiar wolf's head logo. I'm going to leave here tonight with a raging headache—that's a given—and if I can avoid being puked on by a drunk fan—that's a thing that happens at games, right?—then that will be a bonus.

I don't want to be here. It's noisy, it's crowded, the rink smells a little mildewy and wet. Even the air feels damp against my skin. And people—like my dad—shell out beaucoup dollars to be here.

The crowd presses toward the metal detectors and I pull my ticket up on my phone. I tilt the screen toward the security guard and hear the faint *beep* as the barcode registers. He makes a weird gesture, twisting his hands in a circular motion, and I look down at my light blue jersey.

Correction, my dad's. Is it the most fashionable outfit I've ever put on? No. It isn't particularly flattering either. The gray sweatshirt underneath helps pad my already wide belly and hips, but that's okay. I'm not here to impress anyone. I'm just here for… how long is a hockey game? Three twenty-minute periods plus two fifteen-minute intermissions? I should be here for about an hour and a half. That's not too long in the grand scheme of things, but long enough to want the sweatshirt. I've seen some men in shorts, but I know how cold ice needs to be.

The man circles his fingers again, like he's tracing the outline of the wolf. I have no idea what he wants from me, so I shrug as I pump one of my hands into the air. "Go Arctic."

"I need to see your bag, Ma'am."

Right. That makes a lot more sense. I should have realized that's what he was after, except the level of noise in this place is making my teeth ache and my brain skitter away from logical thought.

I shrug the tiny backpack off my shoulders to unzip it, and the security guard uses the end of a pen to flip through the contents. There isn't much. My wallet, a pack of hand wipes, a knit hat, and a pair of black gloves. The man pokes at the small rectangular device at the bottom of my bag.

"What's this?"

"My e-reader?"

He pauses, staring down into the bag, and then frowns back up at me.

"You're going to read during the game?" He sounds shocked, but I'm not sure why he should care. I paid for my ticket—okay, it's my dad's ticket—fair and square. It shouldn't matter what I intend to do during the game. I could burp the national anthem or do some basket weaving. As long as my clothes stay on and my language stays appropriate, who cares? And let's be real, I've also seen shirtless guys painted in their team colors and they almost always end up televised. Not thrown out.

I zip up my pack, looping it back over my shoulders.

"Only if it gets boring," I say, and the security worker blinks at me as if I'm speaking in a foreign language. "Like if no one scores and there's a shut-out thing." I clarify.

Immediate groans from the people all around us.

"You fucking jinxed it!" The words come from a man a few feet behind me. He has his arm around a tiny blonde who rolls her eyes. And right. "Shutout" at a hockey game is like "Macbeth" in the theatre. Bad luck.

"Why even come here if you don't understand the game?" Blondie presses a manicured hand to her partner's chest.

Because I can. I want to say, but there's no point in antagonizing the locals, so I just shrug and turn away from her.

"You can go." The ticket worker gestures through the metal detector and even he looks pissy. I guess it makes sense that people working at a hockey arena during a professional hockey game are hockey fans. Whoops.

The thing is, I don't hate hockey. I don't. There might be a little resentment over the fact that my dad has never missed a game in over thirty years. With over eighty games crammed between the months of October and April, that's a lot of evenings that I spent being watched by Jess, the high schooler who lived down the block. That eighty does not include preseason games, or the all-stars break, or playoffs. Or the Olympics when Dad filmed and watched every match. I just don't see the point of men strapping knives to their feet and ramming into each other over and over. It's pretty violent, not to mention chilly, and there are too many rules to pretend to understand.

To be fair, I'm not a fan of most organized sports. Never have been. I played volleyball in high school, but even then my only real asset to the team had been my height. Even at sixteen, I was already six feet tall. I never had the innate athleticism or passion that my teammates had. I needed gym credit, and the volleyball team was always looking for new players, so I was in no danger of getting cut.

But Dad... Dad is a huge hockey fan. An Arctic fan. He's a season ticket holder. One who's never missed a home game. Ever. Not in the thirty-five years he's followed the team. Honestly, it's a good thing I wasn't born during hockey season, or he might have missed my birth. Considering he's the one who picked my name, I wonder if I still would have been Quinn Cooper. Maybe my mother would have picked something different. Maybe I'd have *been* someone different. I don't know my mom well enough to know what she would have chosen. Probably whatever was most popular twenty-seven years ago.

I used to join my dad for some of the televised away games, but I never paid attention. A few of the players were fun to look at, but usually I sat on the end of the couch and read. At least it was a way to share the time together. Pride kept me from asking for explanations of the plays, and Dad was too engrossed in the action to notice that I wasn't. I'd never considered inviting myself to an actual game.

But here I am.

This is the first game my dad has ever had to skip.

When he asked me to go for him, I couldn't say "no." That would be shitty daughter behavior. My dad, despite his obsession with this sport, is the best anyone could ever ask for. He held down the single parent fort my whole life. He never forgot birthdays, he encouraged my passion for art, he paid for college. So no, I hadn't been about to turn down his request; but I still packed my e-book just the same.

I let the crowd pull me down the aisles lined with concession stands. It's hard to make sense of the seating. The Stand labels each section with blue and white signs, but the numbers don't always go in order and I don't know if I'm headed in the right direction. It's a good thing the place is an oval. It might take a few laps, but I'll figure it out. Maybe I should grab a snack? Will the crowd die down once the game starts? Is there anything for sale here that won't bankrupt me? That pretzel was almost ten dollars. Is that normal? Imagine if I wanted alcohol?

100, 101, 102, 103, 104.

There.

I exit the mass of moving people and head down the right hallway. It's like walking through a train tunnel, the sound muted, before I'm blinking out into the bright lights of the arena. The ice comes into view and I shiver. It gleams with a slick, wet sheen, stark blue and red lines cutting it into neat sections. The team logo sits right in the center, a white wolf with its head tipped back as it howls at a non-existent moon. For a moment, it feels like I'm at the edge of a cliff. Something monumental. I don't have to be a hockey fan to feel the excitement pulsing all around me.

There's still time before the game starts, but most of the seats are already full. The air is crisp, but not frigid. It smells of metal and popcorn, with a sour undertone of beer and sweat. And okay, it's already better than I expected. Better than the mad crush of people lining up to get inside. It's not great. I'd still rather be home, but it's only one evening. I can handle anything for a few hours.

I pick my way down the rows, keeping a close eye on each end seat. There are no letters, just numbers, and I can't figure out if the seats are counting up or down. I feel the stares of the other people following me. I'm used to staring. I'm used to commentary. That's one perk of being tall my whole life. I was the tallest in my class by first grade, and I'd held onto that title until two boys surpassed me in my senior year of high school.

Six feet is tall for everyone, but it isn't just my height that draws attention. I'm big everywhere. Not willowy, not waiflike. Solid. Ursula from the little mermaid. I have rounded hips and a soft belly that folds when I sit. My thighs have dimples. My copper orange hair draws attention too. It's supposed to be curly, but it can't decide what to do most days and frizzes around my shoulders and down my back. Who has the time to constantly blow dry and straighten? Okay, many people, but not me.

I'm not expecting the buzzer from the Jumbotron, although I should be. It's not like I didn't see the numbers count down. I feel my foot slip on the edge of the step and I grip the center railing for support as I sit down hard on the cold concrete. Better than falling face-first down the steps, but still embarrassing. I glance around to see if anyone is staring, but everyone nearby has their heads buried in their phones. Small miracle. I use the railing to lever myself upright and dust off the back of my leggings. Nothing wounded but my pride, and even that is relatively unscathed, since no one appeared to have noticed.

"Good thing you weren't holding a beer, eh?"

The voice startles me all over again, but this time I stay on my feet.

I look up into a pair of hazel eyes, mostly brown with green streaks fanning out from the center of the dark pupils. Pupils that shift and expand as I stare up at him. The lashes are a dusty blonde color, but so long that it's genetically unfair. He is looking right at me, not up, not even from a step down, which means he's tall—well over six feet—besides having gorgeous eyes. His hair is shorter on the sides, almost spiky, with a longer swoop of sand blond falling over his forehead. A stylish cut that he probably perfected before coming here. His face is clean shaven, jaw and cheekbones sharp enough to slice bread. Something hot and liquid unfurls in my belly, and it's enough to make me snap out of it.

I turn away, staring past his shoulder at the slick of ice. "Uh yeah." I'm ever the picture of eloquence. "Good thing I don't drink beer."

The man's lips pull up as if he wants to smile.

"What is your drink of choice?"

"Rum and coke," I try not to let the statement sound like a question, but he's attractive enough to fluster me. Hot enough that I'm struggling for words. I thought that kind of thing only happened in books.

"Good choice." He nods, stepping around me to continue his walk up the stairs. "Careful the rest of the way."

He gifts me the last words when we're shoulder to shoulder. When he's close enough that I can feel his body heat even through his clothes. Anyone else might consider this moment a meet-cute. Locking eyes with a handsome stranger, exchanging some banter, feeling the tingles start low. They're all classic signs, but there aren't any romantic possibilities here and I won't see him again. Not with nineteen-thousand other people here to watch the game.

I refuse to turn and watch him go, instead focusing on the confounding seat numbers. I'm headed in the right direction, but I'm also nearing the glass partitions that block the ice from the crowd. That can't be right, can it? Hockey-illiterate or not, even I know that this is exceptional seat territory. If only that couple at security could see me now, they'd for sure be pooping themselves. Even if it were true that I am less-deserving of an amazing view of the game than, say, a genuine fan, my dad is one hundred percent deserving. He should have the best spot in the house.

He might have one.

The seat is in the second row, one spot in from the very end. There's barely enough room for me to crabwalk past the first seat. My thighs touch both the back of the chair in front of me, and the folded plastic seat next to me. I stare down at my spot, and just know that I'm going to feel those armrests cutting into my body. My knees are going to touch the seat in front of me, too. So not comfortable at all. I've been on commercial airlines with better economy seating and in smart cars that have felt roomier. *I'm doing this for Dad,* I remind myself. He'd much rather be here, and he isn't a tiny guy either. If he can stick out games multiple times a month, then I can suck it up and survive one.

I'm right. My knees do press against the seat in front of me, and I have to bend my legs at an unnatural angle to avoid kicking the person in front of me, too. My shoulders are wider than the seat back and I'm increasingly aware that I'm taking up more than my allotted space, but honestly, who were these seats even made for? Children? Maybe no one will sit next to me. Unlikely, but not impossible. How many single seats sell? Aren't people more likely to watch the game in pairs? Maybe whoever bought the end seat would swap? It would at least provide extra leg room.

The music changes and men in bulky padding and arctic blue jerseys trickle out onto the ice. Someone throws handfuls of pucks out in front and the players skate looping circles as they send the black discs barreling towards the net. At the far end of the arena, white jerseys edged in red and black are doing the same thing. It's kind of cool to watch, like holding a kaleidoscope up to the sun and spinning the wheel to watch the patterns shift. I like this better than the bare-knuckle brawling. It's also nice to see where the puck is as the players move. Everything goes too fast for me to follow during actual gameplay, and then I feel like an idiot.

My phone vibrates in the pocket of my leggings and I dig it out, swiping to answer the call.

"Hi Dad. You didn't tell me you have the best seat in the house." His seat looks right out on the Arctic bench.

"You made it!" He sounds tired even through the phone.

"Of course I did. The little hockey men just started skating and I swear I'll watch some of the game before I pull out my book."

Dad laughs, and it's a boom of sound I'd recognize anywhere. I can almost see him with his head thrown back, mouth wide, nose scrunched as he belts his amusement into the air.

"You're a good girl, Quinnie Bee," he says, and I feel guilt sucker punch me in the chest. I'm not good. I can at least pretend to be enjoying this a bit more. An amazing seat at a professional hockey game? There are people who'd pay through the nose for this opportunity.

"I love you, Dad," I say instead, heat prickling the backs of my eyes.

"I love you too. Go. Have fun. I'll see you tomorrow."

The call cuts off and I snap a few photos of the players on the ice. If nothing else, at least they're fun to look at. Okay, some of them look like infants, but a few of the older ones are handsome in an oozing-testosterone-and-sex-appeal kind of way. I read somewhere that the average height of NHL players is six foot one, but at least one player—for Boston, maybe—is six foot nine. I've seen enough advertisements with chiseled abs to know that hockey players are in incredible shape, but with all the padding it's easy to forget. I've gone feral over my fair share of fictional hockey players, but I'd never understood the appeal of the real thing. Maybe tonight will change that. Not that I have time for any of those pesky things like feelings or relationships. Not right now.

My dad's favorite player stops by the bench and smiles at one of his teammates. I try not to feel like a stalker as I zoom in and snap his picture. He's probably used to having fans take his photo, but I still cringe as I send it to my dad. The response I get back is full of unintelligible emojis. Dad's not the best texter.

The buzzer goes off again and the players file off the ice. A glance at my watch tells me we're about fifteen minutes from the start of the game. A family slides into the row on my left, an elementary-aged kid taking the seat next to me. I give him a friendly smile and nod at the harried looking parents who are shepherding two younger kids into the row as well.

"I like your jersey," the kid says, and I laugh.

"I like yours too," he is also wearing a baby blue Arctic jersey, but his swallows him whole.

"Varg's my favorite player," the kid is bouncing in his seat; "but Dad says I can't get his jersey until I outgrow this one."

Considering jerseys are sixty plus dollars—I know because I bought this one for my dad for Father's Day—I can understand his dad's point of view. I don't say that, though.

"He also says we got to make sure Varg doesn't get traded first." The kid grins at me. He's got his two front teeth, but he's missing a few others and it makes me think of the players. I know some of them are missing teeth, too. "I think he's gonna stay forever."

"Well, whose jersey do you have on now?" I ask. Hockey jerseys only have names on the back. There's a little number on the front chest, but I don't know the roster well enough to recognize them.

"This one is Oakes." The kid shows me the back of his jersey where the number sixteen is stitched on in perfect lines. When he turns to face me, his face twists into a glower.

A cup appears under my nose. It's held in a sinewy, masculine hand. A golden-tanned hand that is attached to a red and black jersey from the opposing team. No wonder the kid's glaring. The drink-giver is clearly enemy number one.

"A virgin rum and coke," the deep male voice says, and I recognize the cadence even if I shouldn't. I snap my eyes up to see the man from the stairs. The one who'd seen me trip. The same man who is lowering himself into the seat next to me.

"It's just a coke." He smiles a crooked grin. He has perfect teeth to match his perfect hair and face. Perfection shouldn't do anything for me, but there's that heat again. "I'm not sure The Stand sells liquor."

How big of a fan do you need to be to wear your team's jersey to an away game? How big of a fan do you need to be to travel to an away game alone? A pretty big one, right? So great. Not only am I going to spend most of the game crammed into a seat that is two sizes too small, I get to do so while sitting between two people who love hockey.

The kid leans right over my body, his lean frame pressing into my stomach, and I suck in air to avoid any more contact.

"You suck, sir." He points an accusatory finger at the drink-bringer.

So yeah. On my right is a pint-sized super fan. On my left is one of the most beautiful men I've ever seen.

Fuck.

2 ERIK

I don't know why I felt the need to buy the redhead a soda, except that she looks as miserable as I feel and that is something I can appreciate. I settle into a seat better suited for an eighth grader and try to send her my least creepy grin. She still hasn't taken the cup, more concerned with shushing the kid sitting next to her. I don't think the tiny human belongs to her, considering he's the spitting image of a woman sitting on his other side, but Red seems invested enough in his manners. It's cute. She's cute. Not why I bought her a drink, but still cute.

She looks up into my eyes and, just like on the steps, my stomach heats and my breath gets shorter. She has the kind of eyes only seen on cartoon princesses. A little too big for her face, round with a color that looks like it's been painted on. Lighter green around the pupils with a darker green band around the irises. Her lashes are red, orange-red like her hair, and they curl. I noticed those eyes right away. Most people probably do. Those eyes and that hair and that height. No wonder she almost took me off my feet, too.

"Look." Her smile is all sugar sweetness, but her eyes stay wary. "It's not that I don't appreciate the gesture, and I hate to accuse you of anything, but I know better than to take a drink from a total stranger."

I can't fault her there. I am a complete stranger offering her a drink that I could have done anything to. I didn't, but she doesn't know that. She's right to be cautious. I lift the cup to my mouth and take a long sip from the straw, letting the icy sweetness burst over my tongue. Then I fish an extra straw out of my pocket and hold the drink out again. Just in case.

"If you still don't want it, it won't offend me," I say, but she takes the cup from my hand, making sure our fingers don't touch. Then she turns to the kid next to her.

"Do you know how to call 911?" She asks, and he rolls his eyes.

"Duh, it's 9-1-1."

"Great. If I fall asleep or out of my chair, then take my phone out of my pocket and do that." She grins at me, "no offense."

I'm not offended at all. I have a sister. Anna is older than me by about five years, and already married to a great woman, but I'd have lost my mind if she'd taken a drink from a stranger without mitigating some risks, too.

The kid rolls his eyes again. "I have a phone, you know."

"Of course you do," the redhead shakes her head at me as if we're sharing some private joke.

The announcers call out the starting lineup, and I force myself to watch as the home team players take the ice. They file to the bench as the announcer asks everyone to stand for the national anthem. I get to my feet. The cold always makes my thigh muscles ache and I rub my fingers into my left quad as everyone around me crosses their hands over their chests.

Vic is out at center ice, but I catch his eye. My brother grins at me and then rolls his eyes, probably at my choice of jersey. So sue me. I'm here. That's rare enough as it is. I don't need to wear his name plastered across my back. That brings back too many memories I'd rather avoid.

The music finishes and the organ launches into the *O Canada*. Roughly forty-two percent of all NHL players are Canadian and I've known the words to both anthems since I was a kid, but not every team plays both. The redhead sings along. Her voice is husky and deep, with a soothing lilt. I want to turn toward her, cup a hand around my ear so I can hear her better.

"I'm impressed you know the Canadian anthem," I say as the last notes bleed away.

"That's what happens when you've been watching Arctic games since birth."

The teams separate and take their positions for the first puck drop.

So she's a super fan. That's not a surprise. Not only is she wearing a jersey, like most of the arena, but she's here alone. Not with a date, not with a friend, not with a family member. She clearly came to watch the action, and that's fine. Even if I'd been hoping we could chat more over the next few hours, it's not like I don't know the game. I can hold my own and I can always strike up conversation during intermission. If she's interested.

I didn't want to come to the game tonight, but I should have known better than to fly into town and think I could avoid this. My mother had been appalled to hear that I had planned to stay on the couch of my hotel room and not even put the game on in the background of whatever else I planned to do. I'd planned on working, I always plan on working, but even I'm not immune to my mother.

I wonder if she knows I don't watch any games. Not Vic's, not my hometown, not the All-Star Break or the Olympics. The last game I watched was Vic's professional debut, but even that was from the comfort of my home. The last time I set foot into an arena was… damn. Almost half my life ago.

None of that matters in the face of maternal guilt. My mother had a single ticket waiting in my email in a matter of hours. This is what I get after avoiding my family for so long. All those carefully maintained boundaries crumble. I do better at a distance. I do better via text or email. But it's easier to make excuses from a thousand miles away.

The Arctic takes possession from the face-off, and I settle back into the too-small seat to watch the action. The worst part about hockey is how much fun it is to watch. The snick of blades cutting through fresh ice, the slap of sticks hitting the puck with each pass and shot, the boom as the boards rattle under the force of a hit, and the siren when the rubber finds the back of the net. Music. It's a tune I'll never forget. One that plays on repeat in my brain whenever it finds an opening. And as thrilling as that song is to hear, as fun as hockey is to watch, it's more fun to play. Too bad I didn't get a choice there.

I shouldn't have come tonight.

In front of me, Vic stands and hops over the boards, skating onto the ice with the speed and power he's known for. My brother plays right wing, and a long time ago I played opposite him, left wing on the same line. We'd dreamed of playing in the NHL together, with our best friend Robbie Oakes—Bo, as the hockey world now knows him—playing center. We'd been invited to the USHL draft the May after we turned sixteen and no amount of caution from the adults in our lives could convince us that this wasn't it. The break. We'd play two years in the top Juniors League in the states, then put our names in the NHL draft.

And then... well, it *had* been the big break for Vic and Robbie. The two of them taking on the world.

I hadn't made it to training camp.

The lines change again, still no score, and I chance another look at the woman next to me. I expect to find her glued to the game, bright green eyes following the line of the puck as it moves back and forth from stick to stick. I have no intention of trying to impress her with my hockey knowledge—a douche move—and I definitely want to steer clear of mentioning my brother—an even douchier move. Is douchier even a word?—but I want to talk to her, and I can't explain why.

I couldn't have been more surprised, not even if the redhead morphed into my mother and told me this was all a dream, to look over and find her nose buried in her book.

Fascinating.

She's pulled a knit Arctic hat down over the top of her copper hair, and the bottom of her curls twist away from her body as though trying to escape. I wonder if they'll be hot to the touch, like an open flame, even though that makes absolutely zero sense. Hair doesn't take on body heat. It stays at room temperature. Ice rinks aren't nearly as cold as people think. It's colder closer to the ice, colder with fewer fans in the stands, colder if it's cold outside, but Red is bundled from head to toe with a bulky sweatshirt, the heavy jersey, and a hat. Maybe she's always cold. Or maybe some part of me is still used to this even years later. I'm in a Chicago jersey and jeans and still feel perfectly comfortable. My gaze slides over the smooth curve of Red's cheek. Actually, I might be a little overheated.

"What are you reading?" I can't help the question. Not even when she jolts like I poked her with a cattle-prod. She meets my eyes over the top of the device and a blush stains her neck and cheeks and even her forehead until she is as red as my jersey. I can feel myself smiling. The wide, uncontrollable smile that shows all my teeth and makes my cheeks ache. She really is absolutely fascinating.

"Nothing." Her voice slips over me, just like I remembered. She snaps the cover of her reader shut with an audible click and looks out over the rink, busying herself with a study of the back of the Arctic's heads.

I hold both my hands up in self-defense. "No judgment. I'm all for reading."

Her blush doesn't dim, not even a little, but she flits her eyes back toward me. She opens her mouth to respond, and I can't wait to hear what she's going to say when a small voice from her left breaks into the conversation.

"I hate reading." The kid makes an exaggerated face of disgust. "It's boring."

"It's important," Red says without missing a beat, like maybe it was me who took the words away from her. Me, she couldn't respond to. Her complexion returns to its normal color. Maybe it was me who made her blush. I shouldn't like that thought as much as I do. Not about a stranger.

The kid's eye roll is so dramatic that even I can't miss it, and I'm surprised that his face doesn't get stuck that way. Then he winces, since clearly he's heard Red's point before now.

"No," the kid shakes his head. "I'm eight. I think I'd know by now if reading was important."

"Well…" Red shoots a help-me glance in my direction and I shrug but temper it with a raise of my brows. Red looks highly unamused, but soldiers on. "If you couldn't read, you wouldn't be able to read your favorite books,"

I try to hold back my laugh because even I know that was a lame response. An elbow presses against my ribs as the kid sighs.

"I don't like books," the kid's tone is that of a beleaguered parent trying to explain the obvious to an uncaring toddler, "because reading is boring."

"If you can't read, you'd have a hard time following the hockey game." Red beams at the kid like she'd put him in checkmate. I have doubts, but it's a valiant effort.

"Got to read those names somehow," I try to help, "and the trivia on the Jumbotron."

"I can look at the numbers and my mom reads me the Jumbotron."

Well shit, we're being out-logicked by a second grader, but at least we're going down together.

"Reading numbers is a kind of reading," Red tries again and the kid rolls his eyes…again.

"No, it isn't. When I read, the letters get all jumbled up, but that doesn't happen with numbers."

"Graham," the woman sitting on the other side of the kid—clearly his mother with the same dark skin and honey-colored eyes—says. "I'm so sorry he's bothering you. Graham, you can't just talk to strangers."

Next to her, one of the smaller kids upends a box of popcorn and starts crying.

"I'm not bothering them." Graham rolls his eyes again. So at least that's something he dishes out to everyone. "They're my friends."

"Do you even know their names?" His mother asks and if this leads to me learning Red's real name, then I will offer babysitting services free-of-charge. Or I will hire someone to babysit for her. I've been waiting for an opening to ask.

"I'm Quinn." She holds her hand out to Graham's frazzled mom. "It's nice to meet you, and I definitely consider Graham a friend."

Quinn. I test her name in my head, and I like it. Quinn. A good Gaelic name. It suits her with her copper hair and Kelly-green eyes.

"Erik," I say, and Graham's mom glances past Quinn to look at me. I mostly offer to be polite, but I really want Quinn to know it. Erik and Quinn. Quinn and Erik. When Quinn looks at me with a small smile, I can't help but feel warm inside.

"See?" Graham says to his mother. "Quinn and Rick say we're friends."

"Erik," the two women correct, and I try not to laugh as the kid rolls his eyes yet again.

"Look, if he bothers you, just let me know," Graham's mom says as a juice box hits the floor, too. "I'm sorry."

"So we're friends now?" I'm just happy to be in this conversation with her, even if it involves an elementary schooler.

"No, I'm friends with Quinn, not a traitor."

I look down at my jersey. Fair enough, I'd have felt the same way at seven or eight. Anyone cheering for another team was public enemy *numero uno*.

"Maybe Erik's not friends with people who can't say his name right, or who call him traitor." Quinn says and Graham shrugs.

"I'm not his friend then. I'm your friend."

Again, fair enough. The kid's fine, but I also want to be friends with Quinn. Just for the game. Just to pass the next, I glance at my watch, two-ish hours. Then I'll finish my business in town, fly home, and now and then, when I'm feeling mopey about my lack of an NHL contract, I'll remember that I had fun at *this* game. This once.

"Maybe I'm only friends with kids who like to read," Quinn says, and I can tell she's proud of circling back around to this.

Graham sighs long and loud, as if every single injustice in the world is being committed against him right at this very moment.

"Fine," Graham concedes. "But I'm not thrilled about this." He turns his attention back to the ice before I can ask him to clarify if he's agreeing to be our friend, or cutting us off. Us. I shouldn't be thinking of me and Quinn as an "us." Although maybe I'm so drawn to her because I'm desperate to avoid thinking about why I'm here at The Stand.

The game cuts to commercial and players migrate toward their benches. The ice scrapers skate out with their shovels as the music changes. There's the Arctic's mascot, a big white wolf named Howl. He's up on the Jumbotron, dancing with a bunch of kids. Next to Quinn, Graham jumps to his feet and starts imitating the mascot's moves. It's like watching an overcooked noodle do the limbo, but the kid's having a blast and Quinn is clapping her hands, cheering him on. One of Graham's siblings hops up to dance too, and at their prompting Quinn shakes her shoulders to the beat.

"You're really good with them," I say, dipping my head a little to talk directly into her ear. Her hair tickles my nose and lips and she smells amazing. A bit like the rose soap my mom always stocks in her guest bathroom, but with something spicy underneath. I don't have to duck much, which is a rare relief.

"I should be," she turns until our gazes collide.

"Kids of your own? Siblings? Cousins?" Not that it matters. We're just chatting. I'm being friendly because she's fun to talk to, and she smells nice and it doesn't hurt my neck to meet her eyes. Her stunning gemstone eyes.

She laughs, full on guffaws—head thrown back with teeth and gums on display, a real smile—as she shakes her head.

"No. No, no, no. No kids of my own. No siblings or young cousins."

I try to hide my confusion. There are tons of reasons someone doesn't want children. I don't want kids. Not with my genetics to fuck things up, no matter what the doctors have promised. She doesn't owe me any kind of explanation. I'm just curious. Inappropriately so.

"I'm sorry," she wheezes out the words between extra bites of laughter. "I forgot we don't know each other that well. I'm a teacher, elementary art, and as much as I love my job and love my kids at school, I never see myself having my own. I'm too tired by three o'clock."

"That's fair," I say. "For the record, it's the laughter that threw me, not the answer. I don't want kids either."

I'm not sure why I share that last part, other than to make her feel better about the piece of herself I'd practically forced her to share. Quinn smiles at me again. I hadn't noticed before, but her bottom teeth overlap just the tiniest bit in the front. It's just another little thing I like. Something that makes her different, unique. Another little detail that pulls all my focus until I can't see beyond red hair, and green eyes, and white overlapping teeth.

It's no excuse for what happens next. I should have shaken off my Quinn-induced stupor and noticed. It may have been years since my last NHL game, but I still know what it means when Cher pumps through the loudspeakers. I know the "Shoop-Shoop-Shoop" and what comes next. And yet it isn't until I glance at the bench and met my brother's eyes, until Vic points up to the big boxy Jumbotron, that I realize that not only has The Stand brought out their Kiss Cam, but that someone with a sick sense of humor has turned in on a couple wearing jerseys from the opposing teams.

Me and Quinn.

3 QUINN

At first, I'm not sure what causes Erik to freeze up on me. We've been chatting. I'm going for broke with my flirty smile because he's hot and I deserve to have a bit of fun—especially when he seems interested too—and then he looks out over the ice and his muscles lock down one at a time.

"No pressure." His lips barely move as he forms the words.

Erik tips his golden head towards the center of the rink, and his pink tongue brushes along the edges of his mouth. I copy him, wetting my lips before I realize what I'm doing, and his eyes drop to follow the movement. And yes, Viking gods like Thor can afford to be picky about who they kiss, and strange girls wearing their dad's jersey to a hockey game they don't want to watch rarely fit the bill, but I know that he's at least thinking about slicking our mouths together. I am too.

"Pressure?" I ask, but instead of an answer, Graham makes an exaggerated gagging sound.

I flinch and spin, hands out to—I don't know—catch whatever is coming, but Graham points at the Jumbotron and makes the sound again. I can't even be mad about the scare. I'm just grateful he didn't lose his cookies all over me. That would cut the flirting and the fun time off at the knees.

"Ew," he says to me, "You aren't going to kiss him, are you?"

I *had* been thinking about it. I'm pretty sure Erik had been thinking about it too, but I follow Graham's finger and now I know what had Erik so weird. Centered on the giant screen are me and Erik. We're surrounded by a big red heart frame and the words KISS, KISS, KISS blink along the top. The camera slides away to another couple, bored waiting on us, and the crowd roars its displeasure at the missed opportunity. An adorable older couple shares a quick peck and then the camera pans back to us. I watch camera-me wave, looking confused and stunned. Next to me, camera-Erik looks pissed.

It's strange staring at myself and not seeing me stare back.

I don't know where the camera is and I don't want to look for it. I'm more interested in looking at the man sitting next to me. He seems smaller on the screen. Or maybe I do. Not as imposing as he is in person, although that glare isn't something I've seen before. This should serve as a friendly reminder that I don't know Erik as well as it feels like I do. The covert smiles, the heat in my belly, the connection and chemistry are well and good, but they can't take the place of understanding someone. Knowing them.

On screen-Erik shakes his head in a slow but firm "no" as the Arctic players bang their sticks against the boards. A chant that sounds a lot like "Do it, do it, do it" practically rattles the teeth right out of my head.

"Is it just me, or are people overly invested in whether we kiss each other on camera?" By people, I mean the hockey team. I'd have thought they'd have more important things to worry about. Like the game. The hooting and the catcalls pick up steam.

"We're cheering for different teams," Erik says, and I frown. Is that really that exciting?

I must ask out loud because Erik looks a little less murdery as he says, "It's more fun for the crowd if its two people who aren't together. Teammates, siblings, anything to get the crowd riled up."

So perceived enemies would do it.

The kiss cam ends as play resumes and everyone's attention turns back to the game. I breathe a sigh as Erik and I leave the spotlight. Two players speed down the ice, light blue and red spiraling together as they slam into the boards, battling for dominance. The crowd seems to hold its breath until the Arctic player emerges from the scuffle with the puck. He makes a break for the net and the crowd goes wild. My heart is pounding and my palms are sweaty and watching at home from the couch feels nothing like this. Not that I ever watch.

The Chicago goalie stops the puck and despite the roar of the crowd, the silence between Erik and me feels heavy. I want the smiles, the flirting, the fun back.

"The Kiss Cam is weird anyway," I say. "Why force strangers to kiss each other? By strangers, I mean people you don't know, because even if you think they're a couple, they might not be. And it's all so hetero-normative. They only show men and women, but what about queer couples or nonbinary fans? Don't they deserve the chance to participate in the tradition?"

"I thought you said it was weird?" Erik's mouth twitches and I know he's holding in a laugh.

"It is, but then everyone should have an equal opportunity at being humiliated."

"So that's what it is? Weird and humiliating?" He sits back in his seat, his bicep brushing mine. There is real muscle there. Heat and muscle and I lean away to give myself some space. It practically puts me into Graham's seat, but the kid is small and doesn't seem to notice me taking the lion's share of the armrest.

Erik is looking at me with shadows in his hooded hazel eyes and I can't figure out what he wants from me. Had he wanted a kiss? Well shit. Kissing him wouldn't be humiliating, not when he's fun and funny and he looks like that. But rejection? With an arena of fans watching? Well, if I'm wrong and he doesn't want a kiss, if he's weirded out that someone thinks we'd be an appropriate fit, then yes. Humiliating would be the understatement of the century.

"Yes," I say. "No. Depends on the person I'm supposed to kiss. I guess."

Erik nods as if my jumble of words makes perfect sense and turns back to watch the game. Two players collide along the rail and a helmet goes flying as the Chicago player slams back into the ice. The crowd's volume crescendos with approval as the Arctic player takes control of the puck and leaves the man lying there. The Chicago player rolls to his hands and knees, but he doesn't get up. He stays there, forehead pressed to the rink, rocking back and forth. The other players continue to battle out the game as if someone isn't injured.

"Oh my god." I clutch Erik's arm as more players skate right past the downed man. "He's hurt."

"Don't worry, they'll take him off and check him before allowing him back out." Erik covers my grasping fingers with his opposite hand. His thumb rubs over the back of my knuckles.

"Why haven't they stopped the play? Shouldn't you care more? That's your player there." I can hear my voice getting shrieky, but seeing a grown man fly off his feet and slam on a rink of ice is a lot more gruesome in person than on a television screen. It never occurred to me they wouldn't blow a whistle and stop the game. Aren't they going to get him out of here?

"It wasn't an illegal hit," Erik says. "The refs can't stop play until his team has the puck."

Graham can have his whole armrest at this point. I'm halfway in Erik's lap, my stomach in my throat, because the Chicago player, number 12, still hasn't gotten up.

"Fuck you, man," someone yells from a row behind us and I let go of Erik's arm as if he'd spontaneously caught fire. I also catch the gleam in Graham's eyes at the bad word and I have to fight the urge to lecture the asshole on language usage in front of other people's children. "That was such a dick move. Maroni clocked that guy. Totally illegal. The refs are fucking blind."

"Wasn't an illegal hit," Erik repeats to the angry man whose red and black face paint is bleeding down his neck into the collar of his jersey.

"He hit him in the head!"

I might know nothing about hockey, but I want to agree on that one. A hit to the head seems like something that shouldn't be allowed, even with helmets. My knowledge of football might be even less than my knowledge of hockey, but I know bad things happen to people who take too many hits to the head.

"Head wasn't the intended point of contact and they both had eyes on the puck, not Maroni's fault that Thompson had his head down."

"Fucking traitor." The guy yells back and I'm a little worried we're going to have beer thrown at us, or something worse.

"Ignore him," Erik says, which is easier said than done. He turns back to the game as the opposition finally intercepts a pass and the whistle stops play. The injured player has managed to get to his feet and a few of his teammates bolster him as he weaves toward the bench and off the ice.

"You know a lot about hockey," I say as the thumping beat of classic rock pumps through the arena. "Are you a ref?"

Erik laughs, but it sounds off. "No. I never reffed, but I played for a while. Back in high school."

"Why do I just know that is an understatement?"

He winks at me. Honest-to-God winks. But then he doesn't look away. He's holding my gaze and heat unfurls in my stomach like a shot of liquor. My limbs feel heavy. I feel the blush climb my neck and spread across my cheeks. This is unreal. It must be the thrill of being here, the energy of the crowd. Lust at first sight isn't a real thing.

"I'm a man of mystery," he says and then raises his hand to my face.

Erik's fingers curl then flex as if he wants to brush them over my skin, but he's stopping himself. Maybe there's something on my face? I scrub at my cheeks.

A catchy fifties girl group belts through the loudspeakers and I recognize the song moments before the Kiss cam fires up again. They get three quick hits in succession as the image pans over the crowd. And yes, I'll be the first to admit that it was adorable when a tiny woman with white ringlets grabbed the cheeks of the equally tiny man she was sitting next to and planted a smacking kiss on his smiling mouth. Not humiliating or weird at all.

"I have to warn you," Erik says, his voice hushed and rushed. I turn my head to look at him and we're so close our noses almost bump. "There's a high chance they're coming back for us."

Coming back for us? I suppose it makes sense that they'd try again. The crowd had seemed almost manic with glee over the prospect of me and Erik being thrown together. And while I'm deciding what I'm going to do if he's right, there we are again, framed in a pulsing red heart, my hair clashing with the animation. Erik is already looking at me, his face turned toward mine. The stadium erupts again, catcalls and jeering as people chant for us to kiss, kiss, kiss.

"They're probably going to keep coming back for us until we fall in line." Erik says and I can barely hear him over the pulse drumming in my ears.

"Fall in line," I echo, my eyes dipping to his wide mouth. His lips are pale pink and they're wet from where he swiped his tongue over them.

"Or we can just keep ignoring them. I can even resort to drastic measures and flip them the bird." He tips his head down to find my eyes.

I snort at that, and Erik smiles.

"You can't flip off the camera. There are children present." And I don't mind kissing him. I want to, actually.

"So you're saying—"

I'm about to tell him to kiss me, about to grab his ears and pull his mouth to mine. His hazel eyes are flitting all over my face. His hair is falling over his forehead, making him look young and boyish and approachable. His jaw is rock hard, flexing as he watches me. I can see the muscles contract and relax. I would give almost anything to know what thoughts are running through Erik's head right now.

"That's right, traitor. Betray your team some more and kiss the Arctic-loving bitch."

That's the same angry fan as before. I not only recognize the voice, but I find it hard to believe Erik could have made multiple enemies in one hockey period. Erik sucks in his breath, his nostrils flaring, and I know he's about to do something rash. Not entertaining, once-in-a-lifetime rash either, something heroic and probably stupid. On camera. I'm going to have significantly less fun if he gets himself ejected from this game.

The camera tires of waiting and moves on to another couple, but Erik doesn't seem to notice. His eyes have gone glacial and his brows pinch together. His shoulders are tense. Other than my dad, I've never seen another person so angry on my behalf. The players hit the ice again and Erik doesn't even notice.

"Hey," I say, leaning closer and placing my palm on his granite thigh. He flinches at the contact, and I almost lose my nerve except that I'm desperate to distract him. "Joke's on that jerk. I don't actually love the Arctic at all."

I get through to him, just like I intended.

"What?" Erik says with a laugh. He pulls back to look at me, but not enough to dislodge my hand.

I nod. "My dad's the fan. This is his season ticket seat. This is his jersey for his favorite player—Victor Varg—and his hat. I'm here because he was going to miss his first game in thirty-five years and that was unacceptable to him." Thoughts on the team aside, it was unacceptable to me, too.

"So, which team do you follow?" Erik asks and I'm about to break his darling heart.

"None of them." I shrug. "When I still lived at home, I'd read when my dad put the games on."

"That would explain everything." Erik grins and nods at my reader.

"Don't knock reading, I'm only friends with people who read. Ask Graham."

"So you'd say we're friends?" Erik asks.

"Would you not?" I don't give him a chance to answer that question. "I know we don't know much about each other, but I'd say we're friends. Don't tell me if I'm wrong, just let me die in denial."

"We can be friends. Quinn," Erik says. God, I should have just written him a note. *Do you like me? Check yes or no.* It would have been less juvenile than this conversation. "So your dad's favorite player is Varg?"

I nod. "Yup. He's followed him since *your* favorite team traded him here." I'm assuming he likes Chicago, but maybe the jersey isn't his any more than this one is mine.

Erik's watching the guys battle it out for the puck at the centerline. All I see is a dog pile with a few stragglers hanging back waiting for scraps. Number twenty-five from the Arctic, Varg, breaks from the pack and makes a beeline down the ice. People jump to their feet, cheering as the goalie skates out of the net. With his big red pads on his legs and his hands up to block the puck, he looks like a giant crab.

ON ICE

Varg slashes the puck to a teammate waiting to the goalie's left.

The minute the goalie turns to block the new threat, the puck is fired back to twenty-five and then the siren blares as he puts the little black disc over the goalie's blocker and into the back of the net. The vibe in the arena is intoxicating. The players slap each other on the back as the Jumbotron replays the goal. Music blares out of the speakers as most Arctic fans stand to cheer. Graham is screaming at the top of his lungs, arms stretching above his head.

"Arctic Goal from number twenty-five, Varg, assist from number sixteen, Oakes."

The Jumbotron zooms in on Dad's favorite as he skates towards the bench. His teammates pat him on the back as he goes by. For a moment, Victor glances up at the camera and winks. His hazel eyes stand out in stark contrast to his tanned face. His jaw and cheekbones could slice bread, and even from under his helmet and half shield—even under the patchy late-season beard—I can tell he is a dark golden blonde. I also recognize him. Not just because he's our top goal-scorer this season. Not just because he's my dad's favorite. Not just because I drive past his shirtless body on a billboard every morning on my way to school, but because he looks just like…

"Brothers." I whirl on Erik, who isn't smiling, isn't frowning, isn't celebrating his brother's goal. His *twin's* goal. God, they have the exact. Same. Face. Are people that blind? Am I? Erik is watching me as if he's waiting to see my reaction. "You have to be brothers. Twins."

"Yep," he says, his eyes never leaving mine, "Twins."

4. ERIK

The clock runs down the first period, and I still can't pull my eyes away from Quinn. My brother files back into the locker room with the rest of his team, but the Jumbotron still displays his face and stats. I don't need to wonder how Quinn figured it out. I'm more surprised that other people haven't. Vic and I share a damn face, for fuck's sake, but even Graham hasn't noticed.

Our family has always downplayed the twin angle—according to his bio, Vic has two "siblings"—and I avoid going to games, but it still surprises me when I go undetected. When you spend the better part of your life being mistaken for someone else, it feels strange when people stop connecting the two of you. It feels like I've left something behind, except I don't know what it is or where I might have left it.

I didn't lie to her. I shared my name. I can't hide my face, but now that she's put two and two together, I feel guilty.

"Quinn..." the apology is on my tongue, ready and wrapped for delivery, but she cuts me off.

"How did I not figure it out sooner?" Her brows and nose crinkle in the cutest look of confusion. "Are you here incognito?" Her voice drops to a whisper. "I won't say anything. Promise. Except to my dad. I'm sorry, but I have to tell him I sat with a Varg."

"It's not a secret," I say. I feel lighter now that she seems giddy instead of pissed. "It's just not advertised. Sorry I didn't tell you sooner."

"Sorry? God no." Quinn shakes her head until her curls bounce into her face. "You don't owe me any of that. We barely know each other."

She's right, of course. We barely know each other. We've been sitting together for a little over an hour now and beyond her name and her occupation I know she loves her dad and loves to read. I want to know more. I want to know everything, but I can't ask. Not unless I'm willing to share some information of my own. That's a terrifying thought. Beyond my therapist and my family, we don't bring up the past. Not ever. Especially not with the strangely beautiful woman that fate threw into my path.

Not that I put any stock in fate or destiny. I can't. Both have screwed me over far too much for me to be a believer now.

On Quinn's other side, Graham's family has left the row, probably in search of food or souvenirs or the bathroom. She hasn't made a move to leave her seat, but I could move and offer her an escape. It would be easier for me to step out of the row and let her pass than to make her pick her way through the rest of the narrow seats. The people behind us have cleared out too, and even with the music playing over the speakers, it's about as calm as arenas ever get during a game. I don't want to waste this relative privacy. Not for a moment.

"Hi." I hold out my hand for Quinn to shake. "My name is Erik Varg. I'm a thirty-one-year-old therapist from Chicago. I have a twin brother, an older sister, and a giant cat named Loki. I've run the Chicago marathon twice, and both times felt like I was dying. I hate flying and I have a complicated relationship with my family, so I don't see them as often as I should. I'm in town for work, but if I had to spend the evening at my brother's game, I couldn't resist repping my hometown just to mess with him. Clearly it isn't working."

"Hi Erik. It's nice to meet you." Her grin is blinding in its intensity, all full lips and white teeth, and warmth. "I'm Quinn Cooper. I am twenty-nine, an art teacher and I work at my old alma mater. It's always been just me and my dad, although I currently live with my roommate Jen--she's one of my coworkers--and my cat Tesseract. Tessie for short. I do not run. I played volleyball in high school and sometimes I dance while vacuuming. I spend my free time reading or painting. I don't know if I like to fly because I've never been on a plane, I've never been ice skating and, despite my dad's season tickets, this is the first time I've ever been to an NHL game."

"How are you liking it so far?" I ask, and my heart is in my throat as I wait for her reply.

"So far," she holds my gaze for a moment before looking back over the ice, "So far I've been pleasantly surprised."

I have been too.

I suck up every piece of information Quinn lays down and immediately want more. Would it be weird to suggest a cat play date? Tesseract and Loki sound like a match made in heaven. Even if I'm losing my mind. It's absolutely ridiculous. We don't live in the same state. I haven't even asked for her phone number yet. Or permission to contact her after the game. I'm going to ask. Soon.

"I'm six feet tall," she says, but it sounds like a question, the cadence of her voice lifting at the end of the phrase. Like maybe she wants to know how tall I am but doesn't want to ask.

"My brother and I are six five," I say.

"That's it?" She raises one copper brow and for a moment I consider protesting that I am significantly taller than average, but it feels too damn good to smile with her.

"Can I have your number?" The words fall from my mouth before I mean them to. I wanted to ease into the request, ask when I knew she wouldn't mind. Or at least wouldn't be stuck sitting next to me for the next two periods if I made her uncomfortable.

She blinks her big green eyes as she studies me. Someday I will go to my grave convinced I can feel her gaze like a physical touch. She starts at my forehead and traces the lines of my nose, my mouth, my chin, my throat. I swallow reflexively, feeling the familiar weight of arousal sink into my groin. I like her, genuinely like her, and I'm attracted to her. Wildly so. Enough that I want to press my lips to hers, camera or no camera. Enough to want her naked, which means there's something else I have to tell her.

"You can give me yours." She pulls out her phone. "I'll decide if you can have mine after the game."

She is a goddess.

Fucking magnificent.

I rattle off my phone number and watched her type it in. She has long slender fingers tipped with short, rounded nails. Each one painted a different color, with tiny black lines along the top. I lean closer for a better look. Crayons. Each of her nails looks like a different crayon. A little rainbow as she taps the numbers on her phone's screen. I bet everything she wears is bright and colorful. I bet her whole life is rainbow hued. I want to see her outside of the arena. In clothes that suit her personality, chosen from her own wardrobe. Not a borrowed jersey that fifteen thousand people are also wearing tonight.

Quinn slides her phone back into her pocket and my phone buzzes in my pocket. I pull it out and swallow hard at the little green bubble on the screen.

776-555-2368

> Quinn Cooper, seat mate extraordinaire

I bite the inside of my lower lip to stop from shouting in triumph.

"The game isn't over," I say. In fact, the second period is just about to start.

The clock on the Jumbotron hits zero, and the buzzer sounds as fans shuffle back to their seats. Vic skates onto the ice and takes his place for the face-off and the Center skates into the circle to wait for the ref to drop the puck. Ahlstrom is a solid player and I know Vic enjoys playing with the Swede, but sometimes seeing them work so cohesively rankles. It was always supposed to be us. Me and him and Robbie Oakes.

"Prove me right," Quinn says, drawing my attention back to her, and I barely notice when The Arctic loses the face-off and the game gets back underway.

The teams trade the puck back and forth like a game of hot potato. Wayne Gretzky, hockey legend, once said "skate to where the puck is going to be, not where it has been." Unfortunately for both teams on the ice, they seem completely confused about the puck's travel plans. It's as if they're piling off the plane in Paris, Florida instead of Paris, France and wondering why they can't find the Eiffel Tower. It's painful to watch. One of the Arctic players dumps the puck down the ice and as both lines hurry after it, the linesman raises his arm and blows the whistle.

"Why'd the play stop?" Quinn asks and for the first time in a long time, I'm excited to share what I know. Happy to talk about the sport that dominated so much of my past that I vowed I'd keep it out of my future. Or at least a minimal part of my future. I can feel myself smiling, my shoulders pulling back as my chest puffs out. I try to squash both, sure that any amount of smugness will have her regretting the gift of her phone number.

"Both teams are playing sloppy. Johannes shot the puck towards the opposite goal as a stall tactic so the team could get their skates under them, but you aren't allowed to do that—delay the game like that. Any time a team passes the puck from one side of the center line over the opposite goal line, and no one touches the puck, the linesman blows the whistle, and the offending team has to take a face-off in their defending zone."

Both centers skate into position and the linesman drops the puck near the Arctic's goal.

"So why do it?" Quinn asks as Ahlstrom wins the face-off and tips the puck to my brother.

Vic sends the puck to Johannes, their passes connecting with precision as the line swaps at the bench. Even from the second row, I can see the sweat pouring down the back of Vic's neck. Stamina, I want to tell him. Sometimes those forty-five second shifts turn into a full minute or more and Vic never worked on his long game. Even years later, I remember the screaming agony in my muscles after too many long shifts on the ice. Agony only made better with conditioning. Then again, Vic has trainers and coaches now. It's their job to prep him. Not mine.

"They needed a minute to reboot, and since the Arctic has won approximately eighty percent of the face-offs tonight, they deemed it a necessary risk." I point to the crowd of players circling the opposition's goal. There's a scramble for possession and then the buzzer sounds as the Arctic increases their lead. It isn't a pretty goal, but points are points.

Quinn doesn't jump up when the rest of the fans do, but she claps and smiles as the announcer names Tyler Gage as the goal scorer.

"I probably should have paid more attention to all the games when my dad had them on." She wraps her arms around her front and cups her elbows. Her shoulders curve in too, and I want to tease out why she's caving inward, hiding herself. I want to understand. She seems to feel guilty, although I can't figure out why. Does it have to do with her dad? If that's the case, what are the odds that we'd end up sitting together? Two reluctant viewers with complicated families? Probably higher than I think. A lot of people have family guilt nipping at their heels.

"I bet he just enjoyed having you with him," I say because it's something most people have heard over and over and over again, but there's also at least a morsel of truth to it.

"Maybe," Quinn shrugs. "Is this therapist Erik coming out to play?"

I hadn't meant to channel my professional side, more like my own personal experiences. I hadn't even considered my background with Quinn. Most of my daily work isn't with support systems, but with the patients themselves. With the teenagers I see, we work on worrying less about other people, since they're outside their control, so they can focus on their own healing and fight.

Empathy is a wonderful thing to have, but putting yourself first is necessary. That's something a lot of oncology patients forget. Especially kids. They forget they aren't fighting for their mom, or dad, or grandma, or siblings. They aren't surviving to spare the people in their lives some type of heartache. They're fighting and healing and doing what they can for themselves.

"I'd prefer not to think of you as my client," I say instead.

"Right," she nods. "Can't be friends with your clients."

Friends. I try not to chuckle. That's definitely what I'm most worried about. The ethical implications of spending time with her. I think the ethics board would be significantly more concerned with the fact that I've already pictured her naked. That I want to press my mouth to hers.

"Or more." I watch her brows furrow and then smooth almost faster than I can process. Her mouth twitches too, a picture of confusion. Like she's trying to convince herself that she misunderstood me or that I didn't mean what I'd said. I'm willing to give her some time to catch up, even if my ego aches a little over the idea that she might not have even considered the possibility of something. I've only been writing sonnets in my head based on the color of her eyes and hair since I first saw her. Okay, maybe not sonnets, but I've been thinking about them.

"Right, if the Kiss Cam comes back." She nods like she understands, but she doesn't.

"Even if it doesn't."

I'm putting the ball in her court. It doesn't matter that this is crazy, that it can't go anywhere. I *like* her. I think she likes me too. And no matter how juvenile that sounds, it's not something I've experienced in longer than I like to admit. If I don't shoot this shot now, I'll still be thinking about it in my meeting tomorrow, when I board my flight home, probably when the playoffs start in a few months.

Quinn's teeth worry her bottom lip, but she doesn't look away. My skin feels tight, my abdomen heavy and full. I'm dangerously close to a semi. Just from the thought of pressing my mouth to hers.

"That's good to know," she says.

There's a bang as two players hit the boards just to the right of the Arctic bench. The glass shakes and around us everyone jumps to their feet for a better look. The view is obscured as the two men grapple for the puck, tied up on the rail. I can't see any of the action, but the fun part isn't the hockey. It's having Quinn lean into me as she tries for a better view, too. For someone not very into hockey, she seems to be having a good time. I hope that has something to do with me because I'm having a good time too. No mean feat considering I've avoided rinks since I was sixteen.

The players clear the puck, moving out towards center ice, and people regain their seats as the whistle blows to stop the play.

"I'm so sorry," Quinn says, and she's staring down in horror at where her foot rests over the top of my left shoe. "I should have paid more attention to where I was stepping and—" she moves her foot back even though I never felt the weight. She's blushing again and I shouldn't think it's cute when she feels embarrassed, but it really doesn't matter that she stepped on me. It wouldn't matter even if I *could* feel her weight. "I'm making this a bigger deal than it actually is." She finishes and then she's looking out over the ice as if I'm not even there anymore.

"It's okay," I say, because it is. And this might not have been how I planned on sharing the information, but I knew I needed to say something. If there's any chance for us beyond this game—even just for tonight—well, I should tell her now. Yes, I know it's up to me when and with whom I share personal pieces of my history, pieces of me, but sometimes getting the news out sooner rather than later is the quickest way to weed out the rotten apples. Not that Quinn's a rotten apple. I already know she isn't, but it doesn't stop me from putting this off.

Quinn scrubs a hand down her face, loosely banding her hand around her own throat. She's trying not to look at me, and I wait a beat—for the game to pick up and the people around us to be distracted—before I reach over and offered her my palm. She drops the hand from her neck and slips it into mine, twining our fingers. Her hand is warm and dry. Solid.

"It's really okay, Quinn." I wait for her to look at me. "I didn't even feel it."

"Yeah, okay." She rolls those pretty green eyes. "Thanks for being so cool about me not only stepping on you but freaking out after."

"I'm not being cool about anything." I pull her hand to the top of my thigh, watching her for any discomfort. I move slowly so she can pull back at anytime. "I really didn't feel it."

Using both our hands, I gently pull on the leg of my jeans. I tug the denim until she can see the mechanical components that make up the ankle joint of my prosthetic as it disappears into my boot.

And then I wait.

5 QUINN

I have no idea what to say or how to react.

Erik has a prosthetic leg.

Do I care if he has a prosthetic leg? No, of course not. He's the same person I've been talking to for the past hour. It doesn't change the lust he sends spiraling through my veins with his crooked smile and heated glances. I want to tell Erik it doesn't matter. I don't care that he only has one leg, not in the way he might think, but this is a part of him he's chosen to share with me. A part he might have made it through the entire game without sharing. A part he could justifiably have withheld for weeks or months as we got to know each other through late night text messages. And look at me getting ahead of myself here, but sharing this still means something. Right?

"If you want to tell me, I want to know," I say.

My brain is crackling, the kind of static that accompanies a bad television signal, as it comes up with scenarios and backstories. He's young. Only in his thirties, and yet comfortable on his prosthetic. Comfort and confidence I can only imagine takes a significant amount of time to master. I want to dig into his past and ask for all the details.

The words are bursting on my tongue, eager to ask about the leg, what happened, how it affects his daily experiences, how it affects his…women. But I don't know if that's okay. I don't want to do this wrong, so I won't ask anything without him guiding the conversation. Insatiable curiosity might have killed the cat. It will definitely kill the possibility sitting between us.

Erik lets his pant leg fall, covering the metal, and I feel the rasp of the thick denim as if it's dragging against the inside of my skin. I squeeze my fingers around his and rub my thumb over the meaty flesh where his thumb meets his palm. He's watching the game, hazel eyes following his brother as he takes a shot on goal, but the corner of his mouth twitches up in a small smirk. The cockiest little movement that has my stomach flipping over on itself as if I've spun out on The Scrambler at Six Flags.

"You're dying to ask me questions right now, aren't you?"

"No." My voice breaks on the word and I know that I'm the worst liar, but now Erik knows it, too.

"You're the worst liar." He shakes his head, but he's smiling even bigger now.

"Okay, I want to ask." I admit, "I want to ask a lot, but not all my questions are about your leg."

He turns to look at me. A blank expression masks his features, and I want to swallow my words or rub my hand down his back. I don't think it's the leg that's putting his guard up, not after the teasing affection and the smiles. I think it's me saying I want to know more. There's something else he's worried about discussing. I try to turn my body to face him, but it's difficult with the little plastic armrests already pressing into my hips. He goes back to watching the game.

"Just because I have questions doesn't mean I'm going to ask them." Our fingers are still linked. "I am lethally curious, but I'm like that with most things. And I can wait until you want to tell me. Whatever you choose to share is up to you."

Erik tilts his head and looks at me from the corner of his eye. His hair glints gold in the lights and his cheeks are pink, although it's not a blush, more like a reflection of his jersey. His mask is gone and in its place is something deep, fathomless. Something that pulls at my heart until I feel the physical tug like the moon with the tide. His eyes drop to my mouth, and he straightens, angling in the seat with ease, turning so his chest faces me. It feels like we're balanced on two ends of a pole held by a tightrope walker. I suck in a breath and let it sit and burn in my lungs, too worried that I'll ruin the moment if I gasp for another.

I lift my chin, even though I don't need to look up to see into his eyes. Seated, we're just about the same height. I wet my lips and close my eyes. Taking a moment to center myself. It feels like I'm melting from the inside out. Drowning in heat. When I open my eyes, Erik is so close that each breath pumping through his chest almost pushes his nose into mine.

"You okay with this?" He asks and I can taste the sugar-soda on his breath, feel the warm air break over my chin. I can't find words over the thrum of my pulse and all I can do is nod. Erik's next breath sounds like he's run a marathon. Or played a shift on the ice. "You're okay with me putting my mouth over yours and sucking your taste into my soul? Because I've been wanting to. Almost since the moment I saw you."

"Yes." The word is out before I realize I've spoken. Thank God. That kind of question needs more than a nod. I already know Erik is the kind of guy who won't assume. I sway toward him. My eyelids feel heavy and my lips are tingling. Then Graham jumps out of his seat. Fists held up in front of him.

"Fiiiiiiiiiiiiiight," the little voice yells over the crowd and the moment between Erik and me snaps in two like a bar of chocolate.

Erik blinks, his brows furrowing as he shakes his head. He looks like he's trying to reorient himself. Shake the cobwebs out of his brain. I do too. Graham is still screaming, throwing mite-sized punches into the air in front of him as two players faceoff in front of the net. I look back at Erik again, but he's got his arms propped on his thighs as he watches the tension unfolding on the ice. I wonder how high up his prosthetic goes.

"Maybe the refs won't let them?" I say and smile when Erik snorts out a laugh. The two players circle each other. Up on the Jumbotron, their mouths trade anatomically questionable barbs, and I hope the kid hasn't mastered the art of lip reading.

"They're saying bad words," Graham says, eyes alight with devilish glee. "This is the best thing ever."

"Your team's up by two, and this is your favorite part?" I try to gesture towards the angry players, but Erik is still holding my hand and I'm not quite ready to let go, either.

"They've been circling forever now, I bet the ref will—" but I don't get to finish that sentence because the Chicago player throws his gloves down on the ice and slams a fist into the jaw of the player in blue.

Everyone is screaming, maybe even louder than after a goal. Fans along the boards are pounding on the plexiglass with the flat of their hands. The Arctic player, Spaeglin, is taking the brunt of the beating, but he isn't down. His opponent has him by the collar as he hits and hits and hits.

"Why haven't they broken it up yet?" I whisper to Erik, wincing with each punch. The stripe-shirted refs and linesmen are there too but watching from the edges of the altercation just like the fans in the arena. It's a train-wreck I can't look away from. I don't want to see the Arctic player hurt, but I can't seem to close my eyes.

"They have to wait until it's safe for them to go in," Erik says.

"It's a bloodbath," I say. "I don't think nine has thrown a single punch. He's just taking them all." As if he hears me through the crowd, Spaeglin grins and sends a punch hurtling into the jaw of the man holding on to him. And okay, maybe if the refs had tried to slide in there, the Chicago player would have punched them instead. "I hate the fighting," I admit as the two men crash down to the ice, the Arctic player landing on top of his opponent. "It just seems so unnecessary."

"It's strategic." Erik rubs comforting circles into *my* hand this time. "You can't let the other team walk all over you. If there's a perceived slight, or a mistake, your enforcers handle it for the good of your whole team. Sometimes a fight can change the momentum of the entire game."

"What was the 'perceived slight?'" I ask. "I was...suitably distracted before the gloves came off." Not that I'd have any idea what happened, even if I'd been watching. A flush reddens the tops of Erik's ears and damn, that's adorable. I'm in danger of liking almost everything about this man. It feels like I know him. Feels like we've known each other for years, not just an hour. Then again, knowing the man wears a prosthesis doesn't mean I actually know anything about him. I have to stay honest with myself, but it's hard to stay grounded when he smiles at me like that.

"I uh—I wasn't paying attention either," Erik says, as the refs separate the players and escort them off the ice. "But a scrum in front of the net usually means someone took a run at the goalie." He pauses and listens as the refs announce the penalties. "Both players are getting a five-minute major for fighting. That's normal, but the Arctic is going on the power play because Riles is getting an additional two minutes for starting it."

"Why aren't they going to the penalty box?" I ask as a different player from Erik's team skates across the ice and takes a seat in the penalty box.

"Less than five minutes left in the period. They'll go straight to the locker rooms and one of Riles' teammates will serve the instigating penalty."

"You don't seem all that worried that my team is ahead and now has an extra man on the ice and a better chance at scoring." I bump my shoulder into his.

"We have a pretty good penalty kill percentage," Erik says, "but win-or-lose today, I'm still going to be forever grateful that my mom bullied me into coming."

He means because of me.

It's there in the way he looks at me. In the words he said about wanting to see where things between us went. Long term, there's nowhere, but today? Tonight? I'm not the woman who goes out and picks up a partner for a one-night stand. Not because I'm opposed to having a single tryst, but because they seem to take a lot of time. Usually, I spend my free time at home, sleeping or reading, or with my dad.

Could Erik be a psycho killer who wants to skin me and wear my intestines as some sort of hat? It seems unlikely. Possible, but unlikely. So far, he's been nothing but kind, respectful, sweet. He hadn't drugged the soda he'd bought me. He's given me some personal details about himself. Even if he is dangerous, I doubt Vic Varg's twin brother would troll for victims at his brother's hockey games. That seems a little too obvious. Does it even matter? He won't do anything right here, surrounded by people, and he hasn't asked me for anything beyond the game.

"Are you miserable being here?" I ask, my heart aching as it runs away with all the reasons his mother may have had to guilt him into supporting his twin. Reasons that all center on the metal ankle joint he'd showed me.

Erik hunches his shoulders and he frowns, but he pulls our hands from his thigh into his lap.

"I thought I would be." He looks at the bench, empty of Arctic players now that the period is over, but where his brother sat mere feet from him. "But I was wrong."

"For what it's worth," I say, "I also thought I'd be miserable here. I was wrong, too."

"I'm too charming for my own good," Erik says, and he's right. I couldn't have a bad time with him if I tried.

"Nah," I shake my head. "I'm glad I got a seat next to Graham."

The kid in question has escaped to the bathroom now that we're once again between periods. On the ice, two men in inflatable hamster balls are trying to run from the center line to the goal and back without falling. Howl is on the Jumbotron, letting a group of middle schoolers in hockey jerseys teach him how to do some dance moves I don't think my limbs can imitate.

"I'll take second place. That's fine with me." Erik pulls his buzzing phone out of his pocket and it must be a crazy coincidence, but mine goes off, too. I hold mine up to see texts from both my dad and my roommate.

Jen's message has a grainy, blown-up photo of a red and blue blob sitting with a white and blue blob. At some point, Erik and I had made it onto the game feed and my roommate has a screenshot of the evidence.

Jen Peterson

> Did you kiss that beautiful man? Because I have so many questions. And a lot of jealousy.

I'm not sure how Jen determined Erik is beautiful. He is, but the picture looks more like pieces of play dough smashed together than actual people. My dad's message is similar, and I can practically hear him teasing me through the phone.

Dad

> I think I saw you on the feed. Hard to tell with these damn tiny televisions.

> Are you sitting with the Varg brother?

Of course Dad would recognize Erik, even on the tiny television in his private room. Next to me, the man in question lets out a bark of laughter and tips his phone in my direction. He has a similar message, too.

Mom

> Looks like you're having fun. I'm glad I got you that ticket.

She also attached a photo. It looks like the same one Jen tried to send, but with better quality. We're angled toward each other, both smiling as he holds both of our hands against the top of his leg. The details in the picture are still hazy—I can't see the shade of his eyes or the sparkle in the irises—but it's a sweet picture, intimate. It looks like two people on a date. Two people who are crazy about each other.

"We've been discovered." I show him my messages, including the abstract photograph. Erik's eyes flare as he reads the lines on my phone.

"Your dad," he laughs, one big hand cradling the back of his neck. "No pressure or anything."

"He's a teddy bear," I assure him. "My roommate is the one to worry about."

"I thought you said she was a teacher," Erik said.

"That's why you should be scared. She teaches kindergarten. She can find out anything anytime and get you to do whatever she wants without you even realizing that it wasn't up to you. Kindergarten teachers are some of the most terrifying people I've ever met. Except for anyone who willingly teaches middle school." I grin because it's true. Jen has one of the best-behaved classes I've ever taught. And every single one of those kiddos adores her. "Besides. I don't think you get to throw rocks. What about your mom?"

Erik nods, lips pursed together. "Yeah, you're going to need to move to Siberia and change your name."

"What?" I rear back, shocked. "But she thinks you're having fun!" I point an accusing finger at his phone. It shouldn't matter at all if his mother approves of me. This isn't a thing between us, but now that her name has crossed his screen, I want her to like me.

"Exactly. You'll have to move or she'll probably file a marriage license for us and send out the invites."

"That seems a little premature," I say, but relief has my heart pounding so hard that I can feel it in my throat. I'm absolutely ridiculous.

"You made me smile in the photo." Erik shrugs his shoulders. "My mother will do more than commit a crime to try to make me happy."

There's a frown teasing the edges of his mouth, and I'm not sure what to make of that. My dad would do the same thing. There's something I'm missing. About why he rarely comes to games, the flat look in his eyes when he mentions his mother or brother. There's history there. Something most likely intertwined with his fake leg and as much as I want to press, want to know everything about this man sitting next to me, that line of thought is absolutely ridiculous.

Three hours ago, I didn't know his name.

"She won't actually do anything," Erik says. "She just uh—" he rubs the back of his neck and looks out over the ice. The men in the balls are gone, replaced by a teeny tiny figure skater leaping around in a floaty blue skirt while Idina Menzel sings about the cold.

"My leg's the reason I stopped playing. I had surgeries and had to take time off right as my brother and I were drafted into United States Hockey League. It's been a bit of a sore spot for me over the last decade. I love seeing my brother succeed, but it was supposed to be both of us. We aren't as close as we used to be, but my mom is still fiercely protective of me. And my siblings. I guess most moms are."

"I get it," I say as the little girl curtsies and leaves the ice. "My dad has some health stuff going on, and this was the first game ever that he was going to miss. I might not love hockey, but I love him. I think it's okay to be a little crazy for the people we care about."

"This is the first game I've come to in a long time," Erik says, voice low and hoarse, and I know—I *know*—that he's telling me something important. "In theory, I know I shouldn't still avoid these after all this time, but—"

"Feelings aren't always logical."

He turns to face me. Not just his head, but his entire body, twisting at the hips to look into my eyes. He isn't watching as the camera turns on, the animated hearts appearing as another song about kissing blares through the speaker. He's completely focused on me, his eyes on the hands I'm twisting in my lap.

"My mom was right, Quinn." Erik twines our fingers together. "I wasn't happy about coming tonight. But I'm glad she made me."

"It's nice to support your family," I say, hoping that I'm missing his point. Desperately wishing that I didn't misread him. "Even though it also sucks to admit that the people pushing us are sometimes right."

"Silly woman." He shakes his head. "My brother has nothing to do with it. I'm glad I came because I met you."

Good boy, I think. I just needed to be sure. Just needed another couple of seconds for the camera to catch up. I was banking on them being just stubborn enough to try again. Erik squeezes my hand just as I catch the two of us framed on the Jumbotron. He hasn't noticed yet, and this time I don't hesitate.

"I'm glad I met you too, even if this damn camera won't leave us alone."

Then I lean in and press my mouth to his, smiling into our first kiss.

6 ERIK

Her lips are cool against mine, thanks to the chill from the ice, and I lean into the pressure of her kiss. I want to catalogue each individual feeling. The warmth of the breath escaping her nose and breaking over my cheek. The crackle of her curls as I slide a hand around the back of her neck to hold her to me. The silk of her skin under my fingers. She's made up of a million textures and I could spend years exploring each one.

The sounds in the arena bleed away and all I can hear is the blood rushing through my ears and down my body to pool, heavy, between my legs. Her scent is everywhere, sunshine and roses overpowering the metallic ice of the rink and the sour tang of beer. I angle her head with the hand I wind into her glorious curls and sweep my tongue along the seam of her lips. I just know she's going to taste even better than I imagined. She opens just enough to release a little sigh, enough to give me the barest taste, and then she pulls back.

Quinn is whispering something as I chase her mouth with mine, pressing our lips together a second time. I swallow her words as I kiss her again. Her hand is on my chest, and I want her to slip it either up into my hair or down to my fly. I'm not picky. She leans into me for another searing heartbeat, two, and then she pushes me back again. I'm ashamed to admit that I almost lunge for her again as I watch her lips shape words I know I'm supposed to understand.

"Family. Friendly." The four syllables clang around in my brain like single cymbals searching for their mates.

The noise from the crowd filters back into my awareness. There's hooting, catcalls, and foot stomping. I glance up at the Jumbotron to find that we're still there, putting on a show for The Stand. I can't find it in myself to care. I try to locate the camera across the ice as I slide my arm behind Quinn's back, cupping her shoulder and pulling her to my side. I feel every bit the caveman I appear to be.

As the players file back onto the ice, my brother looks up into the stands, ignoring the fans screaming his name. Vic grins at me and Quinn and I know he didn't see us on the camera, but he can also count on one hand the number of times I've engaged in public displays of anything. I can't resist pressing a kiss to the knit hat covering Quinn's temple. Vic winks.

"Still feeling okay about giving me your number?" I ask.

Quinn's mouth is kiss-swollen and red, her lips wet from my tongue as they split into a wide smile. "Yes," she says, and I smile back.

Keep her, my brain whispers. It takes real effort to come up with any reasons I shouldn't. I know they're there. Nothing has changed, but every con has pushed to the farthest reaches of my brain as if hiding among my gray matter.

"I'm only here a couple more days, Quinn." I hate breaking the cozy little bubble cushioning us, but I have to be sure she understands. I can't offer more than this game, this night, maybe a few extra days. It's not that I don't want to. And maybe, if she's willing to see me, we can get together whenever I make it to town. Except I don't come to town. This time was an exception and long-distance relationships are hard on couples even with a solid foundation. I met Quinn less than three hours ago. We can't be anything more to each other than a great memory, and I'm fine with that. I think.

I have a few more days before I fly home. Back to my high rise in Chicago, back to my practice, back to ignoring as much of the NHL as it's possible to do in a hockey city during hockey season. I don't come here often. I should. Or I should at least make more of an effort to visit. Try to spend more time with my mom, with my twin. Technically, I'm here for them this time. I'm in Quarry Creek as a favor to both of them, but it's a favor that involves minimum face-to-face interaction. Remote relationships. They're our new normal. Have been for years now.

I'm here to talk to a local hospital that is making a name for itself as a pediatric cancer center. Their oncology department is already well known, but they've seen a significant uptick in pediatric cases and want to provide the best possible care. They also have a serious hole when it comes to the mental health of their patients. Most pro athletes have a philanthropy cause, something they support and champion, something they raise money for. Money and awareness. It helps build ties to the community, helps paint the team and organization in a good light, and helps a worthy cause. These kids are my brother's cause.

I agreed to help because it's my area of expertise, and it meant seeing my family. Something that I rarely manage since Vic left Chicago. I've been consulting with the hospital board. Helping them create a new department for an in-house focus on the mental health support young patients need. It's more complicated than shunting them off to other practitioners or into the psych department. Not that both don't have their merits, but there needs to be more than that. A full-scale collaboration. Everyone putting these kids and their goals first. I'll have at least a few more trips to help them straighten out everything they need in order to get things up and running, but the end goal is worth the legwork.

Now I'm thinking of how to draw things out a bit more so I can schedule a few more visits. Maybe she'd want to see me again. Is that too forward?

"Are you saying that as a brush off?" Quinn goes still under my arm, but she doesn't let her smile slip.

"I'm saying that because I want to spend every minute I can with you, but once I leave, I can't promise anything else."

The blush starts on her throat and spreads up her cheeks like someone airbrushed it on. I think we might be on the same page. At least about the here and now. I think she wants what I'm offering. I hope she does.

One-night stands aren't my MO, but I hope she wants this, too.

"I have to work tomorrow," Quinn is watching the game like she follows hockey for her job. Can she hear my heart thundering in my chest? "When is your flight home?"

"Not until Sunday night."

Friday doesn't have to be an issue. I have meetings too. I can pick her up after school, take her to dinner. I wonder if she wears bright colors and clothes splattered in paint and sequins. I wonder if the kids call her Ms. Cooper or if she lets them call her Quinn. I wonder what her lesson plans are for the next day and what medium she prefers to teach. And despite the fucking hypocrisy of knowing I can't make her any long-term promises, I hope she gives me the chance to find out.

"My dad's in the hospital," Quinn says, and I want to fold her into my arms at the hitch in her voice. "That's why I'm here for him tonight. If he doesn't come home tomorrow…well, I promised to bring him good food and entertainment every day until he does."

"I understand." I might not have the relationship with my family that she does with hers, but I get it. I do. I also understand what she's not saying. She has weekend plans. Plans she is not about to drop for a stranger. I like that. Her care for her dad is an attractive trait. I still can't help but push, just the tiniest bit. "Do you think you could fit me in for a coffee or something?" Anything? I'll take anything.

"I can do that." She says, and it feels like my heart skips a beat in my chest. "There's a decent coffee cart at the hospital if you want—"

"I want," I cut her off before she can talk herself out of it. I twist my fingers in the bright curls hanging down her back and watch her smile.

Chicago scores a goal and then the Arctic returns the favor almost immediately, leaving the score at three to one with half of the third period already gone. I have to admit that I've stopped paying attention to the game. I'm just grateful to see Quinn hasn't reached for her e-reader once after I caught her the first time. The game is getting choppier, and the fans rowdier, as the clock runs down, and Chicago gets desperate. She's still a little jumpy when the players slam into the boards, but nowhere near her initial reactions. She's having fun. It's hard not to find that infectious.

Would it be inappropriate to invite her back to my hotel room? Yes, all the blood in my body is still making my pants tight. I had to adjust after that kiss and the problem hasn't self-corrected, but extending an invitation doesn't have to be about sex. I want to spend more time with her. I don't want the final buzzer to go off in seven minutes and thirty-two seconds and we go our separate ways, even if it's only for twenty-four hours. We have less than seventy-two hours before my plane taxis down the runway and catapults me back to my apartment and my melodramatic cat. I want to spend as many of those hours as possible with her. More kisses, joint orgasms—both would be a bonus. The real treat is Quinn.

Another Arctic goal, this time on the power play after a high stick that is going to require stitches, and this game is basically over. A lot can change in a few minutes on the ice, but the Arctic has a solid lead and Chicago can't seem to pull their sticks out of their asses long enough to put up a decent fight.

A pair of small dark hands wrap around Quinn's waist and I drop my arm as she shifts away from me.

"Bye Quinn. Bye Rick," Graham says, hugging her as tight as his little body can manage. "We're leaving now 'cause Naya and Grayson have to go to bed."

"Erik," Quinn corrects, patting his skinny arm. "Don't stay up too late reading. Tomorrow is a school day."

Graham rolls his eyes and waves at us both as he follows his mom out of the row.

"He's not one of your students, right?" I ask. In the row behind us, several people file out of their seats, too.

Quinn shakes her head. "There are three elementary schools in town, but he either skipped every single art class since kindergarten or he doesn't go to mine."

"Hopefully his teachers appreciate his newfound love of reading," I say, and she winks at me. She is too damn cute.

"Here's hoping." Quinn glances around as the stands continue to empty of fans. The clock still shows four minutes remaining in the game. "Why is everyone leaving?"

"Trying to beat the traffic," I say as the Arctic huddle around their bench for a pep talk during a commercial break. "The end is pretty guaranteed, so they'd rather not sit in the never-ending lines to get out of here."

Stupid. What if she heads out now, too? I haven't locked down her time for after the game.

"Good thing I parked like ten blocks away," Quinn is watching me out of the corner of her eye. "Did you need to get going early to avoid traffic?"

I shake my head, "I took an Uber from the Marriott, so I can order a car whenever. I may have to wait a little. Too bad I didn't think to bring a book."

Quinn's mouth twists as if she isn't a fan of my answer. "I like you, Erik, but I don't lend my e-book out to anyone," she says, tucking her hands underneath her thighs.

"Do you want to grab something to eat after the game?" I didn't mean to ask like that. I meant to be smoother.

She smiles before she makes eye contact, green eyes shining.

"I could drive you back to your hotel." Her blush streaks across her cheeks. "And I know a few local spots where we could grab something—"

"I'm not hungry." I cut her off. "Unless you're hungry, but the Marriott has room service until midnight. We could just go there and—" and fuck. I don't want to sound pushy or creepy. The only thing I want to taste is her, but I'd also willingly order her one of everything on the menu and listen to her talk.

"Yes," Quinn nods and her flush deepens. "Let me just text my roommate. Promise you're not a serial killer?"

"Scout's honor." I hold up two fingers and she rolls her eyes as she pulls out her phone.

"Why do I just know you weren't a Boy Scout?"

I wasn't one, but that's because I've been playing hockey since my seventh birthday. I didn't have time for Scout meetings or projects when every day was practice, and every weekend was a game or a tournament. The older Vic and I got, the further we had to travel for games. There had been nothing but hockey. We hadn't wanted anything but hockey. Right until my life came to a screeching halt. Then there was nothing but hospitals and pain.

"The Marriott downtown?" Quinn asks as she taps out a message on her phone, and when I nod she asks, "Room number?"

"Three Oh Four."

She laughs at something, types another message, then slips her phone away.

"Jen has your name and room number, so if anything happens to me, you're going to be in big trouble."

"I promise I won't do anything to you that you don't ask for," I say, trying and failing to keep the blood north of my groin when she flushes.

I fish out my own phone and open the camera. It's the most unflattering angle ever, but even with the clear shot up my nose, no one could miss the grin on my face. I'm... happy. Being here makes me happy. Quinn makes me happy. I can't remember the last time I'd felt more than just content. I might have forgotten how to feel this way.

"What are you doing?" She asks as I stretch my arm out to center us both in the shot. The photo is going to cut off half of our heads, but our faces will be clear.

"It's your insurance policy," I say, moving closer until her satin cheek brushes the stubble along my jaw. I count down but can't resist snapping the photo a beat early. On "three," instead of after it. Taken off-guard, Quinn's smile is wide and genuine and mine is its twin. I took this picture to put her and her friend's minds at ease, yes, but also so I can have a reminder of this night and this game for the years to come. A little piece of joy that showed up where I least expected it. I open my messenger and send the photo first to Quinn, and then, on a whim, I send it to my mother. "Share it with your friend or anyone else you want to. That way, if the police ever had to question me, there'd be proof that we were together and at what time."

She opens the photo and stares down at us in miniature. I expect her to make some disparaging comment about her hair, or her nose, or her shoulders. Most of the women I know would have. My sister would have roundhouse kicked me for not letting her be in charge of the shot, and for pulling the camera up without her permission. The photo of Quinn is stunning and the candid smile she'd sent the camera captures the way she's looked all night. Tempting, and fiery, and wonderful, and real.

"That's a splendid picture," Quinn says as she forwards it along. "You look okay, too."

My brother Vic has been nicknamed the NHL "pretty boy." Un-ironically. Since he and I once split from the same egg, I know that "pretty" moniker can apply to me too. I might not have the experience he does, but I've been around my fair share of gorgeous women. Quinn doesn't do a single thing I expect that she'll do. She is a breath of the freshest air. And she isn't wrong. She looks gorgeous both in person and in pictures.

"You're beautiful," I say, and the final buzzer swallows my words.

On the ice, the teams line up to shake hands and I realize that I've made it through the entire game thanks to Quinn. She's made it fun. She's been quiet about the details, but between the seat belonging to her father, and the mention of a hospital stay, I imagine this hasn't been an easy evening for her either. Hopefully, I've helped her through the last few hours the way she'd helped me.

Now I'm eager to get her somewhere less "family friendly" to explore more of our chemistry.

"I wouldn't call it confidence," Quinn says as the players leave the ice. "It's more like realism. I know what I look like. You know what I look like. Everyone who's ever seen me knows what I look like. Why worry about how that's captured by a camera? I think it's pretty obvious you like what you see—"

"I love what I see."

"So why worry about it? That photo of us? That's two people who look happy because they are happy." She stands up, stretching her arms above her head, and I get lost in the movement of her strong and powerful body. I shake my head to rein myself in. "In all seriousness, thank you for tonight. Whatever does or doesn't happen from here on out…" She's still talking, but I push to my own feet, letting myself find my balance as I take her hand in mine.

"I had a good time tonight," I tell her. "Thanks to you."

7
QUINN

We both know why I followed Erik back to his hotel room, but it's cute how little pressure he's putting on me. The door closes behind us and we're in a standard hotel room. I check out the bathroom and the king-sized bed while Erik turns on the few lamps and shoves some dress shirts into his open suitcase. The room is far from a mess, but his effort to clear even the smallest piles is… sweet. Like he cares what I think. Would he do the same for a regular one-night stand? I'm getting ahead of myself.

"Did you want to order something to eat? Watch a movie?" He brushes invisible lint off the end of the white and gold bedspread. "Do you want something to drink?"

He almost seems…nervous, but that can't be right. Even when he told me about his leg he'd been quiet and watchful, not buzzing with anxiety. Now Erik is almost vibrating out of his skin, in a full-blown panic of some sort. Does he think he'll offend me? That I'll get mad he brought me here for some nefarious purpose? Because I invited myself. For sex.

Maybe I should clarify that I chose this. Maybe he needs a little shove in the right direction.

Erik grabs a bottle of water out of the mini fridge and his jeans pull tight over an ass that could have been chiseled right off a Greek statue. Never have I ever had the urge to sink my teeth into someone's butt, but for Erik, I want to make an exception.

I cross my arms over my front and grip the hem of my dad's jersey, getting a handful of the hoodie under it. I tug both over my head, dropping them into a pile on the nondescript gray carpet. My beige camisole doesn't offer the best support, but the lace trim is pretty, at least. With the double layer over top, I hadn't been concerned about the girls swinging free. Now I'm grateful I'm not wearing one of my standard industrial strength bras. There is nothing fun or sexy about plain white cotton attempting to scaffold me into submission and still barely succeeding. Boobs are boobs. I'm pretty sure this man likes mine.

And the way Erik swallows, his throat bobbing as he locks eyes on me, definitely proves me right. The bottle crumples in his hand, spraying water over his fist and down the front of his pants. He doesn't notice.

"Fuck, Quinn."

His eyes are hot and dark as they skate over the skin of my shoulders and up my throat. I can feel them as if he's touching me. My body is overheating. I'm slick between my legs. We're on the same page and there's nothing else we need to worry about. Not right now.

"Yes. Please." I stretch my arms over my head and gather my hair into a thick band. My curls are tangled by now. It'll take a gallon of the expensive conditioner and another full wash day, but that's a small price to pay for the rest of the evening. "Unless I'm misreading the situation. I can put my shirt back—"

"Don't even think about it."

Erik sets the bottle on the nearest surface, nearly dropping it to the rug with his inattention. He crosses the room in three long strides, the heat from his chest smacking into mine before he even touches me. My whole body is aching when he finally reaches out to take my hand in his, pressing his lips to the ridge of my knuckles.

I go dizzy at the brush of his mouth. I lose the breath from my lungs as Erik dips his thumb and pointer under the slim strap of my tank and brushes the pads of his fingers over more sensitive skin. I shiver, goosebumps rising along the place where we connect and following his touch down over the tops of my breasts.

"You're fucking gorgeous, Quinn. I want to get my hands and my mouth all over you." His words slip over me and I'm drowning.

My head feels too heavy for my neck and it's easier to let it loll back as his hand dips an inch into the top of my cleavage. We haven't even gotten started yet, not really, and already I can't keep my eyes open. This is just the beginning and I'm so far gone I can't see the starting line anymore. I want him to pull the shirt up, or down, or just off. I want his hands on my naked skin. Did I say we're just starting? I was wrong. The last few hours have been tortuous foreplay, and I need this more than oxygen. Need him.

"I want that too."

I push the words out as I reach for the hem of his jersey. Erik helps me pull it up over his head by gripping the back of it and yanking in one fluid movement. He has a white undershirt on underneath, and it's gone before I can ask him to take it off. His body is leanly muscled, smooth, and golden. He's not cut the way his brother is—it's hard to avoid the advertisements all over town—but still firm and strong. There's a patch of dark blond hair between his pecs. Another trail of it leading down to his belly button and then disappearing under the waistband of his jeans.

"I'm going to kiss you, Quinn." He says, and I almost don't notice because my eyes aren't done devouring him, but then his lips are on mine and he tastes even better than he looks.

That Erik is taller than me is something almost foreign. He slides his hand up the column of my neck, his thumb pressing into the sensitive skin until I tip my chin up for him. The angle is better this way and when he growls, the sound vibrates from his chest into mine. I'm on fire, melting inward just from his touch in a few strategic spots. His hand circles my throat and as I open my mouth in a gasp, he uses the opportunity to push his tongue past my lips.

There is no easing into this kiss. The brush of our mouths at the game had been all the build-up we were apparently going to get. Erik devours me like a man starved and I am not complaining, but I want to gorge right back, so I suck on his tongue and swallow his moan. He pins me to the wall behind us, his fingers flexing against my throat, and I relax and let my muscles go loose. Even now he's gentle with me, his free hand cushioning the back of my head as he licks the inside of my mouth.

Erik pulls back to nip at my lips, and the sting sends a corresponding tug and ache to the warm, wet spot between my thighs. He still hasn't touched my breasts, hasn't slipped his hand under the waistband of my leggings. I'm still basically dressed, and he's only shirtless. I'm already more turned on than I've ever been in my entire life.

"Too fast?" He presses the words to my mouth, sipping at my lips and giving me almost no chance to reply. I shake my head. It's not too fast. It's not too much. It's perfect and I've never been hotter. "I don't even have you naked yet, but I need to taste you here," He says, and cups me through my leggings. I'm so wet I know he can feel it through the fabric.

I drag my hands down the front of his chest and almost feel physical pleasure as he drops his hand to adjust himself in his jeans. I can just make out the head of his cock sticking out over his waistband. I want to taste him.

"Don't look at me like that or I'll lose my mind," he says, his body shaking with the force of his words, and I let my gaze rake him again.

"I can't help it. You also look edible." I let the tips of my fingers tease at his erection, and his hips stutter against my touch. Erik bites into the skin of my shoulder and moans.

"Me first," he says, and grips the sides of my pants to tug them down.

He pushes the stretchy fabric to my knees and I shimmy them the rest of the way down. His hands trail back up the outside of my thighs and we both moan together. I'm already a quivering mess, even before he leans forward, dropping his forehead to my collarbone and licking a hot, wet path along the top of my chest. My knees feel weak.

"I'm going to lie down on that bed and you're going to climb up my body and sit that sweet pussy on my face. Got it?"

I hesitate.

"I don't know what you're expecting here," I say and blush. Sex positivity is all well and good, and getting my motor going listening to his words is fabulous, but almost two-hundred pounds of woman is still a lot for anyone to take. "I'll drown you."

Erik walks backward to the bed and lies down on the comforter. He pushes the pillows to the side so he can be flat near the headboard and then he crooks his finger at me. I'm walking toward him before I realize I've moved.

"I'm a big guy, Quinn." Erik says. He looks like he'd rolled off the pages of a magazine with his pants barely concealing a monster erection and his chest slick with sweat. "I can handle you just fine. And if not? Well, I can't think of a better way to go than between your thighs. So hop up."

I'm already on the bed and knee-walking to his prone body. It surprises me how easy it is to straddle his chest. Maybe because, despite my protests, I want to do this. His chest hair tickles the sensitive skin between my legs and I shiver on top of him. The inner faces of my thighs are already slippery with my arousal.

"You're sure?" I ask again, as he loops his hands around the back of my thighs and pulls me higher up his chest. "I don't mind against the wall or lying down and letting you be on top for this."

His mouth is so close that I can feel each of his breaths break over my pussy.

"What if I told you I have some…limitations when it comes to kneeling and putting all of my weight on the length of my leg?" His eyes are solemn as they search mine. The heat banked to a manageable level. "This is the easiest way for me to eat you without spending half my energy trying to balance, but if you aren't sure, then we can figure something out."

I'm an insensitive idiot. I'd honestly forgotten about his prosthetic. Had he said where it started? His pants are still on and for all I know, his knees don't work quite the same way mine do. Despite my complete self-absorption, he is more concerned with my pleasure than anything else. If Erik says he can handle me on top of him, then he can handle me on top of him. I push up onto my knees and let my body move the rest of the way up Erik's until his mouth is right between my legs.

"Make me come, Erik," I say and drop my weight, blocking the giant grin I can feel against my core.

He doesn't respond, simply drags his tongue along my folds and suctions a kiss from my pussy. It's the same way he kisses my mouth, like I'm the only source of oxygen and he's drowning without a hit. After the first few passes and deep, wet licks, I tip forward to grab the headboard. By the second time he latches onto my clit and sucks, I scream and rock my hips against his mouth. I'm not even pretending to hold myself up anymore, riding his tongue towards that ever-elusive peak that is barreling down on me with surprising speed.

Erik's hands have been stroking circles into the inner faces of my thighs, but now one slides to where we are connected and he pushes two fingers deep into my aching center. He pumps them once, twice, sucking the entire time, and my body seizes up like melted chocolate being shoved into the freezer. I splinter into a million pieces all over his face. I come so hard I scream his name. I come so hard I almost black out.

When I regain control, I'm still seated on Erik's face. He's gripping my hip to hold me there as he continues to suckle soft kisses against my over-sensitized pussy. He pulls his fingers out of me, and I try not to moan. My own fingers are white-knuckled as I grip the headboard behind him and my thighs shake as though a magnitude seven earthquake just destroyed every single thing I knew about orgasms. I feel him smile against me.

I slide off Erik's body and slump into a sweaty heap next to him on the bed. I curl around his torso, his chest heaving as he grins up at the hotel room ceiling. His hand finds mine, and he links our fingers. The bulge in his pants looks painful, especially when he drops his free hand to adjust himself.

"We're not done," Erik pants into the room. "Promise. Just let me catch my breath and we'll keep going."

I press a kiss to his left shoulder. I need a minute, too. Aftershocks are still zinging through my bloodstream and tightening my muscles. Erik presses his mouth to our joined hands and then rests them on the warmth of his chest.

"That looks like it hurts," I say, staring down the erection tenting his pants.

"Are you offering to kiss it better?"

I feel the words more than I hear them, and he's joking around, but there's a thread of desperation there. It makes my mouth water.

I slide down his body, my fingers playing with the button on his jeans. I unsnap it one-handed and tug the jeans down over his hip bones until they sit snug along his thighs, offering his balls and his cock up like a gift encased in dark cotton briefs. I trace my finger down the bulge and grin when the flesh jumps under my touch.

"Yes." I press a kiss to his erection and Erik fists his hands in my hair. He's groaning as he shifts his hips under me.

"We'll have to save that for another time," Erik says. He drags me up his body and when I'm staring down into his face, arms propped on his chest, he lifts his head and presses our mouths together. "You put that mouth anywhere near my dick again and I'm going to go off like a bottle rocket. I'd rather do that inside you. Between your legs, Quinn."

I shiver at the promise in his words. "I'd prefer that too," I say and slide a kiss over his throat. "Do you want me on top again?"

"Only if you want to be." Erik palms himself. "I'll take you any way you're willing to give me."

I frown, "I thought you said it was easier—"

He chuckles, the sound turning to a moan as I cover his stroking hand with my own, jacking him myself.

"Quinn," he says my name again, like it's a prayer. He bites me on the chin and tips his hips up to meet my grip as we slide our joined hands up his erection. "I lost my leg below the knee. I can do anything other men can do."

"But you said—"

"I said 'what if I told you.' I'd have said almost anything to get you to sit on my face."

I roll my eyes, but I'm also smiling as I sit up and tug his pants further down his thighs.

"How romantic."

Erik pushes up on his elbows, meeting my eyes with his. "Is that what you want? Romance?"

In theory, yes. Maybe not everyone wants a happily ever after, but I do. Someday. That desire for a future with someone who can romance me doesn't mean that I'm putting unfair expectations on this connection with Erik. I know this is different. We could probably be friends. We get along well enough, but there is no future here. No opportunity for more. We live a thousand miles apart and neither of us is moving.

"Not from you, Erik," I soften the message with a kiss to the center of his chest. I'm still wet and ready and my blood is so hot in my veins it's a wonder steam isn't pouring out of my ears, but if we continue this conversational line, then I'm in danger of losing all those things. I kiss him again, melding our tongues together as I wrap a hand around his dick and stroke.

"You can take these off," I whisper against his lips. The pants have to be digging into his skin and hindering his movements. Denim is rarely comfortable, and his jeans have almost zero give.

"My leg?" He asks and I pull back to look down at his leg. I forgot about it. Again.

"What do you want?" It's probably more comfortable for him to take it off, right? I'm still wearing my camisole, and Erik's pants are bunched around his thighs, so no one is naked, but a prosthetic leg isn't the same as a pair of socks. Right? "I want you to do what you're comfortable with." I say, because if the time I've spent forgetting about his leg is any sign, then neither option bothers me.

Erik hikes me up over his hips until I'm straddling him again. My knees rest on the bedspread as I brace my palms on his chest. My core presses into the thick weight of his erection and we both groan. I rock my hips against him, just a little, and I could come again from this alone.

"Condom," Erik pants out, his hands steadying my hips.

I don't have one. I don't carry condoms with me because first, I'm on the pill and religious about taking it every day, and second, I don't have a habit of picking up strangers for happy naked fun time.

"Please tell me you have one in your wallet." That was something men did, right? Carry emergency condoms? A man like Erik probably has a box stashed in his suitcase. I don't like that thought, but protection is protection. Despite our crazy chemistry, I can't just skip safety with someone I barely know.

Erik shakes his head, fingers flexing against my skin.

"I can call the concierge," he offers. He throws his head back and groans as I shift my hips again, the tendons in his neck standing out in relief.

"We are not calling the concierge for condoms." I say, stilling my hips and frowning down at the beautiful man beneath me. "I guess you're getting your rain check sooner rather than later."

"I'll make it up to you. I swear." Erik grits his teeth as I push off his body to kneel between his spread thighs. I take his erection in my hand and lick the head like a blow pop. He's hot and hard on my tongue, tasting salty and musky as I swallow him down. "Fuck, Quinn." Erik twists a hand into my hair, alternating between watching me with ravenous eyes and throwing his head back to groan.

This is probably for the best, I think, as I suck and swirl my tongue around the length of his dick. He's built in proportion—larger than normal—and I just know my jaw and throat will ache tomorrow. Worth it though. Worth it to watch him curse and thrash under my ministrations. Worth it to feel powerful and sexual and beautiful in bed with him. And this is why sex leaving the table is a good thing. If giving a blow job is this enjoyable, I just know sex would make me lose my head and I'll forget that he's leaving. Sex with this man, with the chemistry we already share, may just tip me over the edge and I could fall in love with him.

8 ERIK

The line to the coffee counter is taking forever, but I have it on good authority—aka the nurses—that this is the only drinkable caffeine in the building. After my late night with a certain redhead, and hours of meetings, I need something to get through the rest of the afternoon. A double shot of espresso will definitely help. So will seeing Quinn later for dinner. I'm picking her up at seven. On an unrelated note, I also purchased an industrial size box of Trojans. Just because.

The line moves forward and I check my watch. So far today I've met with the head of oncology, pediatrics, and psych. I have a meeting with the hospital's CEO in an hour and a half, which gives me more than enough time to grab a cup of coffee and check out some rooms set aside for patient sessions. It also gives me more than enough time to think inappropriate thoughts about the woman I can't wait to see again.

There had been a moment the night before—after we'd both been naked and coming down from the orgasm high—when I wondered if I'd made a terrible mistake. Quinn cuddled up against my side for fifteen minutes and then, as if a timer had dinged in her mind, she'd reached for her pants and slipped them on. I knew she had school this morning. I knew she needed to see her dad, and still the image of her turning her back to me as she pulled the stretchy leggings up over her ass had made me feel dizzy and nauseated. I hadn't wanted her to leave, not even for the less-than-twenty-four hours we would spend apart, which meant I'd made a huge mistake because I already wanted more. Even knowing that the end was looming.

I step up to the counter and place my order, wondering how Quinn takes her coffee. Something light and sweet? A blended drink with no coffee at all? Black? The barista raises her eyebrows, and her jaw goes slack when I give my order, but she takes my cash without comment. It's been a while since I've been mistaken for my brother. It used to happen more when he played for Chicago, especially when I was working on marathon training or dressed in workout clothes.

"Thank you, Vic." She hands me the cup with a blush that's nothing like Quinn's.

"Not Vic," I say, and she blinks at me like I'm lying to her. It probably wasn't worth it to say anything. I doubt I'll ever see this barista again.

The cup heats my hand, and it's a good thing the lid is on tight since I almost upend it over the man behind me when I turn around.

"You're Erik!" The mountain of a man crows, almost knocking over his IV pole as he reaches for my hand.

I'm glad to see that the man isn't wearing an open hospital gown, even if he's clearly a patient. He wears a pair of gray sweats and an Arctic beanie pulled low over his forehead. I'm pretty sure the man isn't supposed to be in the general visitor area, let alone buying coffee and pastries while hooked up to an IV, but I'm not his doctor and it isn't my job to police a grown man. Especially one I don't know.

"Yes, sir," I say instead of "who the fuck are you?" and shake the man's hand. I try to avoid gripping too hard and putting extra pressure on the tubes and bandages.

"I was wondering if I'd get to meet you." the man shuffles to the counter and places an order for three different lattes and an assortment of muffins.

"You can help me carry these back upstairs," he says to me as the barista loads drinks into a tray and pastries into a brown paper bag. I don't really have a choice. He doesn't have enough hands to bring the food and the IV pole with him, and I'd rather carry the tray.

"Do we know each other?" I ask as the barista grins at the man and waves away payment.

"Not yet. I'm Sean."

Sean hands me the tray of coffees and lifts the bag of muffins before giving the barista a hearty wink and moving towards the bank of elevators. I follow, pretty sure that the man is harmless. Sean hits the button for the fourth floor, and it's where I'm headed, anyway.

"Do you know my brother?" I ask as the elevator doors slide closed and the car jerks into motion.

"Doesn't everyone?"

Sean is somewhere between his late fifties and early sixties, although the lack of eyebrows and lashes make his age harder to place. That, combined with the floor choice, leaves me pretty sure that Sean is an oncology patient here at Grace Hospital.

The door slides open on the fourth floor and Sean walks out, pole in tow. He moves more quickly than I thought he would, although he is almost as tall as I am, so his long stride shouldn't be surprising. We buzz our way into the oncology wing and he leads the way down a small hallway towards the nurse's station.

"Mary, my love," He booms to an older nurse with short bobbed hair. "I come bearing gifts." He gestures to me and beams.

"Mr. C—"

"Mary, I told you to call me Sean."

The nurse sighs and props her hands on her hips, but even I can see the smile trying to break through.

"Sean, you can't just go wandering around the hospital. What if you need something?"

"Lu told me to take a hike." Sean motions me forward.

"I don't think she meant literally. I think she was teasing you, but I'll have a word with her."

"You'll do no such thing, unless you don't want this soy matcha latte that Erik carried for you." Sean plucks one cup from the tray and pushes it towards the woman.

"You didn't tell me this was an un-sanctioned trip," I say. "I don't want to be accused of aiding and abetting."

"You're dragging innocent bystanders into your plots now?" Mary rolls her eyes, but she also takes a sip of her latte. "What will your daughter say?"

"You wouldn't dare tell her, but she wouldn't be surprised. My girl understands my free spirit."

Sean gives an exaggerated wink and Mary purses her lips, but even I can recognize the affection in her dark eyes.

"Go back to your room, Sean. I'll get these to Lu and Stacey." She takes the tray from my hands and turns back to her work. Sean leaves the muffins on the counter and starts down the hall again.

"Come on, Varg," he calls over his shoulder and I check my watch again. Still over an hour until my meeting. And hey, I'd wanted to see some of the wing and talk to some patients before then, anyway. I hustle down the hallway after my new acquaintance.

Sean's room is private and quite spacious. Someone either has great health insurance or a good amount of disposable income. That same someone has covered the hospital linens with a baby blue blanket emblazoned with a familiar howling wolf. Sean settles into one of the two vinyl armchairs and gestures for me to take the other. I do, unbuttoning my suit jacket as the chair creaks under me. I have nowhere near the mass that I did when I was playing full time. Even at sixteen I was over six-foot and proud of my strength and my power. Running keeps me active, keeps me in shape, but I'm inches smaller than my twin now. I still feel too big for most furniture.

"You here for anything in particular?" Sean asks, reaching for the water pitcher and cup sitting on a rolling table. "Visiting someone?"

"I'm here for work," I say, figuring it won't hurt to get Sean's opinion on the project. He'd older than my demographic, but cancer is cancer.

"Interesting," Sean offers me a cup, too, and I hold up my coffee as a "no thanks, I'm good" gesture.

"I'm a therapist. My specialty is children and teens diagnosed with cancer." I say and take a sip. "My brother does a lot of volunteer work with the pediatric unit here and asked if I'd come talk to them about building up their in-house therapy options for young patients." It's a piece of their patient care that is often overlooked, but I don't say that to Sean.

"Are you going to be moving here and taking over?" Sean stares at me as though he can see into my soul and my past.

"No, sir," I say. "Just consulting. I have my practice back home. This is just a favor for my brother and my mom."

"You're close to your family?"

This conversation is feeling a little like a job interview, but Sean is nice enough and I know all too well that hospitals are lonely places.

"We aren't as close as they'd like us to be," I admit, and the words seem to bring on an ache in my phantom ankle and shin.

"Why not?"

"That's personal, sir."

Sean nods as if my answer is acceptable to him, which is ridiculous. This is my private life, and I'm allowed to share or withhold whatever information I see fit. Sean pulls a cellphone out of his pants pocket and checks the time before laying it flat on the table next to his water.

"Why cancer?" He asks, "And why kids with cancer? Not an easy job."

It isn't easy, not at all, but it's necessary. Cognitive psychotherapy, supportive psychotherapy, psycho educational programs, and family therapy are all considered standard of care for childhood cancer patients. Studies show they improve the psychological adjustment of parents and patients. That shouldn't have to wait until kids are out of the hospital or off the oncology floor. It shouldn't be left up to referrals that can take months and get lost in the shuffle.

These supports are vital and should be available where the children are most vulnerable and in need of help. Between the pain and the fear, kids are liable to lash out at anyone near them. That most often means family members. I know from experience, too, that the fear and anxiety the family already feels about a child's diagnosis and treatment can prevent them from being the best support their child needs. That isn't all parents. It isn't all families, but I'm a big proponent of therapy for everyone involved in a cancer diagnosis, the patient and their family, and therapy early. A prophylactic measure.

"I was diagnosed with osteosarcoma the summer after I turned sixteen." I sip from my coffee and relish the too-hot burn of the liquid as I swallow. "I was scared, I was in pain, and so were my siblings. So was my mother. I was constantly stuck between lashing out at them when things were rough, and feeling like I couldn't let them know how I felt because it was already too much for them. By the time I found myself a good, qualified therapist, the damage had been done." We don't know how to talk to each other anymore. We don't know how to support each other or be a family. Love has nothing to do with it.

If I'd found Dr. Shire earlier, maybe I wouldn't feel so much guilt around my brother's success. Maybe I'd have been more supportive of Vic's career and less angry at the loss of my own. Maybe it wouldn't take extreme acts of guilt to get me to cheer my twin on at games. Maybe we'd know how to talk, how to communicate. And maybe I'd want to spend more time with a family that I know loves me, but that I still struggle to be around.

"Cancer is a tough diagnosis. It's tough on us, the ones fighting, and it's tough on the ones who love us and can't do anything to change what we're going through." Sean leans back in his chair and closes his eyes. "Thank you for telling me. You didn't have to."

"I didn't," I agree, but I wanted to. Cancer is an exclusive club. No one wants to belong, but the only ones who get it are the ones who live through it. Sean mentioned he had a daughter. One old enough to talk to the nurses. I wonder how she's handling all of this. I wonder if he feels like he needs to downplay the pain and the discomfort and the fear. If he hears her crying outside his room or sees the redness around her eyes even when she tries to hide it. I won't ask. Stark lines bracket Sean's mouth. I know what those lines mean. "Want me to get a nurse?"

"It's just some nausea," Sean says. He's holding his body still in his seat, moving his mouth only the smallest bit as he speaks. "Day three post treatment is always the worst for me. Especially when I forget to hydrate."

I never could stave off the nausea, no matter how hard I tried to force it down. Nothing helped. Not the sea bands, not ice chips, not even throwing up. I had one nurse who would douse a cotton ball in isopropyl alcohol and hold it under my nose. That sometimes brought me a bit of relief.

"I used to struggle from hour twenty-four to seventy-two." I say. I refill the cup on the table so Sean can grab it when he wants to. "Then I'd feel better until my next round."

"How many rounds did you do?"

"I did fifteen cycles of VDC/IE. Every three weeks for about a year. Three rounds before my first surgery and then twelve rounds after." I can still remember the warmth of the drugs going into my body. Treatment often left me feeling lightheaded and sleepy. I dozed through most sessions. Which meant Vic, who came to the first few, stopped sitting with me during treatment. It was mom who stayed and read her mysteries while I slept. Mom, who brushed my hair back from my sweaty forehead as I lost everything in my stomach. Mom, who spent a fortune on foods just trying to find something, anything, I'd eat. And all I'd wanted was for her to go away.

"I come in once a month," Sean says. "The tumor surprised us all, especially my daughter. I was told a few rounds after they took it out would be a good insurance policy."

"I've heard similar," I say. "Do you want me to go?"

"I carry a lot of guilt," Sean says as if I haven't spoken. He takes a small sip of water, eyes still closed. I lean over and dim the overhead lights. The room is still bright thanks to a large window, but at least the fluorescents won't exacerbate Sean's discomfort. "I was sick for months. My stomach, my rear... something wasn't right with my digestion. My daughter knew. She hasn't lived with me in over a decade and she knew something was wrong, but I put off seeing anyone. It was just a bug, an upset stomach, getting older, you know? I didn't see anyone, no matter how many times she asked me to. I just kept putting it off."

I've always been aware that hockey, specifically my invitation to the USHL, was part of the reason I was diagnosed so quickly. When I'd started feeling weakness in my lower leg, followed by some redness and swelling, it was easy to write it off as a game or practice injury. I missed some of the initial symptoms of fatigue and pain because my body was always being pushed to the limit, but by the time I was limping with pain knifing into my shin, I had begged to see the doctor. I needed, I thought, an antibiotic or something, so I'd be healed in time to travel. I'd been in Urgent Care that evening and the on-call doctor had recognized the tumor on my X-rays. The biopsy had been less than a week later.

"My doctors thought it was an infection caused by a fistula, a tear in my insides. No one knew it was cancer until I was naked on the table with them pulling a softball sized tumor out of my bladder. And there's my baby girl in the waiting room, getting the news that it's cancer and that they've removed my bladder while I'm still in la la land." Sean lifts a hand and pats his hip. "I'll have an ostomy bag for the rest of my life, and when I woke up in the ICU, I was embarrassed that my daughter had heard about those parts of my body. Mortified that she'd had to sit there by herself and decide what to do because I'd put off the doctor for so long."

"It sounds like the tumor would have been a surprise even if you'd gone in earlier," I say, imagining the terror Sean must have felt. I've had surgeries. Hell, I had my leg amputated, but never had I woken up without body parts I hadn't expected to lose.

"The heart isn't always ruled by logic," Sean says. "She tries so hard to take care of me, and as her parent I'm supposed to take care of her. I can't imagine what that would feel like if the roles were reversed."

This is the whole reason I do what I do. Each situation is unique and nuanced and terrible, and each patient and family member is deserving of support.

"Have you told her yet?" Sean asks, cracking open green eyes and pinning me in place.

Told who? I struggle to orient myself in the conversation. I don't think I've mentioned Quinn, or not

Quinn. I haven't mentioned any *her*. Mostly because if I mention *her*, then I'll have to think of *her*, and that would mean an erection in a hospital room. Highly inappropriate. Did Sean mean my mother? Shortly after I started talking with Dr. Shire, I'd shared my feelings with my mom. The ensuing tears and apologies were almost as traumatizing as losing my leg.

"I'm sorry?" I say, hoping Sean will give me some sort of hint. Or maybe he's just a tired man who's sick and confused and there is no thread to follow.

"I know it's your story, and I'm normally the first to say that no one needs to know our stories unless we want to share them, but as her dad, I need you to tell her. She's strong and brave and has a heart the size of Jupiter. If you see this going anywhere with my baby girl, then you need to tell her about the cancer. And you need to tell her about your prognosis for the future."

For a moment I frown, and then the gears in my brain click into place. It's a hint alright, and I'm the one who's been confused. The green eyes, the Arctic paraphernalia, the hospital stay. The fact that Sean seemed to know me personally. I'd bet my cat that Sean had once had a head full of copper-colored hair.

"Dad?"

I don't need to look at the door to know who's standing there. Her voice washes over me like sunshine and I suppress a shiver. I get to my feet, hands held out like Quinn is a cornered panther ready to strike. She didn't expect me here and now I'm in her space, privy to personal parts of her life without her permission. She's frowning as she stares between me and her father, her gaze softening a smidgeon when she notices the strain on her dad's face.

"I'm fine, Quinnie," Sean says, smiling as she steps into the room and drops her bag on his bed. She holds the back of her hand against his forehead to check his temperature and ignores my presence. "I found Erik in line for coffee and we've just been getting to know each other. Right Varg?"

I can only nod.

9
QUINN

What is he doing here? In my dad's hospital room? Sitting in his armchair, and chatting as if they're old friends?

I thought I'd been so careful about the information I'd chosen to share. Yes, dad is in the hospital, but I hadn't said why. Or even in which facility. Yes, I'd mentioned the hospital coffee cart, and meeting for a drink, but then we never talked about it again. I was going to text Erik from here and meet him in the lobby. Not in the Oncology Wing. I'm not ashamed of my dad. He's probably the strongest person I know, but he deserves his privacy. It's his diagnosis and his fight, not my trauma to exploit for sympathy or care. He deserved a warning before Erik accosted him.

"How was school today?" Dad asks.

His forehead is cool under my touch. A good sign he might get to break out sooner rather than later. Any fever during chemo treatment means an automatic hospital visit and tests. So many tests.

"It was good," I say, automatically launching into an explanation of our latest project and the kids' reactions. Dad chuckles at all the right times, but the sound is hollow. He's probably nauseated. Day three is always the worst for him, even if he won't admit it. Whether it's the nausea or the story, it's definitely keeping him distracted from the feelings roiling in my gut.

Erik straightened in his chair when I walked in. Now he's alternating between staring a hole between my eyes and studying the off-white linoleum floor tiles. He's wearing a charcoal suit and a baby blue dress shirt with no tie, and I hate that he looks edible. He also looks disturbingly like the publicity shots I've seen of his brother, and I'm not sure how I feel about that. I've never been attracted to a twin before. Would Victor Varg do it for me? Just like Erik? I don't think so. Not that Erik does it for me. Not anymore. Not after finding him here. I don't mind reading about stalkers, but not in real life.

"It was great to meet you Sean, but I'm going to let you two have some time together," Erik says and he pushes off of his knees to stand.

He always does that with his hands, uses them for leverage when he gets up. And he takes an extra moment, shifting his weight from foot to foot to find his balance. I wonder if that's because of his leg, then I look away. I don't want to notice his tiny facets right now.

"You don't have to go," my dad insists, but his eyes are closed and he looks ready for a nap.

My annoyance burns hotter. Not only is Erik here, but he's apparently chatted my dad right into a nap. Maybe I wanted to spend this time with him and now I can't because he's clearly exhausted. Erik rests a hand on Dad's shoulder and squeezes gently.

"Thanks for humoring an old man," Dad says. "And think about what I said."

"I will, Sir."

Erik's eyes meet mine and I can't read the emotion there, but it's fathomless. He pauses on his way out of the room, opening his mouth like he wants to say something, and I don't want to admit that I'm eager to hear what it is. I'm itching for a fight. But he snaps his mouth shut and leaves, closing the hospital room door with a quiet *snick*.

I fluff the pillow on my dad's bed with heavy smacks, straighten his blanket with more force than necessary, and press a kiss to his temple that moves his entire body. I refill his water cup and hold on to the pitcher. It's not empty, but I should refill it too. My whole body feels like I've been zapped with a cattle prod. It's disconcerting and almost painful, tiny electric shocks buzzing under my skin, leaving me twitchy and full of too much energy.

"Leave it alone Quinnie." Dad loosely grasps my wrist in his big hand.

Leave it alone, Quinnie. How many times has he said that to me since I was born? When first-grade me shook all the presents under the Christmas tree, determined to find the Barbie convertible. When tenth-grade me wanted to follow Grady B at the mall because I was pretty sure he was meeting up with Kendra K while dating Naomi P, despite not being friends with any of them.

"Leave what alone?" I lift my dad's hand to my mouth and press a kiss to the thin skin over his knuckles. He bruises so much more easily now. Dark purple spots cover his forearms.

"I ran into him. I bullied him into coming back here to chat with me."

That sounds exactly like Dad, not the bullying, but somehow getting everyone around him to do exactly what he wants them to do without them realizing they've been played. The issue isn't that Erik succumbed to my dad's wily ways. The problem is that Erik was in the hospital to be found in the first place.

"I'm not going to do anything, Dad." I hold up his water pitcher. "I'm just going to grab you some ice."

"Lu can grab ice when she stops by next."

"I don't want you to wait that long."

"I can use my call button." He's really pulling out the big guns. He must have read the tension in my body and the murder in my eyes. And he must like Erik enough to spare him the Quinn special.

"It'll just take a second," I lie through my teeth and then I bolt for the door, leaving both the room and the pitcher behind.

It doesn't take long to find Erik. He's standing in the center of the friends and family lounge, jacket pushed back with his hands fisted on his hips. He's staring down at his fancy dress shoes and frowning as though he's upset. Or maybe he's hallucinating and a tiny dancing pineapple is doing the Macarena on his toes. He probably hadn't expected me at the hospital this early. I typically get out of school around three or three thirty, but there had been a special assembly this afternoon, and I'd ducked out early to see my dad and prepare for my date. With Erik. He probably thought he'd be in and out before I knew he'd been here. What does he want anyway?

ON ICE

The lounge doesn't have a door that I can slam, but Erik looks up the minute I storm inside. Is it unfortunate that he looks like he'd stepped off the pages of a magazine while I'm wearing a pair of paint-splattered overalls? Yes, yes, it is, but I will not let that get in the way of what I want to say to him. He drops his hands, letting his arms hang at his sides, palms up. His face is that blank mask again, his eyes dull.

"Quinn," One hand lifts, reaching for me, before he pulls it back. Good idea, buddy. In my current mood, I'm liable to chew it off.

"Don't" I say and cross my arms over my chest. My anger takes center stage. "Why are you here?"

Erik looks around the room like he's thinking about answering me literally. Like I'm asking why he'd ducked into the lounge instead of why he was in the hospital at all, schmoozing my dad—my dad!—when I wasn't there. Ultimately, he says nothing, doesn't even look me in the eye. It feels like an admission of goddamn guilt.

"Why the fuck are you here, Erik? This is creepy, stalker-level shit." The words are bubbling up, pouring out of me like acid, but I can't stop them. Not even when he flinches, as if I've physically assaulted him.

"I—"

"I purposefully didn't share this info. I didn't share my dad's name or that he has fucking cancer, Erik. We barely know each other and some things you don't blast on a billboard for a random guy you decide to suck off in his hotel room."

He flinches again, his face condensing into a frown.

"How did you find us?" The anger is bleeding out of me like I'm a freaking sieve. Pouring out as hurt rushes in to take its place. "I trusted you," I say, no matter how ridiculous that sounds. I've known this man for less than twenty-four hours. Trusting him with my body is not the same as trusting him with my family, but I was going to get there. This feels likes the ultimate betrayal. Like what I was willing to share wasn't enough. He had to reach in and yank out the private pieces I'd hidden away.

Erik grunts like he's been hit in the chest with a two by four or a pillowcase full of bricks. He says my name again, his voice low and laced with hurt. He pushes a shaky hand through his hair, mussing the neat strands into disarray. He takes a step toward me, then another, stopping only when I throw my hand up like a traffic guard and ward him off.

"I'm an idiot," I admit. "I knew you for maybe all of three damn hours before I followed you back to your hotel room like a dumb puppy. I thought you were safe because I felt some sort of fucking connection to you. How ridiculous is that? How ridiculous am I?"

"You're not," He says and steps forward again, ignoring my hands. This time I step back.

"I may not have men beating down my door," I say, "But I know better than to put myself in a dangerous spot. I let my guard down because I thought we had—something—" I blush, feeling stupid all over again. I hate that I'm still attracted to this man, miserable that I react to his closeness.

"We *do*, Quinn—"

"So I didn't protect me and mine. Stalking someone, finding their personal information and using it without their consent, is not okay Erik. I think you need to leave now." My voice cracks on the last sentence. It feels wrong on my tongue even as I know I have to be firm with my boundaries. If he'd just waited for me to make the plans to introduce them… just because it had been a tentative future plan doesn't change the fact that this feels like a betrayal. One that sits in my stomach like a metal anchor. The worst part is that my dad hadn't known. He'd probably been so thrilled to meet the brother of his favorite player that he hadn't questioned why Erik was there or what he was up to.

"I can't leave," Erik says, and okay, that's surprising. I tell myself it isn't romantic at all that he won't leave. I know it's weird that he's here, but I'd been sure that he wasn't dangerous. Once confronted, I was sure he'd back off. The phone to the nurses' station is just a few feet to my left. I'm painfully aware that he's bigger than me and that we're all alone, but if I call for help, I'll go down in history as the girl who booted a Varg.

"I know this looks less than ideal, Quinn, but your father found me. I didn't even know he was your dad until right before you got there."

That seems like a tall tale. I'm my dad's twin with longer hair and boobs. And just because he hadn't found my dad directly, didn't mean he hadn't shown up at the hospital hoping to get some information on him. Maybe Dad just found him first, but what reason could Erik have for being at the hospital at all?

"Right," I scoff. "Like you have some other reason for being here and he just found you and conned you back to his room without telling you who he was? After seeing us sit together for all of last night."

"Yes." Erik steps closer again and I forget to step back, because that sounded like something Dad would do. "I promise, Quinn."

He isn't getting angry. He isn't raising his voice. He's crowding me, but I still have a means of escape. He isn't letting me ignore him as he tells me...

But if he's telling the truth... If this was all some big coincidence...

"Why are you here?" I ask, my voice barely a whisper. From nerves, from embarrassment, I don't know, but I can barely breathe as I wait for his response.

"For work," he says, and then he reminds me about everything. He tells me about his job, and the kids he works with. About his brother's involvement with this hospital. How Vic often shows up in his pads and jersey and hands out signed pucks and merch while taking photos with any mini fan who wants one. He tells me about the meetings he's been sitting through over the last few days. About how he'd frantically sourced some caffeine and run into a patient who seemed to recognize him, not as Vic but as Erik. About how that patient asked him for help and then wanted to chat. And the worst part is that I one hundred and thirty thousand percent know he's telling me the truth because he told me a good amount of this last night. My anger vaporizes like mist.

Shame floods me as I sink heavily into one of the waiting room chairs. It feels like acid bubbling up in my gut. This man, this kind and selfless man, was a goddamn therapist for children with cancer. And I accused him of stalking me. I've been so self-centered and shortsighted that I accused him of lying to me. Of being inappropriate. Erik. The man who put my comfort and my safety above everything last night. I'm the one who crossed a line. Probably my dad too, for not telling Erik who he was, but definitely me.

I want to sink down into the floor, melt away between the tiles until there's nothing left, but that's not the mature way to handle this.

"I'm sorry," I say.

My stomach sours as I wait for him to tell me to go screw myself, to storm from the room, to roll his eyes as his gaze shutters. Instead, Erik crouches down in front of me and puts his hands on the wooden arms of my chair. He's caging me in with his body, but I don't feel trapped. I like having him this close. Maybe that's part of the problem.

"It's okay to be sensitive about this. It's okay to be protective of your father," Erik says. He's trying to catch my eye, but I'm not ready for that. He's letting me off too easy. I was a bitch, and I deserve for him to yell, to scold, to something. That fact that he isn't makes me feel like I've gone right-side up after being stuck on an upside-down roller coaster for hours. Disorienting, terrifying, confusing.

"I should have let you explain first. I'm sorry I went off on you. I just assumed—" I swallow hard. It hurts.

"Don't apologize for being cautious." He pushes a strand of hair behind my ear, and I shut my eyes at the slide of his fingers. "Just because it feels like we've known each other for decades, doesn't change the fact that we haven't. You've had less than a day with me to get to know who I am, and there are too many people in this world who can lie and cheat and then turn around and hurt the people they say they care about."

And there it is. My gut response laid out in black and white. I hadn't been angry, not at first. I hadn't been scared. I'd been hurt. I had allowed myself to perceive our relationship in a certain light and had assumed that he was overstepping my boundaries without my permission. It didn't matter that I hadn't laid those boundaries out for him to understand. It had still been like a knife to the chest. A sting that choked me up and put me on the offensive. I've read enough books about grief and hurt to know that it's easier to channel those painful emotions into anger; but no matter how many books I read, it's still not easy to recognize when I'm in the thick of it.

I reacted like Erik's my boyfriend, and he isn't. That's the basic truth. He isn't my boyfriend, and he never will be. It's one thing to date long-distance after establishing a relationship in person or expecting the distance will eventually end. It isn't practical to start a relationship with a man who lives in another state. There's no sign he's even interested. He'd said it with no qualms the night before.

I know he likes me, at least enough to fuck me, but the hurt I'd felt as his perceived betrayal? Well, I'm halfway to dangerous territory here and there is only one way out. One way to cut these feelings off at the knees.

"I still should have let you explain," I say. "Then you wouldn't have had to rush out of his room."

Erik shakes his head. "It's okay, Quinn. Your dad wasn't feeling great. I'd rather you get some of that time with him, instead of making both of you feel you need to entertain someone else." He smiles at me, the lopsided one that sends my heart clanging about in my chest like a pair of cymbals. "I have a meeting soon, but I'm still hoping to see you tonight. Should I pick you up from here?"

I try to smile, but my lips quiver. I pull them into my mouth, clamping down on them with my teeth. My eyes burn, but I refuse to think about that. What I'm about to do is going to hurt more, but only for a little while. If I drag this out any longer, it's just going to be worse in another forty-eight hours.

"I don't think tonight is a good idea," I say.

"Sure," Erik nods, "I understand. Tomorrow then?"

"I don't think that's a good idea, either." I swallow past another solid lump in my throat. The burn is just getting worse.

"Sunday morning?" Erik offers and it takes an effort to shake my head. Why can't he just take the hint? How many guys are this persistent? Probably the ones who can overlook a misguided panic. The ones strong enough to lose their dream and still support their brother achieving it. God, he's just so goddamn good. Any more time together and my heart will be bloody pulp in my chest.

"I think this freak out has shown me I'm not in the right headspace for you, Erik. I like you. A lot." *Too much.* "But I think it's better if we go our separate ways now, before you fly back to Chicago."

This is too much. He's too much. I feel too much. It hasn't even been twenty-four hours since we met. This man could devastate me without even trying. I can't give him the opportunity.

Before, I'd thought a few extra days together wouldn't make a difference. A few hours holding hands, kissing, dating. Now I know better. Nothing about my reaction to Erik is logical or normal and I'm in real danger of getting my heart bruised. Best to cut ties now rather than let them tighten.

Erik is frowning, still caging me into the chair when he asks, "Can I still text you?"

I shrug like his words don't feel like a blow to the gut. Like his willingness to fight for even a moment of my presence isn't the reason I'm terrified.

"I don't know." I say, because the thought of him texting me when I can't have him hurts almost as much as the thought of never speaking to him again.

10 ERIK

The icing on top of the shit cake is my keycard refusing to work.

I understand where Quinn is coming from. There's a part of me that agrees this is all too much too fast and will only hurt us both. The other part of me is left with a hollow ache between my ribs. And when the light on my room door turns red, I can't resist plonking my head against the sturdy metal door and growling out my frustrations.

No one had been manning the front desk when I walked by, and now I have to go back down and wait for someone to come help me sort out this key mess. It doesn't help that it's late and I'm hungry and I waited on dinner just in case Quinn changed her mind. Which means I'm also disappointed that she didn't.

I've been on my feet too long. My hip aches and my thigh is cramping up. I lean my weight more fully against the door and try to slow my brain. This isn't the end of the world. Sure, Quinn is beautiful, and funny. She made me laugh more in twelve hours than I have in the last five years. She understands me better than anyone I've ever met, too. There was a moment of connection. And here I am jumping the gun because the truth is I know nothing about her.

I just want to.

I thunk my head against the door again, trying to knock her out of my brain, and I almost fall when it opens under me.

"Keep your panties on," Vic says as I use the doorjamb to catch my balance. "Hey Erik."

"What are you doing here?"

"Hiding," Vic responds, as if it makes perfect sense. As if it's normal for him to show up in my space unannounced. As if we spend any amount of time together. A long time ago it might have been normal, but it's been over a decade now. We used to understand each other without words. Now it feels like I'm looking at him through a steamed-up shower door. His shape is there, but it's hazy, hard to make out under the steam and water. "What are you doing here?"

I lean back to check the number on the door of my room. I was under the impression that it was mine. Vic has his giant house he lives in, but I could be wrong. Except there's my suitcase and my things. I jut my chin towards the dress shirt draped over the back of one chair. Vic follows my look and shrugs.

"Yeah, yeah, but I thought you had a date tonight," Vic gestured around the room, "So I figured I'd come house sit."

"It's a hotel. It doesn't need to be house sat, and what if I brought my date back here?" I hadn't been counting on sex with Quinn. I'd never assume sex with any woman, but I had purchased a box of condoms on the off chance that she might be interested in that rain check. A rain check that would not have included Vic, even if it had happened.

"Eh, I was going to leave before then anyway," Vic drops onto the end of the bed and restarts Netflix.

Except that still doesn't answer why he's here. Or how he got in. Unless…

"Did you pretend to be me to get a new room key? You're leaving it here when you go." Because I'm not about to look like the idiot who'd lost his key more than once.

Vic rolls onto his side and fishes a slim white card from his pocket before tossing it on the comforter.

"That little concierge has a crush on you," Vic says. "Didn't even ask for ID and knew exactly who you were."

Or she assumed I was him.

"Go take a stab at her, then." I drop into the chair near the window. "I'm not interested."

"Because of the redhead." It isn't a question, and Vic levers his body up on his elbows. "What time are you going to pick her up?"

It is because of the redhead, but also because immediately chasing pussy after one woman turned me down is a dick move. It's not like I'll never have sex again, but for now, if I can't have Quinn, then I'm okay with an evening alone. That might sound surprising, considering the speed at which we moved. It probably looked like random hook ups are on the regular menu, but they aren't. That's one thing I don't think Vic understands.

Yes, we have the same face, and Vic can pull partners with just a glance in their direction, but Vic isn't living with the lower half of his leg gone. He doesn't have a stump and a dark bump of a scar tissue along the top of his chest. Not that I mind my port scar. Most of the time I don't mind my stump, either. Both are just a part of who I am. A tangible reminder of what I've gone through to survive, but that doesn't mean that the world is as understanding.

Cancer didn't just take my NHL dreams, or my leg. At sixteen, I'd been a top tier flirt, but my experience with girls was pitiful. Who had time for dating? For stolen kisses? I was too busy working on puck control, sharpening my passes until I could connect with my teammates with my eyes closed. Who had time to cop a feel in the backseat? I was at the rink until they threw me out. I spent my free time coaching preschoolers to march across the ice so I could pay for more ice time. And when hockey disappeared like a cloud of smoke, I'd been sick. Hockey had been attractive to girls my age. Cancer was not. And after that… after that I was too angry, too hurt, to learn how to reel in women.

I've been to enough support groups to know that men tend to do better with amputation and prosthetics. Lower rates of depression, lower rates of pain and discomfort with fit, lower rates of mental-health challenges, lower rates of phantom limb issues. And lack of real-world experience aside, I've been a guy long enough to know that in heteronormative relationships, women are significantly more understanding about appearance than men. But that doesn't mean that I haven't faced my fair share of horrible experiences while courting women I wanted to date or sleep with.

With a below-knee amputation, it's pretty easy to go through my daily life incognito. The right pants can hide my prosthetic almost entirely unless someone is staring at my ankles. Young Erik had set out to hide my leg any chance I got, but I've grown out of that over the years. I don't try to hide, but I don't shout it from the top of the Willis Tower. If

I think sex is on the table, I prefer to tell my prospective partner right away. Everyone has insecurities about their bodies, even Vic, but my leg is a class all its own. It's not so much that I'm insecure, as it is that other people can balk at the idea. Even with sex off the table, anyone who will run from who I am is not worth a spot in my life.

That's why I'd shown Quinn. It hadn't been about sex—not just sex—not with her. I'd been too happy sitting there, chatting about a game that had once broken my heart into infinitesimal pieces. Too comfortable poking fun at her and being ribbed in return. It didn't matter that we have no future. I needed to confirm my suspicions before I let myself even imagine anything else. My suspicions that she wouldn't be phased beyond a general sadness for my loss. And maybe, maybe I prepared myself for the tiny sliver of a chance that she'd take it poorly. Look at me with enough thinly veiled horror that it would be easy to leave the game and not think about her again.

What time am I picking her up? I clench my jaw.

"I'm not." I lean into the hard back of the chair.

"But you were super into her." Vic frowns. "People haven't stopped talking about it."

Of course Vic would have seen just how much I liked Quinn. I may have put distance between us over the years, but Vic is still my brother. My twin. One of the best gifts Vic has ever given me was understanding. He's never forced me to talk about any of it. He went off and signed his contract and never pushed me to go to his games or make any appearances. He's steered interviews away from our formative years and our relationship. He didn't cry or coddle me during any of my hospital stays. When he did show up, he squeezed my hand, and treated me the same as before.

"People?" I know our mother had screen shots, but after a few searching questions—that I'd refused to answer—she'd stopped pushing for information. Who else was discussing my love life?

Vic flushes and reaches for the remote, turning the volume up even though neither of us is watching.

"Vic?"

"The media might have gotten wind of you two canoodling at our game against Chicago." Vic says with a wince. "And Tris might be pushing me to get you to come by the head office and do some sort of promotional feature."

Tristan is the tiny brunette in charge of the team's social media pages. Vic had once described her as pushy, brilliant, and beyond terrifying. Given the things the barely five-foot-tall woman could talk seasoned hockey players into doing on camera for her, I'm glad we've never met in person.

"So that's why you're hiding," I say, and my brother nods.

"I'm avoiding her calls, texts, and emails, which means there is a better than zero chance that she'll call the house and show up. She's obsessed with the idea that people will care about your romance since we're twins. I told her no, but the woman's a barracuda."

I think it's less about Tristan, and more that Vic isn't great at telling people no, but he'd rather take a slap shot to the dick with no cup than put me on display when I've said I don't want it.

"Well problem solved," I throw him a bone since he's probably in physical pain trying to avoid the pretty little marketing guru. "You can tell her that the romance is DOA and there's nothing to feature." Vic squirms on the bed and I roll my eyes. "What?"

"The problem is that she likes you," Vic says. "She likes the twin thing, so I figured if I avoid her tonight, and we fly out tomorrow for our game, she'll be distracted. Then by the time our away set is over, you'll be out of town again."

"Thanks." Gratitude burns through me. Vic will catch hell from the woman when she realizes what he's up to. It won't hurt his contract or his game play, but it'll be uncomfortable. It means a lot that Vic didn't just serve me up on a silver platter.

"Don't thank me," he says. "I know you don't enjoy coming to games. The least I can do is keep you out of the spotlight."

I liked yesterday's game. I want to tell him. Was it only yesterday? Then again, he'll assume I liked it because of Quinn. Would that be even worse? I couldn't bother to show up for my twin, but I had fun because of a woman?

The tv chatters on, the fluorescent lights bathing the room in a warm orange glow, and the heater under the window buzzes as it struggles to circulate warm air. I can't remember the last time Vic and I were quiet together, just like this. I can't remember the last time we were in the same room together. Just the two of us. Last Christmas was the whole family. We'd been inseparable as kids, often sitting in silence that mom deemed creepy. Then both of us stopped standing still, too busy racing along the ice after a small disk of vulcanized rubber. Until one day I lay down in a hospital bed and Vic kept moving.

"How's mom?" I ask, breaking the quiet before it suffocates us both with memory.

That's another relationship I need to try repairing. Most of our interactions are through text or email. I avoid trips here. When I am here, I stay in a hotel instead of at Vic's.

Seeing her in person is the hard part. In the years since my diagnosis, she hasn't even changed her hair. Seeing her—the same worry-lined face that fetched me ice chips and held plastic bowls for me to puke in—the woman who shaved my head and threatened to shave her own until I stopped her, the woman who brought me memoir after memoir of amputee and cancer survivors, the one who'd enrolled me, the minute I received the all clear, in the local branch of the special Olympics... well, seeing her thrusts me right back into my angry, hurting, mean sixteen-year-old body, and the guilt I feel at the way I'd lashed out at her over and over again threatens to choke me. Normally I'd make a note to bring this up with Dr. Shire, but I'm leaving soon and it'll be a non-issue again.

"She wants you to move here." Vic says as the next episode starts on the screen. "Says it would be easier to keep an eye on us both if you were here."

It probably would be easier. For her. The guilt burns hotter because even after my distance, my silence, she still wants me here.

Vic and mom have always moved as a unit. When Vic signed on with Chicago, shortly after I started my PhD at Northwestern, our mother had come along for the ride. It made sense since Vic was on the road a good portion of the season. Mom could keep his house in order. Anna was already married and living her life in Colorado, and I was living in graduate housing in Evanston.

Even when they were half an hour away, I avoided visits and phone calls. I cited schoolwork, internships, boards. Then I was getting my foot in the door, building my professional reputation, making my name with the only thing other than hockey I'd ever been good at.

Mom's been angling, since Vic signed the paperwork on his seven-year contract with the Arctic, to get me to move here too. It's like she's forgotten how often I have avoided family get-togethers. I feel guilty as hell for it, but the joint living situation is half the reason I have this hotel room. Even though Vic's McMansion has more than enough guest rooms, I just can't imagine that much forced togetherness. Not anymore. I haven't even stopped by to see them in person. I should.

"I'm not leaving Chicago." I love my job. I love my condo. I have decent friends and neighbors.

"You get to tell her, not me," Vic says. "We were both hoping the redhead might be an excellent motivator, at least to visit more."

I've been trying not to, but now I can't help thinking of Quinn. Round and hot against me, eyes flashing as she smiles. My body floods with the same warm contentment it does every time I think of her or am in the same space as she is. The pull below my bellybutton feels like a magnet tugging me inexorably towards her, even as it stiffens my cock. Luckily, I get that part under control—there's nothing weirder than an erection next to your sibling—but I still can't help the soft smile that crosses my mouth.

"Yeah." The word leaves my mouth without conscious thought, and then I remember how things had unraveled in that waiting room. "I don't know. We didn't end things on a high note."

"What did you do, Erik?"

What had I done? Been in the wrong place at the wrong time. Put her guard up. I should have put two and two together a lot sooner. There was a reason Sean recognized me, knew my name. It wasn't just a mega fan of my brother's. He had a vested interest in getting to know me. That made sense. And then I'd heard her voice and my stomach had dropped because I knew how it would look.

I'd considered telling her she was wrong. Fighting her initial accusations, fighting the distrust and the anger, but I'd turned around in that hospital room and the fight had gone out of me as if someone had punched me full of tiny holes. It wasn't just Quinn standing in the door, glaring at me, confused and hurt and scared. It was Vic picking a fight with another Juniors player when they asked where I was. It was my mom telling people it was just allergies after sobbing in the bathroom.

Quinn had stood in that doorway wondering if I'd overstepped and sought her father on my own. If I'd invaded his privacy because of something she'd said or done. I wasn't. She hadn't. But it didn't matter. No one is rational when they feel cornered.

I'd been willing to wait her out. To give her time to let her dad explain. Her fight-or-flight response had overwhelmed her, and that was okay. I wanted her to feel like she could fight against me—yell at me, scream at me, curse me—and know I would not scare off. The joke was on me. She scared herself off and there was nothing I could do about it.

"We don't have a future," I tell my brother because ultimately that's what it boils down to.

"Well, you could come visit more, see her then," Vic says, "Make a future."

Our connection was too fast. Too strong. Too dangerous. Quinn was right. Either it was a fluke borne from our proximity at an emotionally difficult game, and it would have fizzled out the minute we were both back to normal, or we would have both ended up bloody and brutalized when I boarded my flight back home. And I was always going to go home. I don't think it's a fluke, though. I don't think this feeling, this tug between us, is stress-borne.

And if the pull had been even a fraction less than what it was, then maybe more visits could have been possible, but this level of chemistry... We'll end up in the same standoff every time. Actually, we'll end up in a worse standoff because there was no way that I won't develop actual feelings if I spend more time with her.

"Long distance only works if there's an end in sight." I say. "I'm not moving."

"Who said anything about long distance?" Vic asks, "Just have some good old-fashioned fun."

We tried that and look what happened?

Fun didn't work when there were feelings involved. That's how things got messy and painful. How relationships got ruined before they began. I'd already shot myself in my good foot by bringing her back to this room. Lust at first sight, and I'd lunged for her like I was starved. Now her taste is still on my tongue and I doubt it will ever leave.

So yeah, fun doesn't work when it's the right person, just the wrong place and time. And if I'm smart, I'll go back to Chicago and pretend this weekend never happened.

11 QUINN

What if I've made a terrible mistake?

I grab another jar of black tempera paint from the closet and drop my forehead to the wooden shelf. I've been thinking the same thoughts all weekend, but if I'm still agonizing over sending Erik away almost seventy-two hours after meeting him, then clearly I made the right call. If saying goodbye haunts me now, it would have only been worse after an actual date. After I let him inside me.

Let's be realistic. That was how the evening was going to end, and if the sex was good—and I was confident it would be—we'd have spent the rest of the weekend wrapped up in each other. Distance is the only thing that can spare us both. Well, spare me. I can't assume that Erik was as involved as I was. Maybe the repeated offers to see me were all about sex. Except I don't think they were.

At least in the art closet, no one can see me doubt my decisions. Except maybe the Googly eyes. The first graders love those darn things so much I'm probably single-handedly keeping the manufacturer afloat. It's a good thing I prepped today's lessons in advance because my head is miles away. Probably in Chicago, sitting at some fancy wooden desk and not even thinking about me at all.

"Tell me all about your weekend of sin and debauchery." Jen's voice floats over from the door to my classroom. "You can't hide from me, Cooper. I know you're in here somewhere."

"Closet," I call back, hoping she'll assume I'm grabbing something and not having a mini freak out. Then I take a deep breath, pick up the paint, and step out into the brightly lit room.

Jen has planted her butt on top of one of the long tables—thankfully I've already switched out the paint-covered paper—and is rearranging her skirt over her legs. She's a storybook teacher. Dark silky hair, small frame, a proclivity for wearing lesson-themed skirts and dresses. Her ballet flats never have scuffed toes, and she wears her shiny hair pulled back with giant floral headbands.

"Just say when." Jen holds her hands out in front of her and drags them further and further apart. "You're not serious," she says as nears the one-foot mark. "Am I jealous? Or do I feel bad for you?"

"When did you become Sofia?" I ask, and Jen rolls her eyes.

Sofia is Jen's other closest friend. They've known each other since birth and if Sofia wasn't such a nomad, I'm sure she'd live with us. Sofia tends towards smacks on the ass, crop tops in neon colors, and zero worries about what anyone else thinks of her. A necessity in her huge Italian family. I want to be Sofia when I grow up.

"Rude." Jen lowers her hands, "But you're right, I don't actually want to know how big his—" she widens her eyes and wiggles her brows as she drops her gaze toward my thighs, "stuff is. I'd never be ever to look him in the eyes."

That won't be a problem since Jen won't meet him.

Not because I wouldn't make introductions. Erik is kind and attractive and Jen would adore him in a supportive friend kind of way—Jen does not poach—but because when would I even get the chance? Erik is back in Chicago and even if he comes back for another visit, I wouldn't know. I cut off communication. It's for the best. Right?

"There was no debauchery," I say, and blush as I remember his head between my thighs. "Okay, there was some, but not as much as you're thinking."

"Was he a dud?" She frowns and pulls a granola bar out of some hidden pocket. The crinkle as she unwraps it sounds like nails down a chalkboard, but she offers me the first bite so I can get over it. "It can't be worse than the time I was set up on a date with Luca."

"It was that bad?" I ask. "I feel like that's standard romance novel fantasy material. Best friend's older brother and all that jazz."

"Maybe if there wasn't physical evidence you knew each other pre-potty training." Jen shudders. "I have never had a thing for Sofia's brother, but even if I did, he spent the whole date completely gone over another girl."

I choke on the bite I'm chewing. "That would be a bad date, yes."

"I've never met Vic, but he seems super nice. I know he does a lot of work with Grace Hospital, especially the pediatric wing, and if he's a good guy, his brother probably is too. Every time you and Erik showed up on tv—" she shrugs, "well you were both laughing and smiling and I thought for sure you were having a good time."

"We had a good time," I say because it was the truth, and I won't lie about that.

"So why not have a fun weekend? I got a text that you were going to his place, then I don't see you before school Friday, and you were gone all weekend."

Dad had been discharged Friday afternoon, and I'd spent the weekend with him. I wanted to make sure his laundry was done, his fridge stocked, the bathroom clean. I also wanted to be there in case his fever came back. I'd only found out about the first one because I dropped by earlier in the week to make sure the teenager I had hired was still shoveling the walkway when it snowed. I love my dad, but I'm not sure I trust him to take care of himself.

I probably should have texted Jen at some point other than to tell her I'd see her on Monday, but I'd been feeling a little raw. That was made worse by the fact that every time I picked up my phone, I didn't see Erik's name or number. It didn't matter that I'd been the one to squash our point of contact. Any other time and I'd be impressed that he was clearly respecting my boundaries, but I still felt the freefall of disappointment every time my phone was blank.

So instead of breaking a sweat while naked and relaxed, I'd broken a sweat deep cleaning my childhood home. Dad isn't a slob, but chemo takes more out of him than I know he wants to admit. The trick is trying to take care of him without him noticing.

I'm not sure why he doesn't want my help. Moving out, being an adult, are just more reasons to let me shoulder some of the burden. Why can't he just let me take care of him, dammit? I'm supposed to be the person he can lean on. We're all each other has.

"Dad came home Friday evening," I say. "That was more important than a fling." And it is, but that wasn't why I'd turned Erik down. I didn't have to choose between them.

"Did they ever find out what caused the fever?" Jen's brows tip together in concern, and I shake my head.

"They started him on antibiotics, but his culture came back clear and his fever dropped. They let him go home as long as he carefully tracked his temperature for a while." Meaning I track his temperature. I spent last night googling fever stickers. They're made to monitor the temperature of toddlers, but it might be my best bet to take care of Dad. I can stick it somewhere he can't reach or see. Too bad the reviews had been less than optimal.

"At least it wasn't more serious," Jen says.

I shrug. "Yes, but it makes me anxious, not knowing what caused it. We can treat an infection, but if we don't know what it is, it could come back again."

"Silver lining." Jen slides off the table and wraps her arms around my waist. "Your dad is okay, and you got to go to a hockey game and sit with a hottie. Will you see him again?"

Not unless I see him again on a televised game.

Even if I'd considered a casual hookup when, or if, he came to town, it was a bad idea. Casual sex is all well and good, but not when you actually have feelings for someone. And okay, I might not have capital F feelings yet, but they're pretty much standing in my front yard, peering into my windows, and trying to catch me doing something embarrassing. They are circling the foundation, scoping out the best window to crack open. They are playing ding dong ditch and hoping at some point I'll open the door and let them knock me flat as they bulldoze into my space. Insta-love is only a thing in romance novels. But instant chemistry that lays down the building blocks for more? Totally a thing.

I had a good night with Erik, both at the game and afterward. I enjoyed our time together. He made me laugh, smile, forget that I was only there because Dad couldn't be. Hockey has always been one of the few things that Dad and I don't see eye to eye on, and yet I'd gone for him and met Erik. The way Dad carried on, you'd think he had gift-wrapped Erik just for me. It just sucks that the gift needed to be returned.

"Our lives aren't exactly compatible," I say. "Plus, he's already back in Chicago and we never even talked about if he was coming back."

"He has family here," Jen points out.

"Family that used to all live there. Maybe he holds down the fort." I shrug. "It's fine. It was a fun experience and now we'll both move on with our lives and meet other people."

"So that's it," Jen says, "You're back to being strangers? Not going to visit, not going to write?"

"Write?" Sometimes I swear Jen was born in the wrong decade.

"Text, you know what I mean." She straightens the collar of her blouse with her nose high in the air.

"He hasn't texted yet," I say, and honesty makes me add, "Because I told him I didn't know if I wanted him to."

"Well, that seems like an oversight on your part." My friend and coworker might be a romantic, but she's usually sensible. Levelheaded.

"Why?" I ask. "What's the point in continuing anything when we can't date?"

"Because you obviously want him to text you." Jen says, which is annoying as hell because she's right. I want Erik to text me. Maybe if he did, it would be some proof that we are in this strange ball of emotion together.

"And he hasn't."

"Because he's being respectful, you ungrateful wench." Jen checks her watch. "My planning period is just about over, but this conversation isn't." She smooths invisible wrinkles out of her skirt and runs a hand over her shiny hair. She looks perfect and approachable and nowhere near the existential mess that I am.

I set the paint down on the counter that runs around the edge of my classroom, smiling and waving as Jen heads to the door. I have three more classes this afternoon and then I can go home and drown myself in a romance novel and pretend real men don't even exist.

"Hey Quinn," Jen calls from the doorway. Her smile is understanding and supportive and everything I know I don't deserve, not when this is all my own damn fault. "You can always text him. It's easier to be just friends over the phone."

"It hurts," I say, meaning the ache that's taken up residence behind my sternum and between my thighs.

"Exactly," Jen says. "It already hurts. It'll hurt when it ends, but it hurts now too. So why not have some of the good parts too?"

The door snicks closed behind her, and I turn back to my prep. I have a million plastic bottles to fill with paint for our paint pouring projects. I unscrew the top of the black, hold the bottle tight in my left hand and lift the paint can with my right. It seeps out in shining ribbons, falling into the neck of the bottle. I fill it about halfway and then move to the next one.

The game was significantly more fun than I'd expected. The after had been even better.

Paint oozes over my hand and down onto the counter, shocking me with how cold it is. I sigh, put everything down, and reach for a rag to wipe up the mess. I toss the paint-stained cloth into the large ceramic sink and reach for a clean one to wipe my hands. There's a large spot of dark, wet color on my chest, but at least tempera paint is washable and I always wear an apron. The new rag is rough against my skin as I scrub off as much as I can. I'll wash the rest later.

Erik's cheek had been rough under my palm when I cupped it in my hand. Rougher still when he'd rubbed it across the sensitive skin of my stomach and the inner surface of my thighs.

I drop the rag, bend to pick it up, and slam my head into the tiny overhang from the counter. I barely avoid cursing—sound travels in the old building and knowing my luck Kelly's third graders will already be lined up outside my door—and I rub at the spot on the crown of my head, remembering too late that I'm still covered in paint.

I don't have time to dig one of the small self-portrait mirrors out of the supply closet, so I have to grab a fresh rag and hope the paint isn't that noticeable. It would have been better if I'd spilled orange. At least that would have blended in with my hair. I'm definitely going to get comments from the students, but I have more bottles to fill before they file into my room. If he were here, Graham would have led the pack in teasing. That kid had had an eye roll never before seen in nature.

Erik had been good with kids. His whole job involved working with pediatric patients dealt an incredibly lousy hand.

I reach for the blue paint and promptly stub my foot against the drawers that hold extra paper. My big toe pulses with white hot pain. Stubbed appendages always hurt way worse than they have a right to. No one likes stubbed toes, but I can't help but wonder if Erik misses them.

I've come full circle. Not thinking about Erik is impossible. I've already proven that I don't have the willpower to avoid his memory. Each time I think of him, I maim myself, spill something, or cause myself more work. I'm inclined to believe that the universe is telling me not to think about Erik at all, except these accidents are causing me to think about him more. Something isn't working.

I could text him, I think, as I switch paint colors to fill up the rest of the bottles.

Something simple to open the door for ongoing communication, I think, as I set the paint and mini canvases out on the tables.

We had fun together, I tell myself as my first class creates chaotic swirls of paint that drip off the end of their canvases into small trays below.

I liked him, I remember, as I help slide wet art onto the metal drying racks and promise the class they can see their finished projects during their next art block.

I wish we'd gone to dinner, I admit, as the kids wash their hands, pile their smocks, and line up to go back to their classrooms.

"Screw it," I say and reach into my pocket for my phone. My principal has okayed my request to keep it on my person—on vibrate—just in case something happens with

Dad. His doctor's office prefers direct access to me in case of an emergency. Technically, this is pushing my agreement with my boss, but there are no students in the room, and I'm going to be distracted until I get this over with.

I swipe my phone open and my stomach pitches again when I notice no new messages. This is even more reason to do this. I'm used to my stomach pitching with nerves and fear when I have missed calls. Calls that could have come from the hospital or the oncologist. I'm not used to disappointment that stems from no one texting me. Usually no one does text me. My friends are all at school too or working. When would they have time to text?

I open my messages and navigate to Erik's number.

What if he didn't want me to contact him? What if that's why he's quiet? What if I'd just been a diversion while he was away, and when I rejected his offers to see me again, he had pushed me completely from his mind? What if I'm about to make an idiot of myself?

But what if I'm wrong? What if he hadn't texted me because I'd told him not to? What if he'd felt even a fraction of the connection I did? What if he's thinking about me, too? What if we could still be friends even if we never have anything physical?

My fingers tap at the keys from muscle memory and I hit "send" before I can talk myself out of it. Either he'll be receptive to hearing from me and I'll get a response, or he won't and I won't. I slide the phone back into the pocket of my black pants and turn back to the prep for my next class. I will not think about Erik anymore. Not even a little. Not even at all.

I'm the worst liar.

12 ERIK

If I had put money on the idea that being back at work would help distract me from thoughts of my week away, I'd be a sore loser. Nothing can erase the memory of Quinn. Which is ridiculous. It was one weekend with one woman. A high-stress weekend at that. My inability to think about anyone or anything else must be based on surging levels of cortisol. The same reason so many people fall in love during times of crisis.

Yesterday I did rounds at Lurie Children's, talking with a handful of my patients who had been admitted and needed a little extra support. Today I'm back at the office, stationed behind my massive wooden desk, and wishing I was sitting in a cramped plastic seat at a hockey rink. Definitely not something I thought I'd feel. Not again.

It has been one hundred and twelve hours since I met Quinn Cooper, one hundred and eight since I made her cum. Ninety-four since I last saw her, and twenty-four hours since my phone vibrated with a message from her. A message that contained two simple words that rocked me on my axis.

Quinn Cooper:

> I'm sorry

I had a response typed up before my heart started beating again. Then I deleted it and retyped it, deleted it and retyped it, deleted it and retyped it until I could imagine even my brother rolling his eyes and threatening to send it for me. So right there, in a hospital lounge—which seems fitting given where she'd halted things—I sent my reply.

Erik Varg:

> It's okay

And then... nothing. Should I text her again? I feel like a fucking teenager worrying about the girl I like. I should be able to just type a message and send it. I'm a goddamn adult. But she'd been cagey when I asked before. I can't push her on this. Not if I want any part of her.

I'm pretty sure this message is an olive branch to reopen our lines of communication, but the no response... I know from some of my teenage patients that double texting reeks of desperation. I don't want to misinterpret her choice to reach out. Maybe she was being friendly. Maybe she was tying up loose ends. Feeling guilty—although she had no need to—over how we'd left things between us.

I'd have much rather spent the weekend wrapped up in her, face buried in the cushion of her cleavage, but I don't blame her for taking a step back. And in the end, it worked out. I had dinner with my brother and our mom, and now she's texted me. Once. I'll take it.

I shuffle some papers on my desk and check my email for the tenth time in the last five minutes. I spin my chair in a circle, something I only do when I'm feeling stressed. I like the head rush I get as the world blurs around me, air whipping at my face. For just a moment, I'm ten years old again and spinning on the metal death trap of a merry-go-round at the local playground. Clinging on for dear life, hoping I won't be the one catapulted into the damp wood chips. At least not before my twin.

"Hey Erik," Kenzie leans around my door frame, and I use my foot to bring the chair to a slow stop.

She's one of the newer therapists in the practice, and as a senior member it's my job to make her feel welcome, but all I can think right now is that her hair is the wrong shade of red. Darker than Quinn's, more of a dark cherry color that gleams under the overhead lights.

"It's nice to have you back." Her smile shows straight white teeth, the product of the right dentist and orthodontic appointments combined with good genetics, and I smile at her because it's the polite thing to do.

"It's good to be back."

It isn't a lie. Loki enjoys having his human servant back, and it's nice to be sleeping in my bed instead of at a hotel. The weather even cooperated for my flight. Cold and clear, but several degrees above frigid.

"I know it's Tuesday, but some of us were thinking about heading to Gino's for dinner and a drink."

My gut reaction is to say "no." I'm not opposed to colleague bonding time, but accepting an invitation from Kenzie just feels… wrong. I open my mouth to turn her down, aware that if she'd been anyone else—like Carl from the next office over—I'd have said "yes," and it's that thought that stops me from turning Kenzie down flat.

"Sure," I say, "I like Gino's." Because who doesn't like a good Italian place with plentiful antipasto and an excellent wine list?

"Great!" Kenzie tucks a strand of her hair behind her ear and her blue eyes peek up at me from under her lashes. I wait for the coquettish look to do something for me. It doesn't. "I feel like we've worked together for months and I barely know you. We're walking over around five. See you then."

She's gone before I can say something like "this is just a work thing, right?" So I pick up my phone and type out a message to Quinn. I just want to let her know I'll be unavailable this evening, but then I don't send it. I don't know if the reason I delete the words is that I will, in fact, be available if she calls—no matter what I'm doing—or if it's because it feels strange to account for my whereabouts when she hasn't asked. Would it sound like I was bragging? I have plans? Definitely not thinking about you? I definitely am.

Two hours later, I'm stepping into the wood-paneled bar in Logan Square. Gino's leans into its rumored historical mafia connections. Gold wall sconces cast orange light over the tufted leather booths, old black and white photos and newspaper clippings hang on the walls. The ambiance is good. The menu is even better.

Carl and Kenzie are sitting in a booth at the back of the restaurant. Carl has his phone out, no doubt showing off photos of his five-year-old twins doing something most five-year-olds do. Kenzie sips a blood-red cocktail and peruses her menu, and my limbs feel heavy as I walk toward the table. I don't see anyone else, but there are still a few empty seats. Maybe everyone else is running late. Kenzie looks up and waves. She smiles as I slide into the booth next to her. For a moment our thighs brush, my dress pants against her tailored slacks, and then I shift to put some space between them.

A waiter in a slick white shirt and red tie stops by and I order a rum and coke. I tune out the conversation around me as Kenzie orders apps for the table. School break is coming up and Carl's both jazzed about and terrified of the vacation his family is taking down to a theme park in Florida. Kenzie has gone every year since she was three. She now takes her niece.

There had been no budget for vacation in my family. Not with two hockey players and a figure skater who all needed gear, skates, ice time, coaches. Seasons had been grueling, and we spent the off-season conditioning. When I got sick, treatment had eaten up all the extra money and time. After he was signed, Vic started going on long vacations during the off seasons. He always took Mom and Anna with him. For years I had a standing invite but after repeated excuses they stopped asking.

I can't remember the last time I went on a family vacation. I can't remember the last time I went somewhere intending to spend time with my family. Even my most recent trip to Quarry Creek had been about a favor I could do for Vic, not about seeing him. Or my mother. I can't remember the last time that bothered me. It does now.

Maybe this year I'll invite myself. Just for a few days. Maybe I'll book a flight out to Colorado to see Anna. Maybe it doesn't have to be the off-season. Maybe I can just go back out to see Vic and Mom. Just for a few days.

Does Quinn ever go on vacation with her dad?

The waiter reappears with trays of cured meats, green and purple olives, yellow and green pepperoncini, an assortment of cheeses, artichoke hearts, and small marinated mushrooms. He also holds a basket with golden slices of crusty bread, steam still looping into the air. I haven't eaten anything since breakfast and my stomach rumbles as Kenzie passes me one of the white ceramic plates.

"I guess it's just us three," she says. Her eyes won't meet mine as she stares down at her drink. On her other side, Carl's phone buzzes an intense staccato, shaking on the tabletop in its fury.

He stuffs a piece of prosciutto into his mouth as he picks up his phone. I try not to eavesdrop. I do, but Carl is at the same table and he isn't a quiet person. From the side of the conversation I can hear, it's pretty obvious that one twin is sick, and he's needed at home stat.

"I'm sorry guys," Carl fishes a handful of bills from his pocket and throws them down on the table. It's more than his third of the food, but Carl grabs his briefcase and is out the door before I can return half the cash.

"Should we turn in?" I'm willing to throw some bills down too and call it a night. I have nothing else to do—going home means sitting in my living room alone with my cat—but I'm hoping Kenzie gives me the out.

"Or we could stay," she offers. "No reason to waste the food when we've already ordered."

It makes sense, especially when I consider the fact that I haven't gone grocery shopping since flying home. My fridge might have some old orange juice, maybe a questionable yogurt, and a molding takeout container.

I could stay. Just to eat and talk to a colleague. Nothing weird about that. No reason to feel like I need to call and apologize to Quinn, as if I'm doing something inappropriate. This isn't a date. Kenzie is a friend—well, a colleague—and it isn't like either of us planned for Carl to leave. There's no need for guilt either, because even if this were a date, Quinn and I aren't even seeing each other. We'd had a memorable twenty-four hours, and that's it.

I'm not twenty anymore. Mooning over some woman I just met isn't the thing people my age do.

I nod at Kenzie and she beams back. Her mouth is painted a bright red, and she has a heavy line of dark makeup around her light blue eyes. Her lashes are thick and long, almost too full to look natural. In the dim light of the restaurant, the subtle sparkle over her eyelids shimmers. She is a gorgeous woman. I know that. The waiter knows that—his wandering eyes give him away each time he comes to the table.

Hell, even Carl, who's fiercely in love with his wife and daughters, knows that Kenzie is beautiful. Her artfully applied makeup enhances the parts she wants enhanced, but the dark fringe of her eyelashes only makes me think of the copper shadow of Quinn's. Kenzie's blue eyes, made bigger and more dramatic with liner, only make me think of Quinn's green eyes. No matter how beautiful the woman in front of me is, I can't stop thinking only of Quinn.

If Quinn wears makeup for special occasions, I bet she uses bright and unusual colors. I bet she's the type of person who draws little designs in her eye liner. Anna used to watch videos of people doing unique makeup looks involving flowers and butterflies and geometric designs. I couldn't draw half the things they did on paper, let alone on someone's face—definitely not on my own—but I bet Quinn can.

"Erik?" I've missed something. Kenzie is leaning into me, and I can see the faint smile lines around the corners of her eyes. She's chewing on her bottom lip as she waits for me to respond.

"Sorry," I try to tune back into her face and the conversation. I can spend hours focusing on what my patients have to say. I can get through one meal without my mind wandering off. "Can you repeat that?"

Kenzie's face falls just the tiniest bit, but she asks about my trip once more.

"It was great." I will not mention Quinn. "We made some good progress with Grace Hospital, and it was nice to see my brother."

I'm surprised to find that I mean it. It had been nice to spend a whole evening watching British baking shows with my twin. It had also been fun to see Vic play in person. And not just because I got to meet…well, it had been fun for more than one reason.

"I hope you had a chance to relax." Kenzie pops an olive into her mouth, holding her hand in front of her face as she chews. "Our line of work can be stressful on anyone, but your caseload is uniquely challenging."

It is challenging, but it's necessary. Therapy isn't just letting people unload their problems and their hardships at a therapist's feet. It's a conscious effort by both parties to create healthy ways to manage and minimize behaviors, pain, stress, trauma, or other mental health difficulties. For my patients, the pain and fear and unfairness of a diagnosis plays a role in sessions—of course it does—but my job is about more than that. I help my patients see their value and their sense of self outside of cancer. I help them find healthy coping mechanisms and boundaries that they can enforce to ensure that the big C doesn't take over every single facet of who they are.

"I caught the hockey game while I was there," I say, and Kenzie gives me a small smile.

"That's nice. I'm not really much of a hockey fan." She sounds almost apologetic, but I don't mind that she isn't a fan. "Did your brother go too?"

"Something like that." I say and reach for my drink.

The bartender was heavy-handed with the rum, and it burns a warm path down my throat to sit in my stomach like a little heater. This isn't as intense as scotch or whiskey, but it still leaves a pleasant heat in its wake. I don't drink rum often, but this isn't bad. I could send Quinn a picture of my drink and tell her I'm thinking of her even now. Except it would be rude to pull my phone out and message someone else when Kenzie and I are the only two here. That would be....

My phone buzzes in my pocket and it takes superhuman skills to reach for the device as if I'm simply curious to see who's messaged me, and not ripping apart at the seams hoping it was Quinn. Knowing my luck it's SPAM or something from the APA about professional development, but there's her name across the front of my screen and I'm trying for nonchalance even as my fingers turn white from the way I'm clutching at my phone, and I can't breathe, and I can't think, and my pulse is pounding in my ears like a drumbeat.

The screen goes dark and I swipe it open on instinct. I pause. I know for a fact that if Quinn wants to open up a real conversation right now, I'll be worthless company. I don't open her message, but I don't take my eyes off the little red notification bubble.

"I'm so sorry, Kenzie," I fish my wallet out. "Something's come up." I'm still staring at my phone as I throw several bills on the table. Between my contribution and Carl's, Kenzie is more than covered.

"It's okay," she says. "We can do a rain check, just you and me."

It's the end that breaks through my Quinn-induced haze. All of my worry over the appropriateness of going tonight hits me again with the force of a six-foot-three, two-hundred-and-eighty-five pound defender. My subconscious picked up on the signals even though I missed them. I'd even studied her makeup earlier and was too distracted by thoughts of Quinn to figure it out. Kenzie didn't just organize dinner and drinks with her coworkers. She was interested in dinner and drinks with me.

A week ago, I would have said I wasn't looking for anything serious. Now I don't know what I'm looking for, just that I'm not looking for it with Kenzie. I owe her a definitive answer.

"I don't think that's a good idea." I say, channeling my soothing session voice. "I didn't think of this as a date, Kenzie. You're smart and kind and I enjoy working with you, but I'm not looking to date you."

"You have a girlfriend?" She smiles, but it looks a little wobbly.

"No."

Quinn is not my girlfriend, no matter how interested I am. But also, turning someone down because of a relationship can send the wrong message. It can send the "if only I wasn't in a relationship with someone else, I'd gladly be in one with you," message, and it isn't fair to Kenzie, or to me, to leave that open for interpretation. "I'm just not interested. I'm sorry."

"Well, I guess I can't fault you for being honest," she says and flips her hair back over her shoulder. "And you can't blame a girl for trying. See you at the office tomorrow."

STELLA STEVENSON

Text Message
Tuesday, 6:32 PM CST

Quinn Cooper:

> I just saw Graham and he asked where Rick was. Didn't have the heart to correct him.

> So I guess that's your name now. Rick.

Erik Varg:

> Good name. Sturdy. An honor to be named by a kid with such conviction.

> Where did you see him? I thought he wasn't one of your students?

> I already updated your contact information, Rick Varg.

> Awe that's cute. Rick & Vic.

> He was at the grocery store with his mom and siblings. Looked at me like I was a dog walking on two legs.

ON ICE

> As he should. Didn't anyone ever tell you that teachers need to live at school?

But I'm not *his* teacher.

Does he even know I'm a teacher?

> He obviously knows everything.

> Maybe he thought you lived at The Stand.

You're right. Graham is definitely omniscient.

> Except for the time he made fun of reading.

Even a running clock is wrong twice a day.

> I don't think that's the saying.

It is now.

> Fair enough.

> I'll update my lexicon with your malapropism.

It's not a malapropism, you've just never heard it before. Not my fault.

> Quinn. Babe. Sweetheart. Darling. Honey. The correct phrase is...

> Even a BROKEN clock is RIGHT twice a day.

The pet names were incredibly condescending.

> That was the point. Bow to my superior knowledge of clock phrases.

You wish.

> Kneel before your Lord and Master! His intelligence shall reign forever for his brain is so smart.

ON ICE

If I got on my knees again, pretty sure I'd be the one in charge.

Rick?

Erik?

> Sorry. You need to warn a guy before sending visuals like that.

Lol. You make it sound like I sent you photos of my kitty.

> Don't say things like that either.

> Your wit is only making you even more attractive, Cooper.

> Is that Tesseract? What a sweet fluffy loaf.

> This is Loki.

> What are the odds that we'd both have feline foot warmers right now?

> Considering they're cats and we're both sitting at home right now? Fairly high.

ON ICE

> I hope I didn't interrupt any big plans you and the trickster God may have had for the evening.

> You didn't.

> I'd rather talk to you than him anyway.

> Charmer

> Only with you, Quinn. Only with you

13 QUINN

I let the door slam behind me as I step into my childhood home. Framed school photos from elementary through high school line the long hallway. There's the photo with my missing three front teeth, where I insisted on sticking my tongue out through the holes as the camera flashed. There's the photo where I tried to cover a massive pimple on my forehead with a neon pink bandage. The photo where I cut my hair into a bob and instead of looking sleek and sophisticated, my thick curls ballooned out from my face, turning me into a yield sign.

The reusable grocery bags cut into the skin on my forearms, but it's a matter of personal pride to carry everything inside in one trip. I place them on the spotted Formica counters and start unloading the food. Dad's fridge is almost empty, so it's a good thing I stopped on the way over. All he has is a package of string cheese, some deli meat, and two silver cans of Diet Coke. Before chemo, Dad had stocked the fridge with a local IPA. He usually only had one or two while watching the Arctic, never to excess, and his grumbling had surprised me when I poured the remaining cans down the sink. Beer might not be expressly forbidden, but chemo and alcohol could not be a good combination. Someone has to be an adult about all of this.

"Hey Quinnie," Dad calls out as I stack yogurts in the fridge. Plain Greek yogurt, low in sugar. Dad will complain, but Susan at the treatment center swore it was one of the few things she'd stomached during her worst bouts of nausea.

"In the kitchen," I call back, sliding a cardboard container of steel-cut oats into the cabinet that serves as pantry space.

The builder-grade oak cabinets are the same as they've always been, with the same ornate brass pulls. Some of my old drawings are still stuck to the front of the small white fridge. I'm pretty sure they're from my middle school era, if the sketches of horses painstakingly created with various ovals are any sign. I think it was sixth grade when I started caring about proportion in my drawings. They're held up by the Santa magnets Dad still collects. I've given him one every Christmas since I was maybe two or three. Now he leaves them up all year long and I've had to get creative finding new designs.

"Tell me you didn't buy me groceries." He busses my cheek as he shuffles into the room and sits heavily on one of his dining chairs. He's wearing a pair of Velcro sandals with white crew socks, the same combo he's been wearing my whole life, and I can't explain why I suddenly have a lump in my throat.

"Just eggs, avocado, oatmeal, some almonds and pumpkin seeds. There's some chicken noodle soup Jen and I made, and a head of broccoli. Oh, and there's Greek yogurt in there with honey in the cabinet."

"Thanks Quinnie." He shifts to pull his wallet out of his sweatpants. "How much do I owe you?"

I wave him off. "Nothing. I was already out and about, and I don't mind."

I pick up the smallest metal pot and add six eggs before filling it with cold water from the tap. I let the water run until the eggs are submerged, then put it on the ancient stove. The igniter clicks when I try to turn the gas on, and nothing happens. I turn it back off, wait a few seconds, then try again. Blue flames softly lick the underside of the pot, and I look around for the lid.

"Quinnie," my dad's voice is gentle, but it doesn't disguise his frown.

"I'm just going to boil some of these up for you so they're easy to grab. I know your fingers have been bothering you recently, especially when touching cold things, so I'll peel them before I go." According to my research, heat sensitivity is a common side effect. I've started keeping a pair of gloves in my purse, just in case he needs them.

"Quinn," Dad says again, and I turn my attention back to the stove. Tiny bubbles are forming along the bottom of the pot, but it's nowhere near boiling yet. "I appreciate everything you do for me, but it's not your job to take care of me, baby girl."

"I know." I say.

I don't want to talk about this. Why won't the damn pot boil or something?

"How would you feel if I showed up at your house with groceries and stocked your fridge? Or came over after work and swept and mopped your living room? Or sent Uncle Harvey to do it?"

"I wouldn't mind." The lie tastes bitter in my mouth. We both know that having someone in my personal space, touching my things, doing jobs I'd planned on doing without consulting me first, would drive me absolutely insane. But even though I'd hate it, I can still recognize when someone does something out of love. Even if I don't want it done ever again.

"You would mind. Probably kick me and Harv right out of the house with clear instructions not to return without calling first." Dad laughs. "And you'd probably donate all the groceries I brought you to the local food pantry just to prove you didn't need the help."

"It's not the same," I say.

The pot has reached a rolling boil now and I take the distraction, covering it with the lid before turning down the heat and setting the timer on the back of the stove.

"Why not, Quinnie?" Dad's hands come down heavy on my shoulders. I didn't hear him move from the table, but here he is, standing behind me. The skin over his fingers is paler than I'm used to, the skin almost loose as the tendons stand out. Dad's hands look old. Older than my memories. Almost frail.

I turn around, dislodging his grip, and wrap my arms around his waist. It's hard to bury my face into his chest like I used to as a kid. I duck my head into his shoulder. He still smells the same, like amber and cardamom and aftershave. My eyes burn and I squeeze them shut. I must have spent too long staring into the steaming pot of water because I'm not about to cry. Not now. Not in front of my dad.

"You know why." I mumble the words into his t-shirt.

He pulls me in closer, arms flexing against my back. He's thinner than before, his shoulder blades delicate under my touch. My nose tingles like I need to sneeze, and a tear leaks from the corner of one eye. Dammit. No.

"I'm sick," Dad says and no matter how I lock my muscles and order myself not to, I can't hold in the sob that tumbles out. "I'm sick, but I'm getting better."

He rocks me back and forth as more tears escape onto the gray cotton of his shoulders. I hope he can't feel the wet against his neck, but he probably can. Either way, it's not like he doesn't know I'm crying. My whole body shakes as I try to stifle the sobs.

I'm not supposed to be doing this. I promised myself I would not make this—cancer, chemo, surgery—about me. I'm not the one fighting. I promised that he'd never see me cry, not unless they're happy tears. I failed. We have months to go and I failed him. Dad murmurs something against my hair, soothing words I can't make out, but the cadence of them helps. He's comforting me. It's supposed to be the other way around, but I can't bring myself to step away. I just let my dad hold me like I'm five years old again and wipe my nose on the cotton of his shirt.

"I know the treatments have been hard on both of us," he says long after the timer has gone off and my sobs dissolve into sniffles.

Dad reaches behind me to turn off the stove, but the eggs are most definitely ruined. I couldn't even do that right for him. Boiling eggs is about as simple as it gets. I feel the tears pool again and I suck in a watery breath.

"I'm exhausted and my stomach is off," Dad says. "I ache, and my brain doesn't always work the way I want it to."

"I j-just want to h-h-help." More tears clog my throat, "I c-can take care of th-th-things for you." I need to. If I could shrink down and fight the cancer cells myself I would, but I can't. This is what I can do. I can make sure he's fed and comfortable. I can make sure he can focus on getting better instead of worrying about errands. If I focus all my energy on what I can do, then I won't have time to think about what I can't. I won't have to think about what happens if... none of this works.

What if the treatment doesn't work?

What if he doesn't get better?

What if one day he isn't here?

"You have always done more than you have to, Quinnie." Dad rubs my back in big, sweeping circles. "It is not your job to take care of me. You are my child. If I need help you have to trust me to ask for it. And to ask the right people. It won't always be you, Quinn. It shouldn't be."

"But your groceries—"

"Can be delivered."

"Cleaning—"

"I can still work the vacuum, and Harv knows how to work it, too."

"So you can ask Harvey for help, but not me?" I sound like a brat, I know I do, but I can't help it.

"He's my brother. You're my baby." He pulls me in even tighter. "All I want from you Quinn, is for you to still live your life and be happy. Spend time with your old man when you want to, but don't let this one hiccup halt your life."

"It's not a hiccup," How can he even say something like that? How can he be so cavalier? My tears morph into anger. "It's cancer, Dad. The reoccurrence rate—"

"I know," he says, "But you were there Quinn. You were there after the surgery when the doctors said they got the tumor. You were there when they said they had clean margins. You were there when they told you that removing my bladder helped to keep it from spreading outward into my body. You were there when the scans came back and showed nothing had metastasized. I can't get through this worrying about it coming back. I can only focus on what we know right now. Right now, chemo is preventative. Right now we're okay."

I push out of Dad's arms and turn my attention back to the stove. I carry the pot to the sink and drain the water, dropping each egg into a bowl of ice. They will be horribly overcooked, but I don't care. I can't just throw them away. I rinse and clean the pot, drying it with a kitchen towel. I put it back in the cabinet and lean my forearms on the counter. If I look at my dad right now, I don't know if I'll cry or scream.

He's so calm about all of this. Like cancer doesn't kill. Like people don't suffer complications in hospitals all the time. Like he isn't the only person I have left. Sure, there's Uncle Harvey and his newest wife, Mary, but I didn't grow up with them. They lived out of state when I was young and I grew up in the era before video calls. I had known Harvey from photos and the Christmas and birthday cards he mailed. They are nice enough, but it isn't the same.

Jen is wonderful too, but we've only worked together for a few years. Jen is younger than me and not only does she have her own family, but she basically has a second family in her best-friend-since-birth Sofia Hill. The truth is, beyond work and my dad, I'm on my own. I don't mind, really, I don't. I enjoy spending my weekends reading. I like being at home. I'm not sure that's much of a life to get back to.

"I can't just pretend this isn't happening, Dad."

I pull one of the eggs out of the ice bath and rub it over a paper towel, pressing down with the palm of my hand to crack the shell. It comes apart in almost two parts, but the stubborn little pieces rip off chunks of the white and I have a sudden urge to throw the egg as hard as I can at the closest wall. It's already ruined. Why even bother peeling them? I breathe in through my nose and out through my mouth then pick up the next one.

"I'm not asking you to pretend it isn't happening, but I would rather that we spend time together like we used to do. I'm your dad, Quinnie. Not your patient."

"The Arctic has a home game coming up." My words have a mind of their own. "I can see if I can get a ticket and we can go together."

Dad sucks in a breath and drops his chin to his chest. For a moment I'm sure I've messed it all up. That when he said he wanted to spend time with me that didn't include hockey. Why would it? I've never shown an interest before. I'm about to offer something, anything, different when he says, "I'd like that Quinn," and the tension leaks out of my body.

Of course I offered too fast and don't know how to get a ticket, but how hard can it be? Dad only has the one. A quick check online shows nothing available in Dad's section. Maybe he'd be okay sitting somewhere else. I can swing two last-minute tickets in the three-hundreds. Erik calls them the nosebleeds, but that has to be an exaggeration, right?

Erik.

I can text Erik. Maybe his family owns the season ticket he'd used or knows who does. If it's owned by the team maybe his connections can get me in touch with them to buy it. Whatever the price, it will be worth it. I'll even leave my e-book at home.

I take out the cleaning solution and spray down my dad's counter. Erik has an important job and I'm pretty sure he keeps regular hours. I don't want to bother him at work. Not while I'm asking him a favor. I grab a paper towel to wipe down the counter and hear my dad say my name. There's a sigh in his voice and I drop the paper towel and spray. I just agreed to stop doing things for him and I'm already going back to my old ways.

"Sorry," I say. "It's instinctive."

"You don't have to apologize," Dad says. "This is going to be a change for both of us. I've let you be the parent for longer than I should."

"Will you still keep me updated on everything?" I ask, trying not to let my voice shake. There have been enough tears for one morning.

"Of course." He chucks me under my chin. "I'm not trying to box you out. I'm trying to make sure the time we spend together isn't all about cancer. I heard from a reliable source that it's important for both of us to have a support system separate from each other. We can't lean only on each other or we'll both break."

There is no need for me to feel like my own dad is dumping me. In theory I can understand what he's saying. In reality, it sucks to hear that I'm not enough. And okay, that isn't exactly what he said, but that's what it feels like right now.

"Who's your all-important source?" I ask. Who had been the one to tell my dad he doesn't need my help anymore? Doesn't need me?

"The hospital is working on a program that provides therapy hours for pediatric oncology patients. When I learned about the program, I asked the hospital for a reference to get a therapist of my own." Dad pulls a business card out from underneath a knit Santa magnet with moveable arms. "Give them a call. I bet they'd have someone you can talk to, too."

"That's—" I want to hold on to my mad, no matter how irrational. I want to say I don't need a therapist. I'm not the one with cancer, I'm just the loved one left at home. The one terrified about the future and aware that I can't ever say anything. But a therapist for my dad is a good option. I'm not a professional and he deserves all the love and support he can find. And something about this sounds familiar. "That's Erik's program," I say and Dad winks.

"Like I said, reliable."

STELLA STEVENSON

Text Message
Friday, 12:15 PM EST

Quinn Cooper:

> Hey, quick question when you have a minute.

Erik Varg:

> Quick answer anytime.

> Cute. That's cute. Adorable.

> But seriously.

> I try.

> What do you need?

> Your seat for the Arctic game...

> It was a great seat.

> Good company. 10/10 recommend.

ON ICE

> Is it your family's seat? Your mom's maybe? The team's? Or did you buy it from someone on the internet since it was last minute, and you needed to go?

> My dad is going to the game this weekend. And I offered to go too. Sitting with him is kind of the whole point but he only has the one ticket.

> If it's yours or your family's I'd like to buy it from you. For this game.

> Please.

> It's not mine or my mom's. She watches from the box when she goes.

> Oh.

> Okay then. No worries. Hope you have a good day.

Friday, 12:59 PM EST

Erik Varg:

> I need your email address.

Quinn Cooper:

> ArtsyFartsy@gmail.com

> Don't laugh.

> Never out loud.

> You should get an email from Andrea Mills. If it hasn't come through by the end of the day let me know. Andrea isn't great with technology but I can ask Vic to give her a hand.

> Um sure. I'll look for an email from a woman I've never met.

> She's my brother's neighbor.

> His neighbor. Okay. Super clear now

> Trust me, Quinn.

> I do.

ON ICE

Text Message
Friday, 7:43 PM EST

Quinn Cooper:

> OMG

> Erik is this for real?

Erik Varg:

> Is what for real? The insane hairball Loki left on my bathmat? Yes. Unfortunately, it is.

> Gross Erik.

> You mean 'Gross Loki.' He's the one who did it.

> You're the one who overshared.

> but that's not what I meant...

> Andrea's the one who owns the ticket.

> How much do I owe her?

> Don't worry about it, Cooper. I have it handled.

Erik

Quinn

Erik

Quinn

> I thought you were busy or maybe I'd bored you off. Instead, you got exactly what I needed.

> I'm never too busy for you.

> I'm never bored talking to you.

> You can trust me to come through for you

> It just took me a minute to call my mom and ask her to talk to Andrea. I'm sorry you thought I'd left.

> You called your mom? I'm flattered.

You should be. She thought I was dying when I called, there were tears.

But when I explained why I was asking....

Our Save the Dates are going out tomorrow. Hope you like summer weddings.

> I can do summer. We have to get married in the off-season anyway. My dad would never miss a game.

That's a joke right?

He would never miss your wedding. No matter when you decide to walk down the aisle.

> It's a joke. Promise.

> Besides, your twin can't miss a game either. We can get fake hitched in July.

If you could pick any month, when would it be?

> You mean if it wasn't you and me? I dunno. Maybe October.

> I love the fall. Like most other girls.

We can get married in the fall.

Fake married.

> Even without Vic?

Just name the day and I'll marry you with bells on.

> You're funny. Thanks for making me laugh.

> And thank you for the ticket.

> Just...thank you Erik.

14 ERIK

Saturday night finds me sitting on my over-stuffed couch and clicking through countless channels on my oversized television. I'm in a weird mood, the kind where I'm not happy, not sad, just kind of itchy in my skin. I start three separate shows before turning them off. Nothing is holding my interest, not a reality show, not a history channel show about survivalist skills, not a laugh-out-loud sitcom. I feel the same way about dinner. Nothing sounds appetizing. I pick through two different leftovers containers before settling on a sandwich and a handful of potato chips. Dinner of champions.

My leg is bothering me tonight too, a stab of awareness that centers in my non-existent left foot. I've already blown through my arsenal of tricks to diffuse the pins and needles arcing through my phantom limb, but I'm only able to dull the edges. I'm not a stranger to this type of discomfort. The phantom pain had been almost unbearable following surgery, but it had tapered down over the first few years of recovery. Now it seems to come back during moments of high stress. But I'm not stressed right now. It feels like I'm forgetting something important, but that's different from stress.

I just need a night to decompress. A night to stay in and do nothing, think about nothing, just catch up on the sleep I keep missing. Work has been steady. I'm caught up from my trip. There's no reason I feel so run down. I shoo Loki off the knee scooter parked next to the couch. It's not a great spot for him to sleep, not when I have to use it to get around. I took my leg off the minute I walked in the door, popping the suction and rolling down the sleeve. I've already hand washed my liner and put on my shrinker. I'm in for the night.

I miss Quinn.

I rub a hand over my chest, as though I can ease the strange ache blooming under my sternum. I noticed her the first moment we locked eyes—red hair crackling, green eyes resigned as she realized I'd seen her slip. I knew she was smart from the first words we'd traded back and forth—conversation flowing like perfectly timed passes. I knew walking away from her would be difficult the minute she pressed her full lips to mine and sucked on my tongue. I knew all of that and still hadn't known how off-center I'd feel between text messages. How I'd think of something random—house cats share 95.6% of their genetic makeup with tigers—and she'd be the first one I'd think of telling.

It is embarrassing and exhilarating and exhausting trying to sort through what I feel versus what I should feel. I shouldn't think of her, need to talk to her, every minute. Not after nine days. Nine days we hadn't even spent together. It didn't matter that we'd been texting. This was too much, too fast, and it was also exactly what it should be. I know that deep in my bones.

Grace Hospital wants me back for another set of meetings. They want my input as they interview candidates for the new department I helped create. I'm more than happy to help. I planned on calling into the meetings from here, leaving the hospital administration to take the lead. I'm worried they're leaning too heavily on my expertise and opinions instead of forming their own. I know I'm well-regarded in my field, but I can't run their department for them, not from Chicago. But now… now I suppose I can spare one more trip to Quarry Creek. I push away the sliver of guilt. Is it selfish to plan this trip even after telling myself the hospital needed to do this without me? Maybe. Am I going to do it anyway?

Maybe I'm looking at this all wrong. Maybe they can use the guidance. I can use one more trip to make sure they have this project in hand, instead of tossing them out onto a frozen lake and expecting them to find their balance before they crash through the ice.

My office will be closed Thursday and Friday while the building upgrades the security system. I've already moved my appointments. Emergency needs can always reach me by phone, and Jane handles weekend rounds so she can pick up anything local. I'm looking up flights and browsing the options before my brain can catch up. There's one out Wednesday night. I can give Grace Hospital Thursday and Friday, and then maybe stick around for an extra day and fly back Sunday. I book a seat and tap out a quick email to the hospital director before I can second guess myself.

This trip doesn't have to be about Quinn, although I won't lie and pretend she's not a big part of my desire to travel. I can see my mom. Maybe Vic too, unless he's on the road. I want to see them. How many times have I avoided my family? How many times have I made bullshit excuses? I can't take credit for helping Vic and my mom's pet project if I also can't bring myself to see them. That's pathetic of me. I'm a coward. I wouldn't have seen Vic beyond the arena if he hadn't let himself into my hotel room and even then I bitched at him. It's time to grow the fuck up and do something about this cavern I've carved out between us.

If Quinn wants to see me, great. If not…that's okay. I have no expectations here. Just an opportunity. Even if it looks desperate. I'll see my mother and do my job, and that's why I'm going. An email pings into my inbox. The hospital is ecstatic that I'll be in town.

It feels good to be spontaneous. It even feels good to think about seeing my family, about taking steps myself instead of waiting for them to ask. They don't put pressure on me for visits or phone calls. Whether we're hundreds or tens of miles apart, they've let me bail on so many family functions. No pressure to be a part of their unit. They never need to know that when I say I'm busy, sometimes I mean at home with my cat.

It was never fear that kept me distant, but there was, is, a constant ache of worry and anger. Worry they will treat me like they did when I was bed-bound and sick. A sort of smothering love that made me feel like every piece of what made me Erik had fractured off and disintegrated while I watched until all that was left behind was cancer and chemo and surgery and crushed dreams. Like I was both a toddler who needed coddling, and an adult who needed to hold it together for everyone else.

I couldn't afford to show how scared I was, how much I hurt. My brother needed to focus on hockey. Anna had college. My mother was holding on by the edges of her fingernails. For a while, it had been easier to want them to leave me alone. Stop touching me. Don't look at me like that. No, I'm not fucking okay. I don't think I'll ever be fucking okay again. Why do I have to be the strong one? We can't all fall apart.

And then when they listened... when they backed off.... Then I felt abandoned and lost and I let the distance grow.

I know now, after years of therapy and almost a decade of education, that it's common for families to struggle through a cancer diagnosis. The wedge I drove between us wasn't entirely my fault. It wasn't because I was a bad person, or because they failed me as supports. Illness is hard on everyone. Even when I'd wanted to yell and scream—how dare they cry? How dare they grieve like I was already dead when I was sitting right there and I was the only one fighting for each day? How dare my twin go off and play with the USHL as if nothing was wrong? How dare my mom sob in the hospital bathroom like she thought I couldn't hear? How dare Anna stay in school as if I didn't matter? — even as I'd lashed out, pain and fear clogging my brain, I'd still known they loved me. I only hope they know the same. I should make sure they know the same.

I dial Mom's cellphone and she answers on the second ring. She's a little out of breath and hard to hear over the weird roar of sound in the background.

"Are you in a tunnel?" I ask in greeting.

"Erik?"

Her surprise hits me like a punch to the gut, even though it shouldn't. I don't call her. Ever. If I want to do this, make changes, it's going to be awkward until we both find our footing.

"Yeah, it's me. What are you up to?"

There's a long pause. She doesn't want to tell me, and my brain clicks into place so I know what she's going to say before she says it. I flinch automatically, not because it hurts, but because it used to.

"I'm in the box." At The Stand.

I forgot Vic had a game tonight. Normally, forgetting wouldn't be a strange occurrence. I only keep a cursory eye on Vic's and the Arctic's stats during the season. I don't watch their games or track their schedules. I should have remembered tonight's game because of Quinn. I'd been the one to get her Andrea's ticket. I'd called Mom for that too, another call with awkward pauses and false starts. We do so much better over text. I should have just texted her... except no. I'm trying to make a change. That starts with the simplest steps. Like phone calls.

The background noise changes and Mom's voice is louder when she says my name again. "I just stepped outside. Is everything okay?"

I try not to bristle at the question. I know it's not a fair response. She's not trying to coddle me. She's asking because I don't normally call her, and this is the second time this week I've changed things up. Anyone would ask what was different. She's not asking about my last PET scan or counts. She's not asking because she thinks I'm sick. Her question is normal, just like how it raises my hackles. I take a deep breath and close my eyes, willing the frustration to bleed away.

"I'll be in town next week," I say. "I thought maybe we could spend some time together. Vic too once I check his schedule."

Mom sucks in a breath, her voice thick when she responds, "Vic is on the road over the weekend, but he's home all week." I can hear her smile even through the weird cell connection. "We can make up one of the guest rooms for you so you don't have to waste money on a hotel. If you want to. You don't have to. We... I know you like your privacy."

Even if the hospital wasn't going to cover my hotel, I could still afford it, but I also recognize the olive branch when it's thrust toward me.

"I have a reservation," I say, because I'm not ready to stay in their space, but we're taking baby steps together. We don't need to dwell on the fact that I could cancel the hotel.

"You're always welcome, Erik," Mom says. "We understand, but you're always welcome."

"How's the game?" I ask, desperate for a subject change.

"It's good. Your brother looks a little sluggish, but he's still doing okay. It's tied one-to-one right now." Even through the phone, the buzz from the arena is loud. "Never mind. Tampa just scored."

"It's still early," I say. "Plenty of time."

The conversation is petering out like it usually does. I don't know what to say and she doesn't want to push. Each silence gets longer and longer until discomfort sits on both of us like an anvil. Ending the call feels like a mercy, saving us both from the distance that we can't quite cross. I'm going to say goodbye. I'm going to hang up and count this call a success. I'll see her, and maybe Vic next week. I'll call Anna. I'll turn on the damn Arctic game and wait to see Quinn.

We'd made the broadcast last time. She's sure to be visible again.

"I saw your friend," Mom says and my brain blanks out like someone dipped it in Windex. "Quinn? Well, I didn't see her in person, but she's behind the bench, so the cameras have panned over her a few times."

"Does she—" I stop myself before I can ask if she has a book.

"She's not on a date. Just here with an older man. Her father?"

"Yeah, Sean. He owns the season ticket for the seat next to Andrea." I clear my throat. "She wanted to go see the game with him."

"How sweet," Mom says, and it's a leading statement. This is probably the only time I still know what my mother will do. She's waiting for me to agree with her, to open the door to the other things I like about Quinn Cooper. The list is long. My mom's determined to partner me up with someone, anyone. Determined to know that I'm not alone even as I hold myself apart. This is when our conversations always end. She asks about dates, I say nothing, and then we say goodbye. I don't want to say nothing about Quinn.

"Does she look happy?" I ask, swallowing past a lump in my throat. "Hockey isn't something she watches."

"And she still came with her father?" If I'm not careful, Mom really will plan our wedding. If I'm not careful, I'll let her. "She looked happy enough when they showed them last time. You can always text her."

I can, but that feels intrusive. I don't want her to think she owes me insight into her feelings. Seeing a smile, or hearing about it secondhand, is different. It's not sliding into her messages and demanding that she talk to me. Something she might feel obligated to do because of the ticket, even if she'd rather keep our distance.

Or maybe I'm wrong. Maybe I don't know how to communicate with anyone, not just with my family. I don't want distance from Quinn, but I don't think I get a choice.

"I'll let you get back to the game. Vic needs his good luck charm." I tell my mom instead.

"He does! I'll talk to you on Monday, and we're so excited to see you again! I love you." She hangs up the phone without waiting for my response. Ending the call like she has places and people to see. For the first time, I wonder if she might run off so fast because she's afraid I won't say it back. I should work on that.

I turn on my TV and flip through channels. I'm barely paying attention to what's on. The itchy feeling is back, and I want to dig my nails into my skin and scratch until I'm raw and bleeding. Until things are back to normal. I scroll right past a hockey game and either I'm a lucky bastard or I'm cursed because I backtrack just in time to see a closeup of the Arctic's bench. There's my brother, scowling and grumpy—his team is still trailing by one—and then there she is.

Quinn's red hair is up in two curling ponytails that swing around her ears. Ears covered with a baby blue fleece headband. My cheeks ache as I smile. I've never met anyone who wears so many layers in a hockey rink. It isn't all that cold inside, especially not surrounded by fans. No jersey tonight. She has on a baby blue hoodie with the howling wolf on the front, her hands shoved into the front pocket. My heart lurches at the sight of her, my mouth goes dry. Sean sits next to her. He has the knit hat and the jersey. Their heads are tipped together and yes, she's smiling. Right as the camera shifts, Quinn glances up, grinning right at the feed.

It's like someone is reaching right into my chest cavity, wrapping a fist around my heart, and squeezing.

The puck drops and focus is once again on the gameplay. I see my brother hit the ice and take possession. Mom's right. He's a little sluggish in his movements. Almost like his left leg isn't keeping up with his right. He probably overdid it at practice, but he's working through it. It wouldn't be noticeable to someone who isn't his twin or his mother or his teammate. Vic's center takes a shot from the top of the crease and Tampa's goalie holds the puck.

My phone buzzes.

Quinn Cooper:

> Thank you again, Erik. I hope you get to watch some of the game too.

The only thing stopping me from jumping to my feet at her name on my screen is the cat curled into my lap. It's a good thing Loki's there, because without my leg on I'd have one-hundred percent eaten shit. Balance on one foot? I can do that. I've perfected hopping around my apartment when I don't want to grab the scooter. But a sudden launch off the couch? I'd be down for sure.

My heart is pounding in my throat and my stomach twists. Should I tell her about my trip? I want to. What if she isn't going to be in town? What if she doesn't want to see me? I haven't felt this nervous over something in… years. That's a lie. If I don't count any of my previous interactions with Quinn, it's been years. She has me tied up in knots every time I even think of her name. I'll tell her later. This isn't the right time. She's supposed to be enjoying the game.

> Just turned it on. Vic is slow as fuck tonight.

Be nice, Erik. He's doing his best.

Did you see me?

> It's a big arena, Quinn. How on earth would I find you?

Of course I've seen her. Of course I know where she is. Even if I didn't, I think I could find her blindfolded. Even if I spun around in three million circles, I'd still turn toward her every single time.

Find me Erik. I have faith in you.

She's flirting, right? This is flirting? This is interest and fun and everything? We flirted before, but this time I can do something about it. We're playing and I want to play back. I want her faith to be put in the right spot. Even if this is all I can give her—flirtatious messages and random trips to town—this is something worth holding on to. At least for now. How can I let her know that I'm in this? That I've found her?

I could keep my camera open and snap a picture the next time the feed pans to the bench. I could tell her I like her pigtails, so she'll know I've seen her. I could…

Smiling, I pull up my brother's contact and type out a quick message. Hopefully, he'll check it between periods, or at least when the game ends. Then I send a text to my mom to put my plan into action. On the TV, Vic sends a shot arcing towards the Tampa goalie. The puck whizzes past his blocker and into the net. I pump my fist from my couch, earning an accusatory glare from Loki, and I don't feel nearly as restless as before.

15 QUINN

The Arctic is up by two when The Stand starts emptying out. It feels like an oxymoron, fans willing to miss the end of the game just to reach their cars ahead of the crowds. Then again, people will miss the end of concerts to do the same. There aren't words for how grateful I am that Erik set this up. Have I watched every second of the game, riveted to each pass and shot? Well, no. Have I spent the whole time reading? Also no.

It's been nice to sit with my dad and understand thirty—okay, twenty—percent of what is going on. Dad has never liked to chat during play. He always assumed I understood what was going on and I never asked for explanations because... well, I'm stubborn. The more someone recommends a book, a show, a movie, the less likely I am to read or watch it. In this town? With my father? Hockey was always a firm no-go. Not anymore. That's another thing to thank Erik for.

So I texted him.

Of course I did.

I'd told myself I was going to back off, give us both some space until my galaxy-sized crush has time to die out. Or at least until it's more manageable. Every time I see his name on my phone, I feel the warmth rush through my body as I remember our one night together. Our one night and the best kisses of my life. I just need my brain to forget that I will never get a repeat because he lives in the goddamn Windy City and I live here. In Quarry Creek.

Except space would mean missing out on talking to the man. I feel like a high schooler again, staying up too late to message the boy I like, hoping I'm coming off calm, cool, and collected. Failing miserably. Analyzing each word, the time between messages. Grinning, tongue between my teeth, as I send flirty little texts back precisely because I'm not going to see him again. I might not have the time—or the headspace—to actually date, but the flirting is fun. Nice even. Good build up for some self-care later.

"Do you mind if we stay until the end?" Dad asks, his gaze riveted on the two men battling it out at the blue line. We aren't in a rush. It's Saturday, next week is school vacation, Dad's been feeling good.

"You've never once left early, have you?" I nudge him with my elbow, and he nudges me right back.

"Only once. You were sick, so I left during the second period and came back to let the babysitter off the hook. Only fair that if someone was getting puked on, it was me."

"That seems fair." I don't remember the game he's referring to, but I remember him pushing my sweaty hair back from my face whenever I got sick. Humming Beatles songs in my ear as he rubbed my back.

The Arctic regains control of the puck and streaks down the ice towards the empty Tampa net. I have the texts from Erik explaining why teams might pull a goalie to give themselves an extra shot at scoring. I asked him if it ever worked, and he pointed out that teams have nothing to lose. They're facing the L without an extra goal. Overtime is another chance to win or at least pick up another point. The downside is the morale killer of having your empty net scored on. On the ice, the puck hits the back of Tampa's net and the lights and sirens blare.

Despite all the hockey tips, I can't tell if Erik is watching. Vic is on fire tonight, getting another assist—he's had a hand in each of the Arctic's goals—and the teams circle up for another face-off. The game's over, the clock running down as the linesman drops the puck. The buzzer sounds and both teams straighten up. The aggression bleeds out of them almost instantaneously.

"All these silly folks more concerned with traffic than with watching the game," Dad shakes his head. "They'd have missed that last goal. Varg is a force to be reckoned with, Quinnie. I told you he was when they signed him. Some people think he's too old, but I think he'll play another decade yet."

Erik had said much the same thing.

"Thank you," says a woman to our right. She startles me enough that I have to catch the back of the seat in front of me to keep my balance. "I know I can't take credit for all of my baby's strengths, but I do like to try. Hi. I'm Maria."

Maria has the same dark blonde hair as her sons, and the same tall build. She does not look old enough to be the mother of the lead goal scorer, and her fitted blue jersey and jeans make her look even younger.

"I don't blame you. I do the same." Dad extends his hand past my chest, and Maria shakes it with a genuine smile. "Sean Cooper."

I know this is Erik's mom, but I'm not sure what she's doing here. Obviously, she knows where we're sitting, but did Erik send her to us? Did she come on her own? I want to check my phone. I inhale messages from Erik like they're oxygen—something I'll never admit out loud—but I don't remember him mentioning his mother. Do I need to tell him she's here? Would it be rude to get my phone out now?

"I was a little worried I wouldn't get to you in time, I've never understood why so many people try to cut out early." Maria shook her head, "But then I saw you on the screen and figured I'd make it. Even if fighting the mass exodus is a little like swimming upstream."

She's sweet, coming to check in. Erik warned me that his mom is nosy, but it's a good nosy. Dad's the same way. The proof is in the matching texts they sent us during the Chicago game.

The Jumbotron isn't the same as the broadcast feed and I can't help but wonder if Erik saw us, saw me, too. I can't help but wonder if he likes my sweatshirt, or if he thinks I look nice. I put zero effort into my appearance for the last game and he liked me just fine. Tonight, I took a little more care, although if pressed, I'll say it's because my dad needed his jersey back and I now know I won't freeze to death in my seat. It definitely had nothing to do with a hope that Erik might be watching. That he might see me on the screen and smile. Definitely not.

I'd asked him and he said he hadn't, but that was a while ago. This can change.

"No need to rush. They take a while before we can get in to see them." Maria slides into the seat in front of me and turns to face me and Dad. "I usually wait at least thirty minutes after they leave the ice. Gives the boys a chance to shower, change, talk to the reporters. If they aren't ready, we can wait in the hall."

"I'm sorry, what?" I try to smooth my face into a neutral expression because I need clarification, but I'm pretty sure that Erik's mom just insinuated she's taking us down to meet the players. And you don't frown at a woman about to give your dad that kind of gift.

"Let me get this straight," Dad says. "You're Mama Varg." Maria nods. "And you came down here to introduce yourself to us because you're going down to see the players?" Maria nods again. "In the locker room?" A third nod. "And you're taking us with you." A wink from Erik's mom and Dad turns to me with an awestruck expression. "Marry Erik. Marry Erik and tell him his mama is a saint."

"Dad!" My face is on fire, burning, melting right off my bones. "We're... friends." Sort of.

"I'm on board with this plan," Maria grins and I don't think it's possible, but somehow I blush even hotter.

"The part where they get married? Or the part where you're a saint?" Dad asks and Maria laughs. It's a big, bold sound. It reminds me of Erik, but I don't think I've ever heard him laugh. Not like that.

I want to.

"Both."

Dad joins in and I get an uneasy, twisty feeling in my gut. There's no match to be made, no matter what these two might think. They know that. Right? Erik and I have made it clear. Even if we wanted to try, a thousand miles separate us.

Work separates us. Neither of us can uproot our lives. No matter how romantic it might be, and while I'm a sucker for grand gestures in novels, I have to be more practical in real life.

I should set the record straight. I should remind Maria and my dad that Erik and I are not a couple. We'd spent twenty-four hours in with each other—and yes, we had some fun without our clothes, and I hope neither dad nor Maria know about that—but we both agreed that there is nowhere else for this thing to go. Flirting is just flirting. This crush is just a crush. I look from my dad's wide grin to Maria's matching one. Maybe I can let him down after the game. Erik can tackle his mom on his own.

Maria and Sean fall into conversation as if they've known each other for years and it makes me smile. They're debating plays like old friends, and I could kiss Maria for not letting her gaze stray to the hat covering my dad's bald head or his missing eyebrows. She throws her head back in another laugh, and her hand comes down on the top of Dad's thigh. How many people have I seen shrink away from him in public as if cancer is contagious or as if he'll break in a strong wind? I once offered to pencil eyebrows on him, but he turned me down flat. He said his lack of hair didn't embarrass him. But there's a difference between disguising his condition out of shame, and disguising his condition to protect his marshmallow heart.

"We're probably good to head down," Maria says. She waits as I hold my arm out for my dad. He gives me a look from under his team hat but hooks his hand on my elbow. "We're going to head up and out to the concession area," Maria says and leads the way up the stairs.

The crowd is thinning out now that the game is over, but the joy is still thick in the air. It sizzles and pops over my skin like champagne, thrilling, energizing, sweet. A few stragglers sling their arms over each other's shoulders, grinning and warbling off-tune eighties rock hits. The wide hallways carry the sour, yeasty scent of beer, the buttered sweetness of popcorn, and the smoky char of brats. It's not as off-putting as the last time I was here.

Maria walks with purpose, cutting through revelers with ease. She's clearly familiar with the layout of The Strand, but she slows her steps to match my dad's stride. Dad is practically vibrating down the hall.

"You're sure Varg, sorry, I mean Vic, won't mind an introduction?" He's just being polite. Vic is his favorite player. I'm pretty sure my dad would consider selling me for the chance to meet him.

"Not at all," Maria waves at a large man standing in front of a nondescript door. The only clue that he works for the Arctic is the clear coil of an earpiece snaking down the side of his thick neck. He's taller than me, wider too, and he doesn't even blink as we go past him and down a flight of stairs. "Victor loves meeting fans, especially on good game nights."

"I must admit," Dad says, "I knew Vic had a brother, but I never knew he was a twin. Imagine my surprise when he showed up with my daughter."

His surprise? How about my surprise?

I'd looked up at the Jumbotron and my seatmate had been in two places at once. I'd walked into my dad's hospital room and seen that same handsome face next to him. I had wondered how Erik stayed off the radar. Sharing a face with someone well known doesn't offer a lot of opportunities to remain incognito. I'd assumed I hadn't recognized him because I didn't know Vic's face well either. I'd met Erik first and had zero expectations.

"The boys keep it quiet for privacy reasons. It's not easy being the brother of a professional hockey player."

Especially when they'd once shared the same dream.

"Did Erik ever play too?" Dad asks before I can stop him. He misses my panicked face, too. Then again, my dad is anything but subtle, and it wasn't like he knew about Erik's amputation. We haven't discussed it at all. I doubt Erik's past is something that's on the interview docket. I'd sat with him for hours and hadn't noticed until he'd shown me, and dad had been a little out of it with nausea when I'd found the two of them at Grace Hospital. "Is it strange for him to see his brother going pro?"

Maria's steps hitch and her smile dims for half a second.. If I hadn't known that this was a hot topic, I would have missed her reaction altogether. Losing his hockey career had been an immovable elephant in the room once, but Erik had indicated it was better now. Getting easier every day.

"They were going to be the next Sedin twins," I say, my words echoing in the dim hallway.

Maria stops walking. She turns, eyes searching my face.

"Where'd you hear about the Sedin twins? You don't even like hockey," Dad bumps my shoulder with his.

I don't look away from Maria. The moment feels heavy, a weight sitting down on the tops of our shoulders and pressing us down onto the rubberized floor.

"Erik told me," I say to my dad, but the answer is for Maria. I know it is. "They both got invited to something."

"The United States Hockey League." Maria nods. "They both got drafted to play with the USHL."

"Amazing," Dad says as we continue down a wide hallway. "That's the only Tier I league in the country. Players who don't go pro right away are almost always recruited by Division 1 schools."

"Both boys planned to play in the Junior League for a few years and put their names in the draft when they were eighteen." Maria's smile doesn't reach her eye and I look away before the twisting in my gut gets worse. We shouldn't be talking about this. Not without Erik here.

Team banners line the walls and sections are cordoned off where fans can stand and watch the team take the ice. I've seen enough televised games to recognize this entrance to the tunnel. They always show Ólafsson thundering down the walk, his black and blue goalie pads eating up all the space, as fans cheer and slap high fives against his blocker.

"Maybe," I poke my dad in the ribs, "we can consider the fact that some of our questions can have off-putting and tender answers before we ask them of someone kind enough to take us to meet one of our hockey idols, Dad."

Maria's still staring at me, not even pretending to be subtle. She keeps her eyes on me over her shoulder as she walks down the dim hallway, and her brows are furrowed in a familiar frown as she eyes me. It's not an angry frown, more contemplative. Like I'm a puzzle she's trying to figure out. I've seen the same look on Erik. I stare back, and the corners of Maria's mouth tip into an actual smile this time.

A few yards down the hall is a set of large wooden doors. The right one is open and through it I catch glimpses of people milling about. No, not people. Players. The gold plaque over the top of the frame has a wealthy benefactor's name and the words "Player's Lounge" stamped out in fancy script. Maria raps on the closed door and calls out Vic's name. I hear a chorus of "awes" and several male voices shout "mama's boy." Maria steps into the room and motions for me and Dad to follow.

I expect the large open stalls for pads and equipment that I've seen on tv, and the wide wooden benches overflowing with hockey players, but this room looks like a college common room after an HGTV make over. An enormous flat screen TV hangs on one wall over an even more impressive stereo system. There are plush couches big enough for eight pro-athlete-sized people, and a bunch of tables and chairs at the back of the room. There's a wet bar built into one wall and a sub-zero fridge.

Milling around the room are a handful of hockey players. Most of them are in casual team clothing, their hair damp. The room smells better than I'd assumed a hockey locker room would, but I guess this isn't the locker room at all. It's a place for the guys to hang out. I'd expected them to still be in their game attire.

Vic is lying sideways on one couch, but he stands up when he sees his mom. In his gray sweatpants and Arctic hoodie, he looks so much like Erik that I suck in a breath. The minute he's close enough, Vic wraps his mom in a tight hug. I feel like I should look away, give them some privacy, but Vic meets my eyes over his mother's head, and I'm rooted to the spot. It's Erik, and it's not. Vic's hair is longer on the sides but even wet from his shower, I know it's the same dark blonde as his twin's. His hazel eyes are the same, even with a line of stitches through his eyebrow. He didn't have those in the last game. He's broader than Erik, his muscles probably more defined, but not by much.

"You must be Quinn and Sean," he says. His voice is the same deep rumble as Erik's, but the cadence is off. Like a tiny sliver of laughter rolling in his words. "I'm glad I finally get to meet you both."

He keeps an arm around his mom's shoulders as he offers his hand first to me and then to my dad. Dad pumps Vic's hand so vigorously I'm worried one of them is about to lose an arm.

"Vic Varg." My dad says. His voice is practically shaking with suppressed emotion. "It is such an honor to meet you. I've been following your career since Chicago. You're a damn fine player."

"Thank you, sir," Vic says, with all the modesty of a man confident in his own abilities. Dad slides his gaze to mine and mouths Vic's name as if it's a prayer. I shrug my shoulders.

"I have about a million questions. Can I ask them?" Well, that's better than my dad bulldozing the poor man into answering whatever he wants. Progress.

"Of course," Vic says, "Come on over and meet some of the guys and you can ask us anything you want."

Vic leads my father around one couch and has him sit down on another as several players come forward. They pull up chairs and I watch the men lean forward and shake Dad's hand. He looks like a king holding court, except his people are a bunch of professional athletes. Peppering them with a million and ten questions, he's talking with his hands, big slashing gestures, and my heart goes soft, rolling over in my chest to expose its soft underbelly because my dad is wearing the biggest grin I've seen in months. Possibly years.

"Thank you so much for doing this," I say to Maria, watching my dad inflate under the attention of his favorite team. After all the unhappy crap we've been through in the last couple of months, if anyone deserves this pocket of joy, it's my dad. "You've made his evening. Possibly his entire year."

"You don't have to thank me." Maria waves her hand like she can swat away my gratitude. "It was Erik's idea. He wanted tonight to be special for you both, and he knows your dad's a fan of Vic's."

It had been Erik's idea? He had said nothing, just handled it. The same way he'd gotten me the ticket.

Even without being here in person, he'd made it better.

My little crush stretches, growing at least another two inches. How could it not? This gift. It isn't just for me. It's for my dad. The most important person in my life right now. Erik cannot have an ulterior motive. I'm not even going to see him again. No matter how much I might want to.

"You have an amazing son," I say, and we both know I'm not talking about the professional hockey player who scored the tying goal of the night and made two assists. "Thank you for coming to get us."

"Oh, it was selfish honey," Maria throws me a wink. "Vic and I have been dying to meet the woman who caught Erik's attention."

"I wouldn't say that." Even as I say the words, I can feel my blush spread and my heart stutters.

"I owe you the thank you," Maria continues. "He's flying in on Wednesday night. He called to let me know. I can't remember the last time we saw him more than once in a year, or the last time we talked on the phone, and now we get two trips in a month. And I got two phone calls this week." She turns to me, her hazel eyes a little wet at the edges, and her smile trembling. "Whoever you might be to him, you're the woman who got him to come home."

ON ICE

Text Message
Saturday, 11:48 PM EST

Quinn Cooper:

> A little birdie told me you're the man responsible for my dad meeting his idol tonight.

> By idol I mean your brother. And by birdie I mean your mom.

Erik Varg:

> She used to be more subtle than that. She's losing her touch.

> I think she assumed I already knew.

> Thank you.

> Don't thank me. If anything it was a favor for Vic. He needs constant ego stroking to function.

> And I like your dad.

> I also hear you're coming to town next week.

I am.

> Your mom seemed to think it was because of me, but I didn't even know you were planning to visit. Not that I needed to know. You're definitely allowed to plan your own trips to see your family without telling the random girl you hooked up with once.

I'm coming to town for work.

> Oh...
>
> So forget I said anything. Seriously

And I planned for next week because I hoped you'd be off work. Chicago has a school vacation but I wasn't sure about you guys.

ON ICE

> It's okay Erik, You don't need to explain...

> I should have realized your mom was kidding.

> Or maybe being inappropriately hopeful.

> Or something.

And I hadn't figured out how to tell you without coming off like a creep.

Especially after you asked me to leave you alone. But then you started texting me and I thought maybe...

> Maybe what, Erik?

Maybe you'd want to see me as much as I want to see you. Again.

> How long are you going to be in town?

> Fly out Wednesday night.

> Fly home Sunday night.

< I'd like that.

> Like what?

< To see you too, Erik.

> I have meetings all day Thursday. Can I take you to dinner?

< I have plans with Jen. She's away for the weekend, but I can reschedule?

> Friday. I'll pick you up at two.

< It's a date.

< I didn't mean a date date.

< Like a friend's date.

< Like two friends hanging out. When one of them is in town.

ON ICE

> It's a date, Quinn.

> Oh. Okay.
>
> Good.
>
> Great, actually.

> See you Friday, Cooper.

> Friday, Varg.

16 ERIK

My palms leave sticky sweat prints on Vic's steering wheel, but I try to ignore them. I've been sweating for almost a week now, all of my nerves focusing on this one moment: Friday, 2pm. Vic left me the Mercedes as he headed out of town on a five-game stretch. When I balked at taking the keys, he reminded me it would be sexier to pick Quinn up myself, rather than call an Uber. I could have told him that Quinn was going to drive, but I didn't like that thought either. I have one chance here. One date, one trip, one weekend. Technically, a second chance. I need to do this right.

I let the car idle in the driveway of a little yellow two-story house—with a wraparound porch my sister would love, complete with a swing—and count down the last ten minutes before I can go ring the doorbell and not look like I'm overeager or a stalker. Quinn already knows I've been counting down the days until this date. I told her as much. She doesn't need to know I'm counting down minutes, seconds, too. Here I am, sweating in a borrowed vehicle, about to take her on a date that I've been planning for a week, but that I am terrified is going to be an unmitigated disaster.

The curtain over the front window moves and I think I see a flash of Quinn's copper hair. Probably just checking to make sure the car parked in her driveway isn't here to kidnap her or proselytize on her doorstep. Less than a minute later, the bright blue front door opens and there she is, stepping out onto the porch. She glows in the early afternoon sun and I'm blinded more by the light glinting on her curls than by the kickback from the snow.

I unfold myself from the front seat and smile at her over the top of Vic's too-small car.

"I'm early," I say.

She cocks her head to the side, smiling back.

"I don't mind."

My heart thunders in my chest as I walk around the front of the car, letting my hand trail over the hood of the vehicle. I draw closer to her, sure in my bones that coming here is the best decision I've made in over a decade. Quinn's eyes drop, raking me from head to toe, heating me faster than the car's luxury seat warmers or a twelve-mile run. I want to drop to my knees and take a bite out of the curve where her thigh meets her ass. I want to grab handfuls of her and boost her up onto the hood of my brother's overpriced car. I want to quit my job, sell my condo, and see her every day. I can't, of course, but it's a nice thought.

She has on a pair of stretchy leggings with crisscrossing black and white lines. They showcase the length of her legs and I try not to stare. A white turtleneck covered by a green chunky knit sweater falls over the width of her hips. Her black puffer coat is unzipped, and she has on a pair of fuzzy gray earmuffs and matching knit gloves. She's covered from head to toe, and she still gets me going.

This is the first time I've seen her in clothes she picked out with me in mind. Wearing team gear to a sporting event doesn't count—everyone wears something in team colors or with the team logo—and at the hospital she'd been covered in paint from her day at school. This is what Quinn chose for herself. For a date with me. This is her, and she looks lush and warm and adorable and my pulse is threatening to tattoo its way out of my skin.

She's in a fucking turtleneck and I'm about to lose my mind.

"How casual are we keeping this date, Quinn?"

My body sways toward hers as if she's a statue made of nickel, and I'm filled to the brim with magnets. She furrows her brows at me, her nose crinkling just the tiniest bit, and I want to shake her and tug her into the wall of my chest. I need to know where her head is at because I want to kiss the fuck out of her right now. Because I remember the way she tastes and what she sounds like when she comes. Because I keep forgetting that this isn't the first of many.

"Last time we both got a little burned when things got too intense. I don't want to hurt either of us again." On Sunday. When I leave.

Startled green eyes slam into mine and a flush paints her cheeks. I know for a fact that flush goes a lot further down her throat and across her chest. I try to suck a breath in through my nose without sounding like I've hit the mile twenty wall during a marathon.

"Sorry." She shakes her head, blinking at me. "Can you repeat the question? I was distracted by your mouth."

Quinn Cooper is going to be the death of me.

The only thing that stops me from kissing her is the fact that once I start, I'm not sure I'll be able to stop. Normally, that wouldn't bother me, but we have places to be. We are going on this date. We deserve this date.

"Don't worry about it." If she lets me, I'm going to kiss her later. I can follow her cues. Casual might protect both of us, but I've fallen too far into my infatuation to not take anything she offers.

I open the passenger door of the car and hand her into the seat.

"Buckle up." I'm pretty sure that if I try to do it myself, I'll end up with my mouth on hers and at least one hand under her sweater. Maybe both.

Fuck. I sound like a damn pervert.

"Yes, sir," she says, and I pull back fast enough to thwack my head against the door frame.

"Quinn."

Her name comes out a growl, and she laughs, cheeks streaked red, as she buckles her seatbelt. I make sure her limbs are in the vehicle before closing the door. I need a moment to get myself under control. I can still see her through Vic's tinted windows. The minx. She's laughing, small lines crinkling around the corners of her eyes. I might need two minutes.

The drive to downtown Quarry Creek is short and uneventful. This is because I kept us on the road by refusing to look at Quinn's thighs or breasts or face. I also recite the team names and numbers on the men's Team USA Hockey team from the 1980 Winter Olympics. That keeps my brain off the way she's singing along with the radio—its adorable even if she can't hold a tune—and off what's coming.

I park along the street, feed the meter for several hours, and steel my resolve. I can, in theory, just take her for a walk through the little park behind city hall. Lights hang from the trees, and while the snow on the ground isn't fresh, it adds to the ambiance. I could hold her hand and buy her a hot chocolate from the tiny red cart and pretend this is the whole reason we're here. Or I can bundle her back into Vic's car and drive her somewhere we can get naked. But given that I've already fed the meter, she'll notice that wasn't the original plan.

No. We're doing this. One, because Quinn is one of the few people I can trust to not judge or pity me if it doesn't go right, and two, because I always assumed—years and years ago—that a date like this would be in my future. This was part of the reason I'd fought so hard for amputation even after my oncologist considered my limb salvage surgery a success. I've learned to do almost everything with one leg I could with two, even some things I'd never tried. I run marathons now. I talk about my feelings every fucking week with my therapist. I can handle this one thing.

"What are we doing?" Quinn asks, lacing her hands with mine. Her gloves are soft against my skin.

I pull open the backseat and reach into the dark cavern of the car. I loop the laces over Quinn's shoulder, gripping the blades of my pair in a solid fist. Hopefully, she can't see the white knuckled grip I have on the metal.

"We're going skating," I banish the worry and doubt from my mind. I have one-hundred-and-eighty-two tabs open on my computer browser, assuring me that this is possible. I won't have the same range of movement I'm used to, but I can do this. I will do this. I want to. With Quinn. "You said you've never been before and I wanted..." I wanted this to be something I did for her. Something that will always remind her of me, even years from now, when she's with some other lucky bastard.

"Erik," she breathes my name as she squeezes my fingers and I wait. I wait for her to ask if I'm sure. Ask if I can handle it. Reference my leg. Ask any number of questions that I had googled into the dark hours of the morning. But she doesn't.

"This is a perfect date," she says and everything inside me loosens as I take a breath.

It's going to be, Quinn. I promise.

The rink is just a circle of ice surrounded by plywood boards. It sits smack in the center of the tiny park, lights twinkling even in the afternoon sunlight. I assume the rink gets packed leading up to Christmas and New Year, the fun part of winter when everyone is happy and festive. Probably on the weekends, too. I'd hoped it would be quiet today. It's a beautiful day, the sun shining on the snow, but it's still cold. Our breath makes little puffs of mist every time we breathe. Only the brave are venturing outside more than necessary.

I steer Quinn toward a bench ringing the ice. No one else is out here right now, just a bored-looking teenager working a stand for skate rentals. I lift Quinn's leg, nudging her to turn and face me as I pull her boot into my lap. It's one of those fuzzy things Anna loves. Ugly, but warm. There's a thin white line around the toe. Stains from the rock salt the city uses to thaw the streets and sidewalks.

"If I'd known you'd be up and personal with my feet, I'd have worn different shoes," Quinn says. I smile to cover up the fact that it takes some real effort to tug them off. "I'll admit, when you asked for my shoe size, I assumed we were going bowling."

"We can do that too," I say, "After we skate."

Her smile is soft, warming me up from the inside like a few good sips of cocoa burning their way to my stomach. I drop her boot on the rubber mat covering the ground and look down at her blue and purple polka dot socks. I can't resist tracing my thumb down her instep and feel her twitch in my grip. She snorts out a laugh, trying to pull her foot away.

"How's your brother? Didn't he get injured?" She asks as I slip the white leather boot over her foot. She was the same size as my mom, who had been more than happy to let me commandeer her skates. If things go well today, I'll buy Quinn a pair of her own. Except…when will she get a chance to wear them? It makes me a selfish bastard, but I don't like the thought of her skating with anyone else. I don't like the thought of her being with anyone else.

"He's fine. Out for the next week or two, but fine. It's a grade one groin sprain, but he's still traveling with the Arctic so the team trainers can monitor his recovery." I probably wasn't supposed to tell her any of that. "I'm not sure if that information's public."

"I won't share it," Quinn says. I lace her skates, tugging and tightening to make sure she's secure. I've seen far too many people out on public rinks with their skates so loose it's a miracle they leave without breaking an ankle. "My dad noticed he was on the reserve list and was worried."

"You can tell your dad." I pat my thigh until she gives me her other foot.

"I'll just tell him Vic's fine." Her eyes are flickering back and forth between mine, and my sternum is aching. "No need to say anything else."

I do her second laces up even faster and then it's time for mine. I've read about some athletes having specially made prosthetics with a blade attached. I suppose if this goes well, I can look into it. I don't have anything quite that fancy today.

Hockey skates open almost all the way to the toes so it isn't too bad slipping my foot in even without an ankle joint. This is one of Vic's back-up pairs. We were always the same size as kids and that hasn't changed. We've never shared before, though. Second-hand equipment wasn't something we weren't used to, but we never had to split. Erik's and Vic's. Two sets of skates, two sets of sticks, pads, helmets. I'm glad he was cool with me borrowing these. There's something demoralizing about renting skates after my history with the sport.

Quinn watches as I rock the boot over my foot and make sure my prosthetic is secure. I was a little concerned about the heel not sitting right, but everything is snug and secure. I lace it up and wonder if she's going to say anything or ask how often I get out on the ice, but she doesn't. She just sits on the bench and waits for me, gloved hands tucked under her thighs.

I secure the second skate and get to my feet. So far, so good. It feels strange not having my ankles to help balance my weight, but my skates are usually tied so tight that my ankles can't move much anyway. I remind myself that it's been… a long time since I've done this. It's bound to feel strange, even if I had two functioning legs. My heart is pounding and I suck a breath into my lungs before letting it out slowly. I hold out a hand and lever Quinn to her feet, too. If I think too much, I'll chicken out. If I name this feeling winging through my chest, then I won't take that first step. Instead, I lead her to the edge of the ice.

"I know this is stupid, but I'm nervous," she says, her hands gripping the plywood as she eyes the smooth surface. It's almost automatic, my instinct to promise that I won't let her fall. That's what boyfriends, dates, do, right? But that isn't something I can be sure of. Not anymore. I feel fine standing here, but on the ice is a different beast. What if I can't catch my balance? What if I fall? I'm not afraid of getting hurt, but the humiliation… I haven't fallen on the ice—without good reason—since I was single digits. Admitting that, even just to myself, sucks a lot.

"We're in this together, okay Quinn?"

"Yes," she says, and we step out onto the ice.

I want to say it's easy, but that would be a lie. The ice is pitted and bumpy under my skates—that isn't uncommon, especially on smaller rinks with no Zamboni—but I don't have the natural give in my lower leg to balance it out. It feels like I've travelled back to those first few months when I was still getting comfortable standing, moving, existing. Everything is heavy from my knee down and the ice feels like it's pitching under my feet. I'm grateful for the hours I clocked walking on sand to help sort my equilibrium. It had been a suggestion from a US Army vet, one I met in my second support group. I'd been too angry to get anything out of the first group I joined. Too busy feeling sorry for myself.

I can make this work. Even if I have to take small, marching steps, the kind mini mites use when they first get their bearings on the ice. It would have been nearly impossible if I hadn't kept my knee.

Quinn is holding onto the boards as she takes tiny baby steps too. Every now and then she wobbles and her free arm flails out to help her re-balance. I reach for her waving hand and link our fingers together. She's going to unbalance herself and at least this way I can cushion her fall if we both go down.

"I'm not sure I can hold you up," I say and she shrugs, but won't look at me.

"Yea, I know. You're a big guy, but I'm not exactly a delicate flower." Together we skate another couple feet around the edge of the rink, but she still guides her way with the boards.

"I meant my leg, Quinn." I try not to laugh at her baffled expression. I really do, but she can't be serious.

"You're what?"

"My prosthetic." There was no way she's forgotten. Most people don't let me forget. Except my brother. He'd offered me up as a stand in on a boudoir photo shoot—aka sans clothes—and hadn't thought to warn the photographer that I only have three out of four limbs. The photographer, Jenna, hadn't ended up needing me after all, which is a good thing because I'm not sure I wanted to strip down in front of another woman, but Vic had seemed surprised when I told him he should have warned her about me.

"Oh right," Quinn's cheeks and nose are pink with the cold and her blush, "I imagine your balance is different now."

Different.

Not worse, just different.

I nod. "It takes more effort to catch myself. It's like locking your knees on the subway instead of staying loose." It doesn't mean you'll fall, but it's harder to stay upright.

"We're in this together," Quinn lets go of the boards. "Maybe I'll fall, and maybe I'll catch you."

Later when I look back on our time together, unwrapping each moment to view it from new and sparkling angles, when I conjure up the memory of her smile and her laugh and the feel of her fingers entwined with mine, this will be when I fall. Not onto the ice, but in love with Quinn Cooper. Distance between us be damned. It's not gradual. I've been sitting on the edge of my seat waiting for it to happen. Like a dunk tank, either no one will hit the buzzer, and I'll climb out dry, or I'll sit and wait until I tumble ass over elbow into the cold water. Except falling for Quinn is like slipping into the cool water when it's one hundred plus degrees out and I've been baking under the sun for hours. It's welcome. Comfortable. Needed.

Thirty minutes later, my thighs burn from being on the ice, and my cheeks burn from smiling. We've made multiple laps and even if my steps aren't as graceful as I'd like, I've found a groove. I won't be snapped up by the NHL anytime soon, probably not going to join a beer league either, but I can do this again. I will do this again. Quinn has graduated toward more gliding steps, too. She still prefers to push off with only her left foot, keeping her right foot planted underneath her, but I can help her work on that next time. We've both been able to focus on conversation and while I know we both need to take a break and warm up, I don't want this to be over.

When the sun hits her hair, glowing copper in the light, crowding her up against the boards is an instinct.

I lean into her space. One hand finds her hip and pulls her into the wall of my chest. I like the way she feels against me, even through our layers, and I suck in a deep breath. My other hand slides around her neck and my fingers spear through her hair. I tip her head back and her lips part in invitation. I want to devour her. I want to stamp her taste and her scent and the way she looks right now, so deep into my memory that even a crowbar can't remove it. Nothing will remove her. I suspect that's already true, as my heart pounds in my chest. Pressed tight to my front, I can feel Quinn's pulse sync with mine. I lower my mouth to hers.

One of us moans.

Before Quinn, I never thought it possible that I could make a sound and not know it, but she makes me lose my mind. I'm so focused on the press of her lips that I do not know which one of us made the noise. Maybe both of us. Her mouth is warm and soft against mine. Her lips clinging to mine as I pull back to tilt my head for a better angle. I brush my tongue over the seam of her lips and she opens for me. I can feel her smile into our kiss, and I don't waste time with tentative brushes of my tongue. I push into her mouth and take everything she has.

The kiss is hot and wet and urgent, our tongues slipping and sliding together, curling around each other. When breathing becomes an issue, I pull back and suck in a lungful of cool air. Then I take her mouth again. Her hands fist in my pea coat and I wish they were against my bare skin, her nails digging into my ribs. I need that bite of something to keep my dick in line. I'm already hard as a lead pipe, cock aching and heavy in my jeans. I'm sure she can feel it pressed against her abdomen as she rocks her hips against mine.

"Let's get out of here," Quinn says, panting her words against my chin. I'm struggling to control my breathing, too. Struggling to think beyond kissing her again. With the boards for leverage, I could hoist her into my arms. My balance is solid now. It would be worth it. "My place?" she asks, and it's a quick reminder that we are in public, even if the rink is deserted.

I press the word "yes" into her mouth, letting her swallow it with a smile.

17 QUINN

We stumble through my front door, Erik muttering a brief "ow" against my lips as his elbow connects with the door frame. We're fused at the mouth, have been since we fell out of the Mercedes. We would have driven home the same way if we could. Never had I ever been happier that Jen was out of town for the weekend. We can fuck on every surface we choose. The evidence of Erik's desire is pressing against me. He's been hard since he pushed me into the boards.

I want his sweater off. I want my hands on his skin again. I want his hands on mine. This might be the worst idea I've ever had. This might make my crush a million times worse, but I'm willing to risk the fallout. We can christen the counter later. I have condoms in my nightstand and it's faster for us to go to my room together.

"Upstairs," I pant against his mouth, but he ignores me to press his tongue deeper. I fist his sweater and drag him to my room, pushing Erik down to sit on the edge of the mattress. I reach for the hem of my sweater. Erik reaches for me.

"Let me," he says. His eyes are dark, hot, as they sweep over my face. "I have been fantasizing about this moment since the last time we were together."

"Taking off my top?"

He nods, his cheeks a ruddy pink as he grips the bottom of my chunky knit and the shirt underneath, lifting it up over my hips. His knuckles brush the skin along the waistband of my pants and I suck in a breath, pulling my stomach away from his touch.

"You did it for me last time." His hands move higher, even with the soft curve of my belly button. "I loved it, but I wanted to take each piece off you, to press—" he kisses my stomach, "my mouth to your skin as I bared every inch."

Erik's mouth follows his hands. He stands up, pulling both my shirts up and until I have to lift my arms over my head. He drops them on the floor and his lips find my neck, leaving wet, sucking kisses against my overheated skin. My hands come down to tangle in his hair and he sinks his teeth into my throat as I tug at the silky strands. Heat blankets my system. I tip Erik's head back to take his mouth with mine this time, pressing my body tight to his as he closes his hand over the curve of my breast. The pressure is exquisite, and I ache and arch into his touch.

We break our kiss long enough for Erik to strip too, and it feels like I've taken a blow to the chest. How can I have forgotten how sleek and strong he is? A smattering of blond hair spans the space between his flat pink nipples. His stomach is flat, ridges of muscle apparent every time he sucks in a deep breath. I want to bite into the skin over his ribs, but I'm not sure I can. He's solid, his body hard everywhere.

Erik slips a hand behind my back to flick the clasp of my bra. He has to help pull the straps off my shoulders, and he presses his mouth to the red lines left behind. His hands cup the heavy weight of my breasts, and his thumbs graze my nipples. They harden into tingling points, and Erik purses his lips, blowing hot air over the sensitive tips. I shudder again, my brain melting into a swirl of incandescent color as his hands slip further down my body and under the waistband of my leggings.

I reach for the button on his jeans and it's Erik's turn to suck in his stomach. He burns under my touch, his muscles tense and hard under the silk of his skin. I slide down the zipper and delve my hands down into his straining boxer briefs to cup him where he's even hotter and harder. I can't resist squeezing his erection in my fist—I hadn't forgotten how big he is—and he moans into the curve of my neck, biting down hard enough to leave a mark.

I think I'm going to lose my mind. No matter how many times I've imagined having him back here, the sight of him dropping to his knees, pulling my leggings down my thighs, has me choking back a moan. Erik leaves nipping kisses along the pale dimpled skin he uncovers, taking great care to lift one of my feet and then the other to pull each pant leg off. I'm not sure what I expect next, but it's not for Erik to prop my foot on his shoulder and trail his mouth up my skin to my knee.

"Wait," I say as his kisses move to my inner thigh. His hair tickles the sensitive skin there and my core clenches down on nothing. "My underwear—"

"No." Erik's fingers stroke my center through the fabric and my hips buck into his touch. "They're staying on to slow us down, Quinn." His fingers dip under the elastic. "Last time we got carried away and these are staying right here over your gorgeous ass and beautiful pussy so that I remember to slow down."

I'm so wet the cotton is well on its way to being ruined, especially when his entire hand slides underneath the fabric to toy with me. He traces my opening and my lashes flutter. I'm swooning like a character from a historical novel.

"Slow is overrated," I pant. "We can take it slow next time."

"Quinn." He stops the maddening touches and pulls away from my core. His eyes turn solemn and I feel weird with my foot still propped up on his shoulder. Erik steadies me with his hands braced on my hips as I let my leg down to the ground. He locks his elbows, pushing back to put some space between us, and looks up into my eyes. "There might not be a next time."

His words are slow and quiet, as if they'll hurt less at a lower volume. Even though I know it's true—I'd meant next time as in "round two"—hearing him say it out loud is like dropping a gallon of paint on my toes. I saw it coming, knew what to expect, and I'm still shocked by the intense pain.

"The hospital is in a good place," he says. He drops his chin to his chest, almost muffling the words, but my ears ring as they clang around in my head. "Any help they need from here on out can be done remotely."

"You have family. You've been getting along better. You can visit them!" I say.

I know I sound needy, desperate, but the reality of never seeing him again hurts. I have a flash of memory. This is why

I sent him packing the last time, and it gives me zero satisfaction to know I'd been right. It hurts more after this visit. After an actual date. After all our messages, and phone calls, and time getting to know each other. Hell, he's become the first person I want to talk to. About everything.

Erik's smile doesn't reach his eyes. "I will." He boosts himself up to sit on the bed again and tugs me to stand in the V of his spread thighs. "I can't promise when, or how often, and it would be inappropriate to expect that you'd drop whatever you have going on in your life to see me whenever I'm in town."

"And if I want to?" I lift my hands to wrap around the back of his neck.

He shivers under my touch.

"Then I'll see you every time until you tell me no, but I don't expect sex, and I don't expect you to shackle yourself to someone who can't give you half the things he wants to."

Even in my limited experience, men who don't ask for commitment are not offering it. I had expected nothing less, not when we won't attempt a long-distance relationship, or label this pull between us, but it still stings to think that he doesn't want to ask me for more.

"Do I still get to have you today?" I ask because, self-preservation or not, I ache for him.

"Yes," his voice is hoarse, and I wait for him to say something, anything, else, but he ends the conversation by sucking my nipple into the hot, wet depth of his mouth.

I arch my back, pressing my breasts closer to his lips and teeth and tongue. Each pull on the aching tip sends a tug down deep in my underwear. Erik switches his attention to my other breast, his hand taking over as he rolls my nipple between his blunt fingers. He surges forward and I step back to avoid falling on my butt—because that would be sexy—and then his hands are biting into my hips as he turns us both and pushes me flat on the bed.

There are very few men in the world that can make me feel small, dainty, but Erik looms over me, blocking out the overhead light. He looks so serious, pupils swallowing the hazel of his irises, mouth pressed into a firm line, but his hands shake as he slides them up my body. He kisses me, devouring me as he presses me deep into the plush blankets. Down, down, down until I can't tell where the bed ends and Erik and I begin.

His lips move over my chin and down my throat, nipping that same spot as before, and my legs shake. He kisses down my front, leaving a soft peck to the tip of each breast, then down over my tummy. Even lying flat, my stomach isn't flat, but Erik just swirls his tongue into my belly button and continues down to the waistband of my underwear.

I shimmy further up the bed and Erik uses his palms to push my knees wide. The air in my room is cool as it feathers across the damp cotton of my underwear. I shiver, goosebumps blossoming along my arms and legs. I catch sight of the wicked grin that crosses Erik's wide lips, and then he pulls the dark, wet fabric to the side and drops his mouth to where I ache the most.

I had almost forgotten how well he does this, lapping at my pussy with the flat of his tongue. He sucks my lips into his mouth, probes my entrance with his tongue, and nibbles on the sensitive bud of my clit. I'm sweating and panting, my thighs quivering as the tension inside me builds faster than I thought possible. He's only been here—with me—once before, but he must have taken notes. By the time he presses two of his thick fingers to my entrance and buries them deep, curving them to find that elusive spot that will send me spiraling into oblivion, there is nothing left on my mind except the pleasure he is wringing from my body.

My pussy clamps down on his fingers, holding them deep as I splinter outward. Each time I start to come down, my body loosening by degrees, he twists those digits and sends me flying again and again. When he finally pulls back, seconds or decades later, I can barely keep my eyes open. My limbs are heavy, weighed down with satisfaction.

Erik chuckles as he looks down at me, the sound rich like melted chocolate as it spreads across my senses.

"You okay?" He asks, and I try to nod.

His chin and mouth are shiny and wet, his eyes bright and glassy. His tongue peeks out to lick his lips, and he grins. He's proud of himself, happy that we're in this together, and I find the strength to push up on my elbows and reach for the waistband on his pants. He'd never re-fastened the button and they sag low on his slim hips. The head of his cock is visible over the waistband of his underwear and it twitches as my fingers brush his bare skin.

"I want these off." I tug at the denim.

He covers my hands with his, twisting our fingers together as his muscles lock down.

"Wait," His voice wavers enough that I shake off my lust stupor to look up at him. "I, uh, kept my pants on last time we did this. I can do that again if you're worried about my prosthetic."

I frown. Why would I care about his leg? I'm way more interested in his dick. Or his hands. Or his mouth.

"Some people find it off-putting, especially if I remove it."

"Are you uncomfortable?" I search his eyes for his honest answer. "It's your leg. I don't care if you have no legs, two legs, or twenty. I like you. I'm attracted to you. I'm hoping to have sex with you."

"What if I only have nineteen legs?"

"Oh, well, that would change everything." I smile as I push the denim down over his hips to bunch at the tops of his thighs. "Do whatever you are comfortable with. Pants on or off. Leg on or off. Light on or off. I want you inside me in about twenty-five seconds. Got it?"

Erik pushes his pants the rest of the way down and steps out of them. He kicks them to the side to join the rest of our clothes and my gaze drops to the dark black socket covering his left knee. I recognize the metal ankle joint and the flesh-colored foot before his boxer briefs follow his pants and his erection slaps up against the taut skin of his abdomen. I'm not looking anywhere else now.

I stretch along my mattress, fingers scrabbling against the drawer of my nightstand. Erik opens it for me, pulling out the box of condoms. He drops it on the bed next to my head and I rip it open, spilling the foil packets all over my body and the blankets. I laugh, a desperate choked sound, as Erik scoops one up and tears it open. He has one hand wrapped around his cock, stroking from root to tip, and he uses his teeth to rip the package. Am I drooling? Probably, but my nerves are too shot to care.

He drops to the edge of the bed, sitting so his hip presses into my arm, and strokes himself once, twice more, before pinching the tip of the condom and rolling it down to the base of his erection. He pats his thighs, smiling down at me. His eyes are burning me alive. I push myself up and over him until I'm straddling his thighs. He fists his hands in the elastic over my hips, mutters a quick apology, and then tears my underwear right off my body, letting the pieces flutter to the ground.

"I'll buy you a new pair." He pulls me closer until my breasts rub against the soft hair on his chest. It tickles.

"You can ruin all my underwear." My words end on a moan as he lines the head of his dick up with my entrance and pushes down on my thighs so I can take him deep.

He rocks his hips up into me and I pitch forward, curving my body into his chest. Erik bands his arms around my back and I grind my hips against his, rubbing my clit against his pubic bone. He is impossibly thick and impossibly hard inside me. I'm stretched beyond comprehension. Unsure of the best way to move, but unable to stay still. I push up on my knees and snap my hips forward, then let them rock back as I sink down over him again. He meets me with an upward thrust of his own, hitting that spot inside me that his fingers found with no problem.

"You're fucking stunning, Quinn Cooper. Inside and out." His words hover over me as our bodies slap together again and again. Flutters start in my abdomen, picking up speed and strength and he drops a hand to rub over the spot where we're joined. "I've been dreaming of you since the first time I saw you. I'm not going to last here, baby. I need you to come with me."

I'm close enough that if he just keeps the pace, another orgasm will not be a problem.

Erik takes my mouth in a rough kiss, pressing his tongue deep as he thumbs my clit and grinds his hips into mine. For one brief second, I am so close to the edge that it's almost painful, and then I fracture outward. Fire spreads through my veins as I tremble and cling to Erik's arms. Either I slam my eyes shut or I white-out for a moment, because when I open them again, staring through the strands of hair stuck to the sweat pouring down my face, there he is. Erik's jaw is stone set. He holds me to him with bruising force.

"You're everything, Quinn." He says and presses his face to my neck, groaning a hoarse curse as he empties inside me.

"You really like me on top," I tease after I collapse off Erik's lap, go to the bathroom, and he'd disposed of the condom.

"I like the view," he agrees.

I pull back my covers and slip underneath them. I pat the mattress beside me and Erik frowns.

"We're taking a nap, Erik Varg. Get over here." It's too early to go to bed—we haven't even had dinner—but I like post sex cuddling.

"I can leave my leg on," Erik says, keeping his back to me.

I wrap my arms around his waist and hug him tight. I can feel his body relax into mine, and it's almost as good as an orgasm.

"I said I don't mind because I don't mind. I'd be lying if I said I didn't notice, but I also didn't really notice because it's just part of you. Can you take it off for a short while? I did some research online and I can offer you lotion. Do you need a special compression sock?"

"I can go a night or two without my shrinker." Erik says. He presses a small button at the bottom of the fiberglass shell and then his leg is off. He unrolls a thick white sock from over his knee. At the end of the sock is a metal pin, one that undoubtedly attaches to the prosthetic. Erik leaves the sock inside out and sets them on the floor next to my bed. He slides into the sheets next to me, and I smile as he hunkers down under the covers. He pushes his arm under my neck and tugs me into his chest.

"This okay?"

He's warm and solid against my body, and I swear he's already gearing up below the belt for round two.

"This is perfect."

I already feel drowsy, my eyelids drooping as his body heat cocoons me. For just this moment, I can let myself believe that this is the start of something real. Something beautiful. I'll pretend that we had a round of hot sex because we're a regular couple—one that can't keep our hands off each other—instead of two people desperate to soak up every second we have together as our time slips from between our cupped hands like sand.

Erik's breathing evens out, puffing warm air over my skin. His eyes close, and even in sleep, the corners of his mouth tip up.

"You're the right person," I press the words into his skin. "This just isn't the right time for either of us. No matter how much I wish it was."

"Don't count me out just yet." He pulls me in closer.

"I thought you were asleep."

Erik hums in agreement and kisses me back when I press my mouth to his. He bands his arms across my hips when I turn away, pressing my back to his front.

"We still have a little time," he says into my hair.

And two hours later when I wake to the soft kisses he presses to the nape of my neck and the insistent piece of him pressed to the soft curve of my ass, I lift his hand to cup my breast and he proves true to his word as he lifts my thigh, hooks my foot over the back of his hip, and slides deep inside me for the second time.

18 ERIK

If I thought my first flight home was tough, this one is going to be impossible. Quinn and I stayed together through the night and most of this morning, and it was glorious. Everything I've never let myself want. She was still asleep when I woke, my body wrapped around hers like a climbing vine. My hand cupping her breast in a proprietary grip, and my thigh pressed between her legs. There'd been a large orange cat asleep against the curve of my back, purring like white noise into the room. Quinn snores a little, the snuffling sound cute in the otherwise quiet house.

We both stayed up late and in bed the entire evening. I lost count of the rounds of sex some time after midnight, but I'll never forget the husky sound of her laugh or the deep moan she makes when she clenches down on my fingers, my tongue, my cock as she comes. We didn't even break long enough to eat or shower. We sat propped up against the headboard as she read chapters of her current novel out loud, blushing as the characters stripped off their clothes.

When her cat joined us, we introduced Tesseract to Loki through photos on my phone.

It's terrifying how easily we seem to fit, and I'm terrified by the prospect of walking away. I can't remember the last time I even considered staying with someone.

Quinn's hair is a tangled mess, falling over her eyes and nose, and shifting every time she breathes. My fingers tingle with the desire to push it back out of her face and press my mouth to hers, but I don't want to wake her. I've been waiting, almost all night, for her to ask about my leg, comment on it, do something other than forget it's missing, but she hasn't. I'm growing increasingly aware that I need to tell her about the other parts of my past. At first, putting it off had been understandable because we had no plans to see each other again. I can't pretend that still applies. Even if this is our last moment together, our last chance, Quinn still deserves to have all the information.

I've gotten so good at not sharing this piece of my past that I'm nauseated at the thought of telling her. I'm terrified that it will change everything between us. It changed everything in my family and now I'm clawing my way back to them millimeter by millimeter. What if she looks at me as an invalid? What if she doesn't? It's going to hurt her. Telling her about my past is going to bring up all the fear and worry she has for her dad. I don't want to do that to her either.

It needs to be soon, or I won't do it. Not until I'm back in Chicago and typing the words out on my phone. The scared teenager I never grew out of wants to tell her over text. The adult I've become, the one with extensive therapy under his belt and fancy degrees, knows she deserves this in person. But as she stirs, her body arching against mine, I decide it doesn't have to be right this second. It can wait a bit longer. I still have time.

Quinn freezes, stiffening as if she's surprised I'm still here, but then she relaxes almost immediately and turns to face me. I give into the need and brush her hair back, letting my mouth move across hers in a gentle sweep.

"What time is it?" She stretches her arms over her head before looping them around my neck.

"Close to ten."

I try not to laugh when she sits up so fast she almost falls off the mattress.

"You were supposed to do breakfast with your mom today." She rolls to her feet, on purpose this time, and drags a hand through the riot of her hair. I prop myself up on my elbow, wondering if I can tempt her back under the covers one more time, but she's already twisting her red hair into a coil and her eyes look a little too wide. Our leisurely morning is over.

I sit up and reach for my sock and my leg. It's second nature to slide the sleeve up over my knee and push the pin down into its socket. I hear the click that tells me everything is connected, and I plant both feet on the floor, getting my bearings. My clothes come sailing over the bed, smacking into my back, and okay, I was not expecting that. Quinn threw them.

"Are you trying to get rid of me?" I ask.

She braces her hands on her ample hips and her head cocks to the side. She isn't frowning, but she gives a long-suffering sigh. The kind that tells me she thinks I should already understand what she's about to say.

"I don't want your mom thinking we were having sex all night." She grabs a pair of light purple panties from the top drawer of her dresser and bends at the waist to step into them. I should one hundred percent look somewhere else. I don't.

"First, I'm a grown adult and my mom doesn't keep tabs on my whereabouts," I say, and while Quinn blinks at me like she doubts every word out of my mouth, it's true. My mother doesn't keep tabs on me. Not after I've pushed her to the outskirts of my life. "Second, we were having sex all night."

I duck as a pillow hurtles toward me. This violent streak of hers is new.

It's cute.

I like it.

"We still need to get you home," Quinn says, and I want to wrap myself in the curve of her smile. "I can't monopolize all your time. I bet she still wants to see you."

My immediate thought is to say that my mom won't care, that we aren't that close, but I don't. She cares. She wants more than I can give her. More time, more togetherness, just more. She gave me space because I once demanded it, and after all these years of putting distance between us, I now don't know how to bridge the gap. I still talk to her via text and email, but nothing deeper than surface-level interactions. Everything I could say leaves my brain and I'm that teenager in a hospital bed again, with nothing on my mind except my pain and fear and the knowledge that I can't say anything because it will hurt the people I love.

How many times had Mom tried to connect only to say the wrong thing or ask the wrong questions? How many times did I bite her head off before she stopped trying?

It's time to work on that.

Maybe we both can.

Quinn grabs a pair of jeans and hops from foot to foot as she pulls them up. I could remind her I have a car here at her house and she doesn't need to get dressed to see me off, but she jiggles so nicely as she buttons the denim at her waist that I don't have the heart to stop her. She picks another one of those delicate tank tops I could rip with my teeth, and shrugs on a plaid flannel. She looks casual, gorgeous, and I'm still sitting on the edge of her bed with my pants and underwear snagged around my ankles.

"Let's move, Varg," Quinn says, yanking her hair up into some form of impossible pouf of copper at the top of her head.

We're in Vic's car, halfway to Vic's house, when she looks across the console at me and blinks her wide green eyes.

"There is no reason for me to be in this car right now, is there?"

I can't help but laugh, head thrown back against the buttery leather headrest. "Maybe I need moral support," I say, and wonder if she can tell I'm one hundred percent serious. Maybe it's because I know Quinn and her dad are so close. Maybe it's because one thing my mom keeps saying to me is how much she adores Quinn. Maybe it's because I'm not ready to say goodbye just yet.

"The good news is that I like your mom," Quinn laughs, too. "But if she asks, we spent the night playing scrabble, and you slept in the guest room."

"Does your house even have a guest room? I thought the third bedroom was an office-library-lounge space?"

Her grin is blinding. "Your mom doesn't know that."

I can't stop my smile. I don't want to. Quinn is a light breeze over sweaty skin after too long stuck in a dank, dark basement. She's the first sip of water, sweet and cool, after waking up with a hangover and cotton mouth. I spend a majority of my day cataloging things to share with her during our next conversation, and then when we talk…well time seems to poof out of existence like the social construct it is.

We pull into my brother's extensive driveway, and I park the car in the middle of the circle. I open Quinn's door for her, handing her out onto the shoveled path, and feel like the lowest of the low. Vic is on the road. I should have been the one here with a shovel, clearing the fresh powder and laying down rock salt. It's likely that Vic pays someone to do it, even when he is home, but… I should have offered. The front door swings open and there is my mom. It hadn't occurred to me to tell her I was bringing company with me. I'm sure this counts as rude, but I can't bring myself to care. I'm not ready to let Quinn go. Not yet.

"Hi Erik," my mom waves, "Hi Quinn. It's nice to see you again. I'll make myself scarce."

"No need." Quinn takes the steps two at a time and envelops my mother in a tight hug. "I forgot it was impolite to show up uninvited until we were already on the way, but we came because someone stood you up for a breakfast date."

Mom looks over Quinn's shoulder and pins me in place with her gaze. I expect anger, disappointment, or maybe just a blank nothing, but there's something else in her hazel eyes.

I try not to flinch at the worry I see reflected at me before she shutters her expression and turns a forced smile back on Quinn. Worry. I should have called. Shit. I didn't think. For a moment I'm sixteen again in that hospital bed, tubes and wires hooked up to terrifying monitors and all I can see on my mother's face is bone-deep terror.

I blink the memory away.

"I'm sorry I didn't call," I say, reaching one of my arms out. I hold it wide, hoping my mother gets the hint. "I missed breakfast, but we'd love to share brunch with you."

There's a moment, time suspended in a glass jar full of sand, and I think she'll step back. It's my fault I let it get this far, this strained. I can't blame the boy I was, creating stone-hard walls to protect the tenderest parts of myself, but those stone walls cut everyone out. My mother, my sister, my twin included. Then my mom melts into me, and this hug is warmer than I'd imagined. It's nice.

"I don't want to impose," Mom says and her voice quiet like she needs to offer both of us an out, but I wouldn't be here if I wasn't... if I didn't...

"I want to spend time with you," I say, and mean it.

"Okay," This time Mom's smile is warm and welcoming and real. "Would you rather make something here or go out?"

Quinn watches the exchange between me and my mother with the kind of avid interest that reminds me of someone preparing to be quizzed later. She must notice the tension ramping back up after my mother's offer to cook. If I am passable in the kitchen, it isn't because I inherited my non-existent skills from my mom. Vic has a meal plan and a chef from the team to prep most of his meals, but I don't think the guy works when the team is on the road.

"I'm a whiz in the kitchen," Quinn says. "Especially with breakfast food. Why don't I set up in there and you guys can have your mother-son morning?" She busses my cheek like we've been kissing each other quick goodbyes for years, and then she's over the threshold and inside the house. "I'll find the kitchen, no worries." She calls out and I duck my head so she won't see me trying hard not to laugh. She is adorable.

"I like her." My mom backs up so I can step inside, too.

"So do I." It might be a bigger understatement than the time I told someone it was disappointing to have to quit hockey just as my career was starting. I'm years into not sugar-coating my feelings. "I more than like her. If we were in the same city…well, things might have been very different for us."

"She makes you happy," my mom nods. She reaches her hand toward me as if she wants to touch my face, but freezes, unsure. I bring her palm to my stubbled cheek and allow her to cup my jaw. Her smile flickers. "I'm glad she does. You deserve someone in your life who makes you smile. It's been a long time since your brother or sister or I could do that."

It's not for their lack of trying.

I thread my fingers through mom's and squeeze her hand in mine.

"That was never about you, or Vic, or Anna." It had been naïve to hope they all knew that. "I put up walls to protect myself, no matter who ended up on the other side of them." I clear my throat because this is important. This is the realization I've been working on for the last few weeks, maybe even longer, and I want to be sure Mom hears it. Quinn's light had blinded me for a moment, distracting me from half my goal. "I want to do things differently now. Try to find a happy medium."

"I'd like that too," Mom says, and she drops her hand and her eyes as she blinks back tears.

We step into the enormous kitchen to find that Quinn already has several large pots and pans on Vic's commercial-grade stove. I watch her move, her arms flexing as she dips a piece of bread into a large white bowl and then drops it into a sizzling pan. Her ass jiggles as she uses a spatula to stir a pan full of eggs. Her tank top rides up as she reaches for something in the spice cabinet, exposing a sliver of her soft skin. She's moved right in and made herself comfortable, her flannel looped over the back of one of the kitchen chairs, and now as I stare at her I can see her doing the same in my house. Not just my brother's. The thought is so appealing that I go dizzy for a moment.

I join her at the stove and take the spatula, commandeering the pan of scrambled eggs. They're fluffy and golden, smelling nutty and delicious. My stomach growls, and Quinn's lips quirk into a smile. She knows what I've done to work up an appetite. I know her brain has gone down the dirty rabbit's hole because she's blushing, redness climbing her face. I could almost blame it on the heat from the stove, except that she'd already been beautifully damp with sweat, her hair curling softly at her temples, long before the blush started. I smile back at her and wink.

I tip the eggs onto a waiting plate and turn off the heat. I reach for a paper towel and blot strips of crisp bacon as Quinn slides six perfect pieces of French toast onto a large platter. My mother starts coffee and pulls a bottle of fresh orange juice from the fridge. I marvel at how perfectly synchronized we all are. Every time I look Quinn's way, she snaps her eyes away as though I won't know she's been staring. I can't fault her. I am happy to stare until she looks my way, too. And if our eyes catch and it feels like being struck by a bolt of lightning? Rooted to the spot as heat explodes out from my chest? Well then, that's even better.

"You have to tell her," my mom says, her voice just above a whisper. At least she has the grace to wait for Quinn to excuse herself to go to the bathroom.

And I know. I planned on it this morning before the clock conspired against me. At first, my cancer diagnosis hadn't been relevant. It's personal, private information that a stranger has no business knowing. But Quinn isn't a stranger any longer. She's a woman I want more than I thought possible, even if she lives in a different state. Even if we have no future, she's still someone I consider a friend, someone who's worthy of knowing this secret piece of myself. But there's also Quinn's dad.

This is a loaded situation, not something to spring on her. I've seen her fears and her heartache with her father being sick. What would it do to her to know that I had been too? Would it help? Show her I have insight? Empathy? Would it hurt? Would she decide that fear outweighs anything else we might have been building to? And I'm still leaving. I told myself I'd share if the moment presented itself and it hadn't. This was something I need to share in person, but the truth is I'm terrified. I've already lost so many of the people who matter to me because of cancer. I don't want to lose her too.

But I'm going to anyway. Whether I share this piece of me or not, I'm going to lose Quinn Cooper the minute I get back on that plane to Chicago.

The problem with secrets is that the longer we put off sharing them, the easier they became to avoid.

Logically, I know most people wouldn't fault me for holding this piece back. Emotionally, I also knew that Quinn's feelings on the matter are tied to her dad. Logic sometimes has no place in how we feel when it comes to people we care about. She could be furious with me for holding this back. Enraged I kept it a secret. What if she assumes it's because I don't trust her? As insulting as I know it is to assume what she can and cannot handle, it's worse to think she could misunderstand.

"I will," I tell my mother, "I just haven't found the right time."

"Sweet boy." she lays her hand over mine, her palm warm from the coffee mug she's been holding onto. "There's never a right time to tell a woman that you're in love with her."

19
QUINN

The car ride back to my house is subdued. I offered to take an Uber so Erik could spend more time with his mom, but he insisted on driving me, claiming I'm on his way to the hotel. It's a blatant lie—nothing is on the way to his hotel—but I appreciate the gesture. I appreciate the extra time together, too. I hadn't meant to infringe on his time with his mom. I hadn't even thought about it until we were half-way to Vic's McMansion. I tried to bow out, letting them have their time together, but that hadn't worked. I could read the tension between mother and son from across the driveway and they'd still teamed up to keep me in the house.

They don't hate each other and they weren't angry—I studied them to be sure that Maria wasn't mad I'd shown up—but there was a hesitation when they talked. A disconnect. As if both mother and son had things they wanted to say and do, but something held them back. Both were muted, the vibrancy of their personalities dim under the bright kitchen lights.

"Is everything okay?" I ask as Erik flicks on the blinker and turns onto my street.

He nods, his mouth set in a grim line I'm not used to seeing. I might not have known Erik for long, but I know this isn't him. Erik might be reserved, but there's a curve to the corners of his mouth, a laugh in his hazel eyes. Now he looks almost pale in the driver's seat, his golden skin ashen. It's better than green, but...

"Are you going to be sick?" I ask, and he shakes his head.

The car slows to a crawl. The odometer reads far below the already-low speed limit. No one drives like this on my street. The neighbors have been complaining for months, petitioning the city for speed bumps. Even I'm guilty of driving a little too fast on the tree-lined straightaway. Hell, Erik pulled out faster this morning, although we were running late. If I didn't know better, I'd think he's stalling. Does he not want to say goodbye?

When he drives right past my house, I'm sure he's stalling.

"Erik?" I place my hand on his thigh, feeling the muscles flex under my palm.

The tiny pool of hope drains away. This is more than nerves. Something is very wrong here.

Well, if he wants to murder me, he's had better opportunities. I'm pretty sure he's about to give me "the speech." The "we're better off as friends" speech. The "it's not you, it's me," speech. The "I'm not looking for anything serious right now," speech. The thought hurts more than it should because a) Erik has every right to tell me any of the above, and b) I don't need it spelled out for me when I already know this isn't going anywhere.

It's my fault for muddying the waters. Not with sex, but by tagging along this morning. He probably wants to remind me logistics aren't in our favor, but he doesn't need to. We've both been pretty clear about not looking for anything serious, and it's not his fault that maybe I'm fantasizing about more. I know he hasn't offered it. I'm not stupid, and I wouldn't have time for it even if a relationship was on the table. I'm focused on my dad…

Except my dad wants me to have a life beyond him and cancer.

Maybe that's why this hurts so much. Erik giving me a brush off that doesn't need to be given…it rankles. Even if he hasn't said anything yet.

Overshooting my house is dramatic. He could have dumped me in my driveway. What am I supposed to do now? Ride back with him? Get out and walk? Call an Uber? He couldn't have thought that part through. Erik isn't cruel, even if he's about to dump me. Does it even count as being dumped if we aren't together?

Erik pulls the car into the parking lot of a small playground. Kids litter the plastic and metal structures, ignoring the snow as they play in the cold winter sun. Most have fluorescent colored snow gear and even from inside the car I can imagine the swish swish swish of nylon as they run. Next to the playground is a battered tennis court, the net sagging and full of holes, and a wide green space where a couple is throwing a bright yellow ball for a brown and black speckled dog.

I don't notice Erik leaving the car until the driver's door slams shut. I jolt in my seat, choking when the seatbelt cuts into my neck, and struggle to climb out too. Erik is already halfway up a small hill, moving toward a metal bench. He doesn't look relaxed or comfortable. He fists his hands on his knees, his throat bobbing as he swallows. Suddenly, he bends at the waist and tugs on the length of his dark blonde hair. It isn't gentle. It looks like he wants to pull the individual strands out from the follicles.

I'd rather be almost anywhere else, but I can't leave him like this. I move closer, sliding onto the end of the bench. I leave a good foot between us.

"Everything is not okay," I say, barely resisting the urge to touch him. "I know I don't have the right to ask things of you, but—"

"You have the right," his voice is guttural, clawing its way out of his throat. "Fuck. You have all the right and I should have told you this sooner. A lot sooner."

Well shit.

A girlfriend? A wife? A kid? Something he'd hidden until he saw me with his mother? In his—no, his brother's—space? My mind is spinning out, trying to figure out what his secret could be. Something his mother wouldn't have blown wide open. So probably not a family back in Chicago… except he and his mother don't seem to be close, so maybe she doesn't know either. What could he have held back? He told me about his leg within hours. Maybe I'm wrong and his prosthetic isn't a deeply personal part of him. I'd assumed it was.

My stomach pitches and the palms of my hands are clammy with sweat despite the freezing temperatures. We're only a block from my house. In theory, I can stand up and walk back home. There is nothing stopping me other than morbid curiosity. If this news tears him up inside, well, he deserves every painful second of explaining it to me. And then I can walk home and rage clean. Or something.

"I didn't intend for this to become some big secret."

Okay, so probably not a secret significant other? To be fair, I'd ruled that out, anyway.

"I should have told you after meeting your dad." Erik is still talking and I try to still my rampant thoughts and focus on his words. There's no need for me to speculate. He's telling me now. If I miss it, that's on me. "But then that was it. We'd agreed not to—I still should have said something."

"So say something now," I'm not about to close the space between us, but my brain is no longer whirring painful and muddled thoughts around like dirty laundry.

Erik nods. He pushes back off his hands and leans against the back of the bench. He surveys the park, his attention drawn to a group of kids who've started a pickup game of something with a ball, despite the snow pants and the foot-tall drifts.

"Do you like sports, Quinn?" Erik asks and I frown, tempted to unravel the thread of where this conversation was going.

"I'm not the biggest sports fan. I played volleyball and basketball in high school since the coaches practically forced me to. I'm learning to enjoy hockey."

"But you've always liked art, right?"

Always.

I'd been the girl with the tiny watercolor set and a notebook I carried everywhere. The set of graphite pencils was stored lovingly in my backpack. Dad gave me an easel at three and I never looked back.

"Yes," I say.

Erik relaxes enough to let his arm fall along the back of the bench and I lean back so his fingers can brush the edge of my shoulder.

"I loved sports. Soccer, baseball, basketball. I played everything, but hockey was supreme." He clears his throat. "Vic, Anna, and I had a babysitter that skated. Her boyfriend drove the Zamboni, so she took us down to the rink a lot and he got us free skate rentals. Vic and I didn't start until almost seven. That's late for kids."

First or second grade was late? What was early?

"Money was tight when we all wanted to skate, but mom made it work. It was pretty obvious, pretty quickly, that Vic and I were good. We had local places willing to sponsor us for equipment and travel. That helped a lot. We played well together. Twin Terrors, they called us. The Terrible Trio when we added in Robbie from next door. We were a novelty in a small town that loved hockey more than anything else."

He smiled as the kids whooped and hollered over a win.

"We played together so our natural competitiveness wouldn't destroy the family, but—"

The way he stops that sentence, like he hacked off the edge of the words rather than say them out loud.

"You were better, weren't you?" I ask, and if I move a little closer to him on the bench, nobody needs to know.

Erik nods. "Quitting was never a possibility. I was that cocky. I just assumed I'd be drafted."

"And then you were injured."

He'd been so close to making it, too. I might not know everything about hockey, but even my dad had been impressed that Erik had almost played in the USHL. He'd impressed on me the importance of the league, that Erik had most likely planned to put his name in the draft the minute he was eligible. Dad had also looked up his stats, was confident Erik would have been snapped up that first year.

To have that all taken away in an instant, while his brother kept playing...that would leave a wound. Leg aside, the pain must have threatened to consume him. Blistering his organs and scalding his veins. I don't fault Erik for not going to his brother's games, not when each match-up probably felt like pouring kerosene on the glowing embers of his ruined dream. The distance that would have created between two boys who'd been inseparable—twins—well, no wonder breakfast had seemed strained. Erik's just now clawing his way back to some semblance of a relationship with his family. It's admirable.

He takes a deep breath in through his nose and releases it in a steady puff of air through his mouth. I catch myself matching my breaths to his. Erik closes his eyes and drops his chin to his chest.

"It wasn't an injury," he says and I have to tip my body toward him to hear.

"I'm sorry. I just assumed—"

"I was sick, Quinn." Erik turns to look at me, his eyes haunted and his cheeks gaunt. As if the words are draining his very life-force as they drop onto the bench between us.

I shiver. It's cold outside. The chill I feel has nothing to do with Erik trying to tell me he was...he had.... I'm jumping to conclusions. It's my dad that has me assuming things before I have reason to.

"Cancer," Erik says, sliding the word into my gut like a hot poker. "I was diagnosed with Stage IIB Osteosarcoma the spring after I turned sixteen. I had an eight point three centimeter tumor on my left tibia."

The pain is spreading, radiating out from my chest, and I can't breathe. I can't think. I can't...

In hindsight, I wish I'd said something affirming, supportive, compassionate. I wish I'd said anything and hadn't just stared at him without saying a word.

He watches me, waiting for... something, and I have nothing to give. Once again I'm sitting in the over-bright waiting room at Grace Hospital, trying not to shift too much on the plastic-covered chairs. The arm rests are cutting into my hips and my e-book holds no interest. The hum of some shopping network television channel has been quiet enough to stop anyone from watching, but too loud to ignore. Or maybe the buzz is the fluorescent lights.

There I am again. Stomach pitching as I count down the hours on my watch, reminding myself that while not routine, this surgery is performed a lot and that my dad has some of the best surgeons in the state. Seeing Dr. Wilcox appear two hours too early, but ignoring the lead feeling in my gut because she must be there for someone else. It's just going to be an update, a quick "everything is going great" and then she'll head back to the operating room. That's normal. Doctors give updates to family all the time on Grey's Anatomy.

Except no one is reassuring me of anything...and then Dr. Wilcox asks to speak to me in another room and I'm going numb. Icing over as he tells me to sit down. Frozen as the word "tumor" bombards my ears and my brain short circuits. And the only person who can make it better, who can breathe life right back into my stalled heart, is under general anesthesia having a softball-sized mass cut out of his body while I'm here.

Alone.

One point nine million new cancer diagnoses a year in the United States. Five point five percent of the population here, and yet I never imagined the possibility of it affecting me or someone in my life. I'd worn ribbon pins and taken part in school fundraisers. I'd sat around countless tables listening to the people around me name the friends and family who'd been affected by the disease, aware that I was one of a dwindling number who had no name to offer. I'd cried when I'd come across the stories of young kids fighting for their lives.

It had been luck that had kept me and my loved ones safe, and when that luck ran out, all I could worry about was what I would do if I lost my dad. I hadn't thought about the pain he was in or the way his life was going to be permanently altered. I hadn't thought about how he would feel when his surgery was over and he woke up not healed but facing an even longer road to recovery. No, I'd thought about what I'd do if he died, and months later I am still reeling from how selfish my response had been.

I'm still selfish.

That's still my biggest fear. That I'll lose the one person I've known my entire life and I won't know what to do next. I promised myself that day in the hospital that my dad would never see me cry or rage or panic. I was going to take those feelings and push them so damn deep that he wouldn't have to worry about me. We were going to focus on him. Making him better, getting through each round of chemo and each surgery. We were going to be a unit, coming out together on the other side. No other alternative.

"Quinn?" Erik's hand slides into mine, long fingers squeezing, and I blink to bring his face into focus.

Sometimes I forget how heart-wrenchingly beautiful this man is. How there isn't a single piece of him that isn't appealing. How unfair is it that the universe put him in my life and then slapped a big "not for you," sign across his torso. But I'd take him alive and well and far away, over him sick. I can't handle that. Not Erik. Not now. I don't have it in me to worry about this, too.

I'd give anything now for the man to be dumping me.

"Sick," my throat throbs around the words. "You're sick?"

"No," Erik says, closing the gap between us but still only touching my hand. "No sweetheart, I'm not. I've been NED for over a decade now."

"NED." I've heard the term before, but my brain isn't working at the moment. "Right."

"No evidence of disease. Surgery took the whole tumor, and I finished more chemo as a preventative measure. All my scans and bloodwork have been free and clear."

That sounds good, but it means very little to me when no one had known about my dad until he was open on a surgical table. The bloodwork, the ultrasounds, the whole battery of tests, and no one had noticed a gigantic tumor testing the limits of his bladder.

"What's the reoccurrence rate?" Is that an appropriate question to ask? I should have waited and googled it later. "Sorry, we don't have to talk about it."

Erik shakes his head. "We do. I don't talk about it nearly as much as I should, which means I'm not as okay about it as I want people to think."

"Yeah, so we'll talk about something else." I take a deep breath. I will not make this about me. Not this time.

"Twenty to thirty percent of osteosarcoma patients relapse in the first few years after treatment." Erik says, pulling me against his chest as he speaks. "I'm ten years past the standard five required for remission, Quinn. I still get yearly scans, but I'm as good as I can hope for."

I take several deep breaths, trying to steady the racing thrum of my pulse. His arm around me is the only reason I don't slip right off the bench and land in a heap at his feet. Disease, illness, neither were on my radar when I thought he was acting strange.

"I should have told you sooner," Erik says into my hair. "I'm sorry."

I shake my head, forehead brushing against his jaw. I'm being selfish. I'm being weird. He isn't even mine. He doesn't owe me this information, not now, not before, not ever, and yet I'm devastated by the news. Because he didn't tell me.

Because what if he relapses?

Because... I don't know if I can do this?

Once again, I'm making this all about me.

"When?" I force the question out, "In an ice rink surrounded by strangers? Naked in your hotel room? When I yelled at you at the hospital? When we thought we'd never see each other again?"

"I should have made time. Once I knew I—" Erik scrubs a hand down his face. He didn't have time to shave this morning, and I can hear the rasp of his stubble under her palm. "Definitely before we had sex."

"Why didn't you?"

I know why. This piece of his past is still painful, still sharp. It changed him. That's not something that just goes away. Now the distance between Erik and his mom, Erik and his brother, makes sense. Two weeks ago, I wouldn't have understood, but two weeks ago Dad hadn't looked me in the eye and asked me to see him as more than a cancer patient, to treat him as the same person he was pre-diagnosis. How many times had teenage Erik had to put other people's thoughts and anxieties and hurts above his own? How many times had he looked at his family and seen their fears and worries blanketing everything else he knew? How lonely must that have felt?

"I don't talk about it a lot," Erik says, "And I didn't want to worry you. You have enough going on with your dad."

Guilt twists my guts until I feel like they're going to pop. This isn't and shouldn't be about me. He should only share what he wants to. My reaction shouldn't be something he needs to worry about. I tip my head back so I can press my lips to his scruffy cheek. His kind, darling, and deeply sensitive cheek.

"I love your willingness to put my feelings and my needs first, Erik Varg." I stare into his hazel eyes. "But this time it's not about me. You don't need to shoulder the burden of my worry or my fear or my grief. The thought of anything happening to you scares me more than it probably should, but that's not your responsibility."

"If you think I wouldn't care about the way you feel—" his fury is clear in his voice. It's caustic, biting. I rub circles into the back of his hand.

"Of course you do," I say because Erik has always held my thoughts and opinions in the highest regard and I didn't mean to imply otherwise. "I understand why you didn't say anything before, Erik. And I'm not upset with you. Fuck cancer. It scares me to think that—" that I could lose you too, that I could watch you go through painful surgeries, and pump literal poison into your veins, hoping it kills the tumors before it kills you. That it's probably for the best that this thing between us isn't going anywhere else, since I'm not sure I can handle the worry every time you get a cold. "I'm not upset with you."

Erik slides a cool hand under my jaw and tips my chin up, his thumb brushing over the apple of my cheek. His mouth against mine is a sweet press of lips and tongues. He sips from me once, twice, a third time, and I lean into the contact. We could have been locked together for seconds or decades before Erik pulls back and his finger brushes across my bottom lip. I suck in a breath, ready to fall headlong back into him. Into the heat he fans inside of me and the bubbles he sets loose in my bloodstream.

"We should get going," I whisper against his mouth as he kisses me again. Erik lets his lips follow the path of his thumb and I can feel the corners of his mouth tip up against mine. "Don't smile at me like that." I don't need to dip my eyes down to the bulge at the front of his jeans to know what he thinks I meant. Erik shifts on the bench. "I meant I need to get home to feed Tessie, and I'm sure you have other things to do."

"I don't." Erik says, but his mouth leaves my skin and he leans back against the bench, putting a few extra inches of space between us.

He wants me to invite him back to my house. Maybe for sex, probably for more than that. It would be easy to do. To lose myself under the weight of his muscles and the heat of his touch. And then what? We're right back where we started. Unable to resist spending time together, but not in a position to make more of this than it is. If I invite him back right now, I'm going to do the unthinkable and fall head over heels for him. I won't be able to help myself.

I can't do that. I can handle being the friend he sees when he's in town, but I'm not sure I can keep sleeping with him. Not without losing the rest of my heart. Next time he comes to visit his mom and brother, we can see each other in public. Maybe bring some friends along, chaperones. We can revert to middle-school dance rules and keep space between us.

It's no longer just watching him leave that threatens to break me. I'd been terrified when he shared his diagnosis. Consumed with gut-wrenching fear that I was about to lose him, too. The same selfish need to turn inward and protect myself. To worry about what would happen to me if something happened to him.

It's the same terror I'd felt the last time I'd learned that cancer was threatening someone I love, and it's not fair, not at all, but I have to send Erik right back to Chicago and I have to do it now. I'm already halfway in love with him, and if he stays, I'll slip and fall the rest of the way down. And then I'll spend every spare moment worrying about his health and safety too.

Text Message
Saturday 5:17 PM EST

Erik Varg:

I can still text you, right?

Quinn Cooper:

Of course you can. Why wouldn't you be able to?

I don't know how to answer that without sounding like a dick.

Because I sent you home instead of inviting you in this afternoon?

Yes

I don't know how to explain without sounding like a dick either.

I wasn't expecting anything, Quinn.

I like spending time with you, but I respect your space.

ON ICE

> Things got heavy this afternoon. I think we both needed a reminder of what this thing actually is.

It's okay Quinn. I'm here if and when you're ready.

STELLA STEVENSON

Text Message
Sunday 5:28 PM EST

Quinn Cooper:

> I don't know what time your flight is, but will you let me know when you're home?

Erik Varg:

> Of course. It'll be late but I'll text you when we land.

> Or when you get home. Whatever is easiest.

> My apartment's about 35 minutes from the airport. I'll let you know when I land so you don't have to stay up.

> Thank you.

> Sorry.

> I just worry.

> That's not something you need to apologize for.

> I can't afford to worry about you Erik.
>
> This was just supposed to be one night and here I am asking you to tell me when you get home safely.

I'm sorry.

STELLA STEVENSON

Text Message
Monday 3:03 AM EST

Erik Varg:

Just walked in the door.

Quinn Cooper:

Finally. I was going to send out a search party.

Shit. Did I wake you? It must be 3am your time.

Go to bed. I figured you'd see this in the morning.

Technically it is the morning and I get up early anyway. How was your flight?

It was pretty standard. Almost everyone slept so just imagine being stuck in a room full of snoring people while you twiddle your thumbs and wait for sleep to take you too.

I don't think I could ever sleep on a plane. If my death is coming I want to stare it in the face.

ON ICE

> Also, the last time Jen slept on a flight, someone bumped into the flight attendant on a mad dash for the bathroom and she ended up wearing a whole can of tomato juice. No thanks.

My sympathies. I usually sleep on flights. Conked out before takeoff.

> Not this time?

No.

I just had a lot to think about.

> Want to talk about it?

Back to you not sleeping either...

No one gets up this early. That is serial killer level shit. 3 am is still considered late-at-night.

> I think I find that offensive. I'm not a serial killer. My criminal proclivities are less murdery.

STELLA STEVENSON

> Should I be scared right now?

> Of course not. I'd never hurt someone I care about.

20 ERIK

Two weeks later, I'm back in Chicago and back into my routine. Well, not really my routine, but I think this may just be my new version of normal. Wake up, check my phone for a grand total of zero messages, hit the gym, work, come home, check again, work more, turn on a hockey game, check one more time, go to bed.

I spent the first week waiting for a message from Quinn, watching my silent phone with rabid intent. After the first few days of nothing, I even put the ringer on. My theory was that she'd be more likely to text me if I needed the phone to be silent—in an important meeting, for example. I was wrong.

It wasn't complete radio silence. I got a quick response when I reached out first, but nothing like the conversations we'd been passing back and forth before my second trip to Quarry Creek.

So as week one ended and week two began, I pulled back, too. Quinn is on my mind from sunup until sunup again, but if she needs space, then that's something I can respect. I'd overwhelmed her, stormed her defenses a little too vigorously, even when I knew I wasn't meant to be more than a footnote in her story. A few nights of brain-melting sex, a few dates that I'd tuck into my memory forever, and nothing more than that. Except...

She cares about me.

That isn't arrogance. It isn't me bragging. It's the knowing that seeps deep into your bones when like recognizes like. She feels for me the way I feel for her and there's fuck all we can do about it because we are not only separated by multiple states, and our jobs, but also by cancer.

Quinn is barely holding on, in her own mind, as she handles the day-to-day of her dad's treatment. She's been pushing her reactions so far down that she's in danger of detonating. Combusting until nothing remains but broken shards of the woman I love. My history, no matter how healthy I am now, is fuel on the fire. Because no matter how hard Quinn tries to pretend that she has everything under control, she cares deeply, worries with her whole being.

So while every fiber of my being is urging me to crush the space between us, there's also a little voice in the back of my mind telling me she's doing us both a favor. It's well past time for us to let this temptation, this pull, die a natural death. Quinn was smart enough to stomp on the brakes. I can try to do the same. Try being the operative word.

My phone rings and I don't lunge for it because I'm trying here, but it's a near miss. I'm not expecting it to be Quinn. I'm not, but my brain still shorts out and warmth spreads through my veins just in case as I answer the call.

"Hi Erik," my mom says down the line, and I knew it wasn't Quinn. I did, but my stomach pitches at the familiar voice. "Is this a good time?"

It is, and it isn't.

Even a month ago I would have said no time was a good time to chat with my mother, but I'm working on that too. Trying here, too. We aren't calling every day. We aren't sharing inside secrets, but this is our third call this week and while I still hold my breath every time the conversation hits a lull, it gets a little easier every time.

"It's fine, Mom." I say and open my refrigerator. "How are you?"

I pull open the crisper drawer and look at all the produce. I don't want to cook anything, I just want to keep busy. It's easier to make it through each call if I'm multitasking. Not because I want to ignore my mother, or get through the back and forth faster, but because I have less time to overthink each answer. I've heard the stories of long-time friends coming back together after years apart, chatting as if no time has passed. That doesn't always apply when the original relationship suffocated under guilt and fear and silence. We're easing into this together. Me and mom. Me and Vic. I have to believe that the results will be worth it.

"The boys stopped by the hospital today and signed autographs, took photos." There's a heavy pause as I take her words in and turn them over to see if they are as sharp as they feel. We try to avoid both cancer and hockey for now. We can't do that forever, not if we're both serious about finding our footing, but for now both topics are too sensitive as we fumble our way back to normal. These words feel tender, but it's like poking a week-old bruise instead of a fresh one. An ache I can stand.

"I'm sorry," my mom says, "I didn't mean…"

She sighs and I know that this is where I need to say something, anything, to bridge the gap.

"It's okay," and it is. Her son plays in the NHL. He moved her in with him. She leveled up to be the ultimate hockey mom, and it's okay that she's proud of Vic. Underneath the hurt, I am too. "I bet the kids had a great time. Did anyone beat Robbie in arm wrestling this time?"

Another pause. We're the champions of awkward silences, and I know she's wondering where I heard that Robbie Oakes likes to throw the competition so that the kids win every time.

"You're talking to Vic?" she asks and I can hear the tremor in her voice. God, we've all done a hell-of-a-number on each other over the last decade and a half.

And while I never stopped talking to Vic—he's my twin, we used to live in the same city—it feels like there's been a shift between us, too. Probably since the night he lied his way into my hotel room and we watched British baking shows together while I tried not to think about a gorgeous, hesitant redhead.

"Robbie told me that one," I say, and I can hear the sniffle through the speaker because she gets what I'm trying to tell her. Robbie was the third in our trio. He's half the reason Vic was interested in playing for the Arctic. *If we can't play together, at least I have Robbie.* That's what Vic said all those years ago as I lay in the over-starched hospital sheets and wished everyone would just leave me alone. There were days I hated Robbie almost more than cancer, because my terrified teenage brain told me he swooped in and stole my spot right out from under me. I was wrong.

"Oh baby," there's another sniffle, and I grab sandwich fixings to distract myself from the itchiness I feel at my mother's distress. It isn't my job to fix this for her. It isn't her job to hide this from me. "How's Loki?"

"Your grand cat is good." I grab a loaf of bread and a knife, debating whether I need a plate, too. "I, uh, hear you got some houseplants."

"Anna told me her greenhouse is her baby, so I figured I should sink into my role as grandma. Get some practice."

I pause, closing my eyes as the tension leeches from my body. We made it through a minefield and are finally back on safer ground.

"And just think," I try to keep my voice light, teasing, "No dirty diapers."

"Anna did tell me about this great fertilizer she likes to use—"

"No," I cut her off. "Lack of shit was a perk."

And there it is. A little watery, weak, like a muscle straining after months of disuse, but my mother laughs into the phone and I smile into my ham and cheese. Baby steps. Each day this will get easier until we won't even remember it was hard.

"How's Quinn?" My mother asks, and the pain from that question is worse than when we try to talk about hockey. Or cancer. "She's such a darling. Her students made cards for all the kids. It was so sweet."

I want to tell my mom that Quinn is good. That's she amazing, wonderful, everything. That I probably love her, am in love with her, would give her forever... but the reality is staring me in the face. Not literally, that's Loki eyeing my sandwich, but the reason I started calling my mom, the reason I started texting my brother, is almost entirely because of Quinn. Half of that is watching her relationship with her dad. Cancer or not, I've never seen a closer bond between parent and kid. Parent and adult kid. We used to be like that. I want that back.

The other half is that I couldn't keep staring at my silent phone without fabricating a reason to be checking it. Every time I couldn't resist wanting to talk to her, I texted Vic. Every time I started dialing Quinn's number, I backspaced and dialed my mom's. I thought nothing of calling my mom if it meant Quinn was happy, if her dad was happy. She's the reason I've made it this far, and as much as I want to tell her that, to thank her for that, it's more important that I tell my mom the truth.

"You know we aren't together, right?" I ask and feel the pinch in my chest at the words. The silence spreads again and I prepare myself for the rebuttals I know are headed my way.

But you love her... I do.

But she was good for you... yes, she is.

You don't want to be in a relationship?... With her? Yes. But I can't.

Wasn't the sex good?... Okay, that question has Vic's voice behind it and yeah, the sex was phenomenal.

"Long-distance relationships are tough," my mom says instead, "Maybe if your job wasn't there and hers wasn't here..." she trails off and I let her.

I've thought about that too. In fact, I have an email flagged in my inbox. One specifically offering me the solution to that very issue...

> From: Adrummond@gracehospital.org
>
> Subject: Future Opportunity
>
> Dr. Varg,
>
> We wanted to share our deepest gratitude for all the time and work you've put into getting our psychology and psychiatry offerings on par with the rest of our oncology department. We are confident that the changes you've helped us implement will make a significant difference in the care and treatment of each of our pediatric patients and their family members.
>
> We'd love to continue the partnership and would be remiss if we didn't mention that the department head position is yours if you are interested. We can offer competitive compensation and would love to have you join the team at Grace Hospital.
>
> Sincerely,
> Andrew Drummond, Chief of Staff

The email doesn't matter. I'm not taking the job with Grace Hospital. I'm not moving my practice a thousand miles away to a new state. I'm not selling my condo or packing up my trickster cat. Because… well, I was a lot more sure of my reasoning before this phone call. I think it had something to do with her pulling back. Quinn is already struggling with cancer and her father. She doesn't need me to add my own variables to that equation.

"Oh," my mom's voice is soft, "I'm sorry. I thought… You two fit so well. You had so much in common."

Did we? Or did we share chemistry and attraction and cancer? Did I go from being the man she fantasized about to the man causing her more heartache?

"It's just complicated, Mom." I scrub a hand down my face and nudge my plate closer to my cat. He can steal whatever parts of it he wants. I no longer have an appetite. "I'm pretty sure I scare her."

I can hear my mother bristling through the phone even before she opens her mouth.

"If she has an issue with your—"

"She doesn't." It's not my leg that scares Quinn. That would be an easy way to put her behind me, but it's not that. Not at all.

"Then what could she possibly be afraid of? You're a kind man. A smart man. You're employed."

Well, when my mother puts it like that, who wouldn't find me a catch? Or maybe run screaming because my mommy is the one hyping me up. The irony, of course, is that we aren't as close as that makes us sound.

"I had cancer, Mom." And just like that, I break one of the few unwritten rules for our phone calls. There's a long pause and I can't tell if that tap-tap-tapping is my heartbeat or her drumming her fingers on her counters. That was always her nervous response.

"But so does her dad," my mom says. "She understands what it's like."

And that's why I scare her.

"When I was sick, back at the beginning, when I was just starting chemo, could you have dated someone in remission? Someone who'd lived through what your kid was experiencing?"

"I want to say it wouldn't have mattered."

"One of her first questions was about recurrence rates." I think I hear my mother sigh, but I keep going, ripping the bandage holding my heart together clean off. "I can't be another thing she worries about. Not when I have nothing to offer her. It's not fair to either of us, Mom."

"You have a lot to offer," my mom insists as I hear the slam of a door and the pounding of footsteps.

Vic's headed out of town for a slew of away games and it sounds like he's running late. I can hear him tromping through his own house like a stampede of confused elephants. There's a rustling sound and I think my mom put her hand over the speaker on her phone because I can hear the murmurings of a conversation but can't make out their words. Everything sounds like it's underwater and maybe I should hang up, but I don't. Vic gets louder and then my mom's hand drops away.

"Erik, honey, have you talked to Quinn today?"

Half of me wants to pitch my phone across my kitchen. Didn't I just explain that we aren't good for each other? That we aren't together? Wouldn't it be safe to assume that I haven't been speaking to her at all? Not by my choice. The other half is tense. Half the distance between me and my mother, me and my brother stems from miscommunication and lack of trust. I can give her the benefit of the doubt. She wouldn't be asking right now if it wasn't important. Something happened. Something Vic knows about, but not me.

"I haven't," I say, and then there's another muffled scuffle before my brother is on the other end of the line.

"Erik," He sounds panicked, I don't think I've ever heard calm, unflappable Vic sound so off-center. Not in years. "When did you last talk to Quinn?"

I don't want to admit that it's been almost two weeks.

"Is she okay?" I ask instead, feeling ice bleed through my veins.

"It's her dad," Vic says, "Fuck! I need to be at the airport in twenty-five minutes and we won't be home for five days."

"Is Sean okay?" I feel like a broken record, only able to skip and ask the same questions over and over again, but Vic is talking to himself and to our mom and he's not focusing on what I need to know. "Vic! Is he—"

I can't bring myself to finish the sentence. I can't put that information out into the universe.

"All I know is he's having another surgery and Quinn has gone radio silent." Vic curses again. "She hasn't been home. Jen can't get ahold of her, I can't get ahold of her—"

"Does she know what's going on?"

"I don't know," Vic says. "Jen called me and asked me to check with you. She's trying a few other friends."

Okay. Deep breath. Where the fuck is therapist Erik when I need him? Okay. Sean needs surgery and no one can find Quinn. Vic has a plane to catch. I can fix this. I can.

"Give the phone back to mom, Vic, and have her call Jen. You go get on your plane. You need to crush Arizona tomorrow. I'll handle this." I take a deep breath myself. "We're going to find her."

She's not alone.

21
QUINN

I've seen this commercial three times in the past twenty minutes. It's for hemorrhoid ointment. The one after it is a promo for the Arctic, and the one after that has golden retriever puppies going camping. I don't know why it's bothering me so much. It's not like the volume is loud enough for me to hear what they're saying, anyway. I could look for the remote, but my arms and legs feel too heavy to move from this seat.

An hour, maybe two. That's how long I was told surgery would take, not including prep time or coming out of anesthesia. Also not including any complications they might find on the table. I've only been sitting here for less than half an hour. I doubt they've even started yet. Dad's probably sitting on a gurney making jokes with whoever they tasked with monitoring him. He'd tried that with me too, but the pinched lines around his mouth were hard to ignore. So was the pale skin stretched tight over his cheekbones.

This is what happens when I take time for myself. I do something dumb like fall halfway in love with the wrong person, and then wallow in despair when I'm reminded that it was a stupid idea. And while I'm wallowing and feeling sorry for myself, I selfishly neglect the person who is supposed to matter the most. I took two days off from seeing Dad. I wanted to prove to him I wasn't hovering, but I also wasn't interested in fending off questions about Erik Varg and the best date of my life.

And because I stayed away, I missed the early warning signs.

It only took one look at his face yesterday to see the strain and I wanted to yell, cry, rage. How could he not tell me something was wrong? How could he not have contacted his surgeon? His doctor? Somebody? The man had the audacity to tell me I was overreacting, but if that's true then why did they put him on the surgical board this morning, dress him in a paper gown, and have the surgeons in his room talking through the potential complications if they don't go in and remove the dead tissue from around his stoma.

I've watched enough hospital drama shows to know what the words "excise" and "necrotic" mean. Would he have called me when they told him surgery was the only option left?

I squeeze my hands around the plastic arms of the waiting room chair, feeling the ache in my bones as I breathe in two-three-four and out again.

Routine surgery. This is all just a regular, everyday occurrence for the doctors. An uncommon, but serious, complication. The surgeon is confident they can fix it.

Don't worry.

Don't. Worry.
Don't.
Fucking.
Worry.

Someone's damn phone is ringing. Not just vibrating, but full-on sound. The marimba grates against my already frayed nerves, and I clench my eyes closed, determined to block the sound from my brain. What I want to do is turn around and glare at whoever couldn't turn their phone off. What could be more important than the reason they're here in this surgical waiting room?

My pulse is pounding, pounding, pounding in my ears and I want to sit here and stave off the waves of nausea by not moving a single part of my body, but I can't seem to stop my leg from shaking. I press my hand down on top of my thigh and it doesn't help. Now the movement is even more obvious. I shouldn't be shaking. There's nothing to worry about. Don't worry. Don't.

The phone goes silent, kicking over to voicemail—although that's even more frustrating. If you're going to let your phone ring and ring and ring while people wait for the worst news of their lives, then the considerate thing to do would be to answer it—and I suck in a lungful of air. The chair makes a god-awful screeching noise as I shift in my seat, but I ignore it. My hips and back are killing me from a night crammed into the extra chair in Dad's room. The nurse was nice enough to let me stay even after visiting hours ended, which was a godsend because I'd been trying to figure out how to wedge myself underneath Dad's hospital bed to avoid being kicked out.

The ringer goes off again, and I look around the waiting room. Maybe a well-placed glare will remind them that the polite thing to do would be to turn off their cell phone, except...except I'm the only one in this particular room.

That can't be right. Who ever heard of an empty hospital waiting room? Even this early in the morning, I expected more people to be packed into the plastic chairs, staring at the door. I'm the only one.

Which means the ringing phone is mine, but it can't be. I have it on Do Not Disturb. Jen's at work. My principal knows I'm unavailable. Dad's in OR 2 under general anesthesia. Who else would be calling? Who else would need me? The ringing stops and starts up again and I fish my phone out of my pocket just to prove to myself that I'm not losing my mind. But I must be, because there's Erik's name scrolling across my screen.

He must have bypassed my do not disturb settings, but I'm not sure why he'd have done that. We never talk on the phone and I haven't texted him in almost two weeks. That choice was a conscious, if painful, one. Space is necessary. It's getting harder and harder to remember that he isn't mine. That he never will be. While I think there's a chance he wants to be more, how would it even work? He isn't here in Quarry Creek and I'm not leaving my dad. I love my job. I love my house. I love Jen. I love all the memories packed into this city and its streets and its people. I even love its goddamn hockey team, something I never thought would be true.

I'm still staring at Erik's name when the phone goes silent and the door to the waiting room swings open. It's okay. I probably wasn't going to answer it, anyway. Even as my thumb still hovers, ready to swipe yes on the call, even as my chest aches and my eyes burn. I can't. I feel like an addict in the middle of a detox. If I give in now, if I hear his smooth honey voice, I'll be right back to where we were when I put space between us. I can't handle that again. Not now. If I thought the last two weeks were hellish, well, it'll be even worse trying again. I don't know if he's left a voicemail, but I'll have to delete that too. And still I clutch my phone and wait for it to ring again. He's tried—I assume they've all been Erik—three times so far. Surely he won't give up now.

I can almost imagine what he'll say.

"Hey, Cooper. Were you going to send me to voicemail again?"

I choke on a laugh, because I can just hear the words in his voice and god I miss him and god this day fucking sucks and I would give a lot to be back on our date. Back on the ice together, or even in his mom's kitchen. Before his past froze me in place and I made things weird. Before I pushed him away again and he went. The burn in my eyes is overwhelming and I feel the hot liquid seep down my cheeks.

What is fucking wrong with me? I'm crying over a guy—even if it's Erik—while my dad is being cut open again. I'm the worst daughter ever. Something could happen to him and when the doctor comes out to give me the gut-wrenching news, I'll be sitting here with tear tracks on my face and everyone will assume I'm crying for my dad. And god that's even worse. Maybe I should step into the bathroom, splash some water on my face, take a lap around the empty halls, something to get myself back under control, but I can't move from this spot.

"Baby, hey, I didn't mean it," the voice in my head says and then a heavy weight wraps around my back, a hand cupping my shoulder as it says, "Don't cry, Quinn."

Because the voice in my head was never in my head. It was Erik, and he's sitting in the seat next to me, pulling me against his broad chest, as his lips press to my temple. Erik, who's still holding his sleek, black cell phone. The one he just called me on three times. Erik, who saw me avoid his call and is still wrapping me up in his warmth. Who knew where I'd be even though it's a school day and I didn't tell him about my dad.

"How?" My question is barely intelligible through the waterfall of tears. They won't stop now. Like someone yanked the cork on the Hoover Dam and now 9.2 trillion—actually with current droughts, it's closer to 3.5 trillion—gallons of water are flooding into all the surrounding states.

How is he here?

How did he know?

How am I supposed to do this?

"Your people were worried about you, so we activated the phone tree." He turns me so I can rest more of my weight against him and it's the most comfortable I've felt in at least forty-eight hours. Possibly the last three-hundred-and-thirty-six. "Jen knew something was going on with your dad, but not the details. When she couldn't get ahold of you, she called Vic for my number, and Vic called me. Actually, I was on the phone with my mother when Vic came in, frantic."

"How are you here?" I press the words to the thick cotton of his Henley.

He's rumpled and wrinkled and smells like an airport, but underneath that is Erik and I snuggle in deeper. All my best laid plans, my reasons for drifting away, and I can't even think of one when he's right here. In Quarry Creek. Letting me sob into his shirt.

"We didn't want you to be alone, Quinn." His hand is tracing circles between my shoulder blades, unerringly finding the knotted ache of tension, and I pull back a fraction of a fraction of an inch. He has to be here for work, and I'd have known that if we were still talking. Jen wouldn't want me here alone and I refused to let her take the day off to be with me, so she sent Erik in her place. This might be the first time I regret not telling my roommate that I've been ghosting this man.

"Right," I say, and sit up in my chair and wipe my cheeks with the back of my hand. I still have my phone out and I push it deep into my pocket and stare at the off-white walls, willing someone else to come in. Anyone. "I'm sure you're busy. I'll be okay. It's supposed to be a quick procedure."

"I don't have anywhere else I need to be," Erik says. He's frowning, but he doesn't pull me back against him. "I got on the first flight that I could. We stopped twice, or I'd have been here sooner, but there weren't any direct flights until this morning."

He... what?

"I'm not here for work. I'm not here because your roommate asked me to be. I'm here because you need someone. I'd have been on that flight even if you were surrounded by people, because I'm here for you."

I'm not weepy. I promised myself I wouldn't be, but even as I press my lips together to hold it all back, the tears leak out again. I didn't have anyone with me the last time I sat in this room. I didn't have anyone to rub my back or hold my hand or wait with me. I'd sat alone in these chairs naively believing that everything was going to be simple, routine, according to plan. And when it wasn't, I sat alone in these chairs and forced down the tears and the heartbreak so that when I went to my dad's room in the ICU, he wouldn't have to deal with my tear-red eyes and puffy face. He wouldn't have to console me after hearing he had cancer.

"It's..." I swallow around the word like it's a hockey puck stuck in my throat. "It's going to be okay. He's going to be... fine."

It's a routine surgery.

We're still within the normal time frame.

Don't worry.

Don't. Worry

Don't.

Fucking.

Worry.

This time Erik doesn't pull me into his chest. He lifts me like I'm not a six foot, two-hundred pound woman and pulls me into his lap. His thighs are thick and strong under me as he shifts them, spacing them out to better distribute my weight and wraps his arms around my middle. I can't remember the last time I showered. I'm wearing leggings I've had since college and there's a hole in the armpit of my sweatshirt, but Erik tucks me right into him and rests his cheeks against my temple.

"Nothing ever feels routine or normal once cancer pulls the rug out from under us, and your dad's method of diagnosis was traumatic." His hand finds mine, our fingers twisting into each other.

"The chair's going to break," I say, because I can't handle the swooping feeling in my gut. I'm terrified that the doctor is going to walk in any minute, and I'm terrified they won't and I'm terrified that I'll never be able to let go of this man.

"If it does, then I'll cushion your fall. I'm a big guy. It won't be the first time I've broken a chair." "Erik," I'm going to stand up. Any minute now. Any minute. Except I'm burrowing in closer to his chest.

"If we go down, then we go down together."

I roll my eyes even as they burn, "Those are song lyrics."

"They are, but I felt you relax, anyway." He presses a kiss to my cheek. "It's okay Quinn. Talk to me. Tell me what's going on. I've got you." And it's there, against his chest, that I realize space was never going to help. Not when I'm head over heels in love with this man.

"Let it out," he says.

Except I can't. He's been here before, on the other side. I can't ask him to carry me through this now. I can't ask him to pitch head-first back into his own history and trauma. He probably wants to run as fast and as far away from me as he can, so he doesn't have to deal with this another minute. Cancer was his reality as a kid. It's even his job now. I can't ask him to make it part of his personal life too.

"I'll start crying again," I say, and this time it's Erik who wipes the salt water from my face.

"Crying is cathartic. Let it out Quinn."

"I can't, Erik. He'll know I was crying, he'll know, and I can't do that to him. I won't. I promised."

He freezes under me, his big body statue-still, before he drops our clasped hands and cups my chin. Erik turns my face to his and his hazel eyes slide back and forth between mine. No one has ever looked this deep into me, like he can see right into the center of my soul.

"Baby girl," his words are whisper soft. "Who did you promise?"

Myself, I think, but I can't say the word out loud, instead the sound that comes out of me is wild and feral, wet with heartache and fury.

"Quinn," my name sounds dark and heavy, ripped from the center of his chest as he crushes me to his body. "You don't always have to be strong. There's no shame in needing help. I can hold things together for you if you just let me."

We're rocking back and forth as I press my palms into my eyes. The pressure from my hands can't stop the shaky tears. Nothing can. Every piece of me aches as if I'm sick, from my toes to my belly button, to my eyelashes. My throat stings as I gasp in breath and after breath. My lungs don't feel like they're getting full enough and I try to suck in more air, choking on each sob.

"Is it another tumor?" Erik asks and I barely hear him over the whoosh of air cycling through my ears. I pause before I shake my head. It's not. At least not yet, but they've been wrong before. "Good." He tucks my face into the hollow of his neck. "That's good, baby girl." Then he lets me cry.

It might be hours later, or seconds, or years, or maybe only five minutes, but Erik holds on through the worst of it. By the time I can swallow between wails, and my body has stopped shaking, the entire front of his shirt is wet and still he doesn't shift me away. I'm tired. Bone-deep tired. It's more than the last two days on red alert, more than a night in an uncomfortable chair, guilt pouring over my head like a monsoon. I'm tired enough that I could fall asleep right here in my ratty clothes. Blink and open my eyes a decade from now.

"I'm sorry," I say, and I mean to sit up, to move off his lap, but my bones aren't working right, they've dissolved inside my skin, so I stay where I am.

"Do you have anyone you can talk to?" Erik asks, pushing my hair back from my damp skin.

My head lolls back when I try to shake it.

"My dad has someone, a therapist. He said you recommended them." I'd blush if I thought I had the energy. "I haven't looked for myself."

"I can recommend some names for you too," Erik tells me. "You deserve someone in your corner. You and your dad deserve that."

"Right. It can't be you." It's not a question, but maybe it is a tiny bit. Maybe he can be the one I call and talk to. Maybe that's what he's offering, and I should say no—we don't need another thing tying our star-crossed hearts together—but maybe, just maybe, I want to be tied to him, anyway.

But Erik shakes his head, "It can't be me, Quinn."

I nod, full of a bravado I don't actually feel. "I know. It would be hard for you to be my therapist all the way from Chicago." My heart has no reason to break, not over a man, not while my dad is in surgery, but it's cracking down the center.

"No, Quinn." Erik leans away from me so I can see the frown creasing his handsome face. "I work with remote patients all the time."

Are those the pieces of my heart crumbling into dust? Maybe. I knew the score. This was why I pulled back. This man can destroy me without even trying. Even when I know there's nothing to destroy.

"I can't be your therapist because it would be insanely unethical."

"Because we fucked." That has to be it, right? I'm sure there's a no-fraternization policy or something. I guess I thought it wouldn't matter if we weren't going to be doing that anymore.

"Because it would be inappropriate for me to offer any sort of treatment plan to someone I have feelings for."

My heart must not have crumbled at all, because there it is, pounding, pounding, pounding in my chest as I stare at this darling man.

"You have to have known." He says as his fingers trace the shape of my lips. "I've been obvious. Even my mother guessed. And my brother."

"Guessed…" I can't get my brain to connect to my mouth. Or any other part of me.

"I'm in love with you, Quinn. Probably since that first night at the Arctic game. I wasn't going to tell you here. Not like this. Not when you have zero mental capacity for what I'm telling you, but you have to know. I love you, Quinn Cooper, and you aren't alone."

"I love you." I couldn't stop the words if I wanted to. A horde of butterflies is winging through my belly. I feel like I might throw up, like I've just reached the top of the tallest roller coaster and I'm about to tip over the edge. "I know I wasn't supposed to, but I do."

Erik's mouth is on mine before my declaration stops ringing in my ears. His lips are warm and soft against my tear-wet ones. His tongue takes ownership of my mouth, pressing deep to curl around mine. His fingers fist in the fabric of my sweatshirt. His other hand circles my throat. I moan into his mouth and feel his lips quirk into a smile against mine. We pass wet kisses back and forth until I can barely breathe. Until I can't remember my name. Until I'm thinking about dragging him to the tiny bathroom.

Then something clatters in the hallway and I remember where we are, shame rushing through my limbs. I'm not ashamed of Erik, or what I feel for him, but this isn't the time or place.

"What happens next?" I say when his eyes blink open and find mine. "You still live in Chicago and I live here." I can't leave my dad and Erik still needs space from his family.

He looks pained as he shakes his head. "Nothing's changed, Quinn. Except now we both know. And maybe next time you can call me directly."

"Won't it hurt too much?" I was trying to get space even before I knew he loved me. Will it hurt more or less to stay away this time?

"I am yours however you want me." Erik says. "You call? I'll answer. You text? I'll write back. You need me? I'll be on the first plane. You want commitment? There's no one else for me." He presses our foreheads together. "You want space? I'll give you whatever you ask for."

I want Erik. I want him with me, and I don't want him with anyone else, but I don't know what I want to do next. I can barely think beyond this moment, this day. Could we really do long distance? Could we be something? If my dad's doing well, I could go out to him in the summers, breaks. He could visit sometimes, too. Is it worth it?

"Don't answer me right now," Erik says. "I'm staying with my mom for the next two days. Right now, we focus on you and your dad. Okay?"

And then he holds me as my mind races, breaking probably every speed record known to humans. He holds me while I tell him about my dad's infection and how antibiotics weren't working as the tissue around his stoma lost blood flow and died. How his surgeon is confident they can fix this, and he'll be as good as a man halfway through chemo can be. But that last time the surgeons promised us it would be quick and routine, they'd found out he was sick. Much sicker than anyone had thought. How he is the only person I have left in the world and I do not know what I would do without him.

Erik holds me until the doctors come and tell me everything went well, and my dad is in recovery. For that, he stands by my side and holds my hand, fingers strong and sure between mine. He waits with me until my dad is ready for visitors and then offers to wait for me, but I bring him with. Letting him into my dad's room as the tears start again. And as I sit there with my head on my dad's starchy hospital sheets, letting his calloused fingers run through my hair, as I watch Erik smile and hold up his phone before connecting my dad to Vic and the rest of the Arctic players via video call.

I realize my dad isn't the only person I have left.

And Erik is definitely worth it.

ON ICE

Text Message
Saturday 2:23 PM CST

Quinn Cooper:

> Thank you for today.

> You were right. Dad hasn't stopped talking about it since you left.

Erik Varg:

> I figured he'd like it. If he wants others let me know. Vic has an extensive hockey movie collection. Actually his whole collection is extensive. I can bring you almost anything.

> I actually liked it. You did bring a movie with Patrick Swayze.

> That was my mother's idea. I'd prefer you keep seeing hockey players as pale, sweaty, and missing teeth.

> Oh.

> Does Vic have missing teeth?

> Cute Quinn. If you want someone who looks like my brother, you have me.

I don't want Vic. Just you.

> I know. I just like to hear it.

The Slurpee cup was inspired.

> You can't watch a movie without snacks. The post-surgery liquid diet makes it difficult, but not insurmountable.

He won't throw it away lol

> I'll bring him another whenever he wants.

It's okay. He'll be good for tonight and they think they'll keep him at least 5 days.

> Whenever he wants, Quinn

You'll be gone.

> Anytime Quinn. I'll get him a cup whenever he wants a cup. I'll send my mother, my brother, I'll hire someone.

> Anytime.

ON ICE

> Ok

> Do you get what I'm saying?

> I think so.

> I'm in Quinn. Even after I fly back to Chicago.

> I'm in. I'm yours.

> I want to give this a go.

> Ok

> I'm in too.

STELLA STEVENSON

Text Message
Monday, 06:42 PM CST

Erik Varg:

> Just walked in the door. I hope today was better. My mom said your dad was in great spirits when she left.

Quinn Cooper:

> I miss you already. And thank you so much. I'd say she doesn't have to spend the day with him, but honestly I'm just grateful he isn't alone. Today was a long day.

> I miss you too, Baby girl.

> Are you at the hospital?

> No, Dad kicked me out. I just walked in my door too.

> I'm sorry we didn't get more time together when you were in town.

> You don't have to apologize. I know you needed to be with your dad.

ON ICE

> Besides, my mom and I had some time to ourselves. It wasn't nearly as bad as I feared.

Feared?

> It's been a long time since we've been... comfortable together. We're working on it.

Do you want to talk about it?

> We can, but fair warning, it's cancer-related.
>
> If that's something you aren't ready to talk about right now then that's okay.

I want to help you in any way I can...

> You're up to your eyeballs right now. Don't worry, things are good for now and you need a break.

Will you tell me another day?

> Yes.

I'm sorry. I'm just exhausted.

I have an idea.

Want to have a little date? Right now?

Lol how are we going to do that?

Go to that giant tub in your master bathroom and run the water just the way you like it.

Light some candles, grab your book, add one of those fizzy things, and get in.

Text me when you're comfortable.

Monday, 07:06 PM CST

Ok. I'm in.

Candle scent?

Vanilla something.

> **Book of choice?**

Wouldn't you like to know.

> ...

Erik?

> **Is it a book?**
>
> **Or Porn?**

I think you know the answer to that.

Not that I can do anything about it. Need one hand to text you, one hand to turn pages.

> **You need your hands free Quinn?**

It might make things more fun.

Erik Varg
Incoming FaceTime Video

22 ERIK

I close my laptop on the apartment listings I've been perusing. I've spent far too much of my free time since my return to Chicago looking up homes in Quarry Creek—near my mom, near my brother, near Quinn. Now that we're giving this a real shot, we're back to texting daily again, phone calls too, but we've steered clear of talk about the future. It's the safest idea. Neither of us can uproot our lives, even though technically, we already have. Which is why I have three different realty sites all open in separate tabs. It's why I have two emails to realtors saved in my drafts.

My phone rings and I pick it up without checking the caller ID.

"Varg," I say, on the off chance it's work and not the woman who occupies my every thought.

"Varg," my twin says right back, "Do you always answer the phone this way?"

I usually answer with "Doctor Varg," especially when taking work calls, but I don't say that.

"What do you need, Vic?"

"I'm just checking in to see how the house hunt is going," Vic said.

I love my brother. I do. And I love that we're talking more, but the disappointment I feel because it isn't Quinn's honey-butter voice flowing out of the phone is nearly overwhelming.

"I'm not moving."

I'm not. Looking at listings is just a pastime. Something to do between meetings, or on lonely evenings. Lots of people do it. Loki is a good foot warmer, but there are only so many one-sided conversations we can have before I feel ridiculous. I've never been lonely before, being miles away from my family. Being by myself, with my own thoughts, has always been appealing. Recently, things have been different.

I used to enjoy sitting alone in the quiet of my living room. Now I reach for my phone to text Quinn. When I see something I know will make Vic laugh, I send him a message and share it. I no longer avoid my mother's calls. Now we have a regular schedule. Just yesterday, she told me about her recent foray into the world of crochet. I even sent Anna an email asking when she'd next be visiting mom and Vic. I'd like to coordinate visits.

"Sure you aren't." Vic's laugh is loud and brassy through the phone. "How many places have you bookmarked today? Five? Ten?"

I only bookmarked one today, but I have ten on my favorites list. Not that it matters, real estate doesn't last long no matter where it's located. Most of those listings will be gone by the end of the week. Which doesn't matter because I'm not moving.

"Three guys on the team have realtor wives." Vic says, "And I can always give you the number of the guy mom and I used. We'll get you all taken care of."

"Why are you so sure I'm moving?" I ask and my brother makes a sound like a disgusted wildebeest.

"Your deep abiding love for me. You're wasting away without quality twin time."

"You're getting needy in your old age." A month ago I would have been shocked to find that I don't disagree with Vic.

"You're the one who's a full minute older."

I miss spending time with my family. I miss seeing them at holidays and on random Tuesdays. I miss sitting in the same room as my sister or my brother or my mom and listening to them argue about what to watch on tv, or eat for dinner. Even in the years when I wasn't involved, I still missed being in their orbit. I always counted myself lucky to have a family that let me have my space, my privacy, my distance. I spent so long wanting everyone to just go away, to leave me alone, to let me worry about my survival instead of theirs, that when I got it, I couldn't imagine ever going back. I should have paid better attention to the fact that I didn't want them to leave me alone forever. I should have noticed when everything shifted.

Something had. The glass wall that had kept out my family and everyone else had cracks in it. Big ones. The kind that groaned under any sustained pressure, threatening to fracture outward into splintered shards of nothing. The thought wasn't as terrifying as it had once been. I used to be worried about what would happen if I had to let anyone back in. Now I'm worried about who I'll hurt as the walls crash. Where will the damage be fixable? Where will it be catastrophic? What can I repair and what will stay broken?

"I'm sorry." I pour decades' worth of anger, self-doubt, pain, fear, and brotherly affection into those two words. Words that I should have said years ago. Hopefully, better late than never still applies here.

"What—" Vic starts, but I push forward. The need to explain is sitting right there at the back of my throat, just waiting to burst forth. It's choking me.

"I'm sorry that we aren't close anymore. That was always my fault."

"We already talked about this not too long ago," Vic says, and I can hear the quiver in his voice, desperation to change the subject. "We both said our piece and moved on. It's fine. We're fine. Things are changing now."

That my brother doesn't want to have this conversation means it's long overdue. Hell, I don't want to have this conversation either, but none of us can heal without some closure on the past.

Loki twines through my legs as I stare out over the Chicago skyline. It's already dark, lights twinkling on in each building. Different people doing different things. 1 out of every 200 people will be diagnosed with cancer this year. That's approximately 13, 485 people in the city of Chicago alone. I wonder how many of their lights I can see right this moment.

"No," I swallow past the painful lump growing in my esophagus. "I'm sorry. I wasted a lot of years being so angry."

"I'm not the therapist here, but I'm pretty sure that's a normal reaction."

Push harder. He isn't getting it.

"I was mad at you."

The silence on the other end of the line is deafening, but Vic's still here. Still listening. Letting me say what needs to be said.

"I felt robbed, cheated. How could we be identical down to our very DNA, and yet I was sick, and you were so healthy? Why couldn't I keep the weight on and the muscle tone despite the chemo? Why couldn't I have had any other cancer than one that would destroy my ability to play? I was the better player. I was the flashy player. We were going to get deals because of me." I take a shaky breath. "I was so angry and then I had to pretend like I wasn't. That seeing you with your USHL team gear on wasn't a slap in the face. Like watching you sign with your first NHL team, and score your first goal didn't set tiny pieces of me on fire."

A ragged inhale on the line. "Erik," Vic says, but I'm not done.

"I knew it wasn't fair. I knew it was shit luck that cost me my everything while you got to live our dream. And the worst part of all of it?" I gulp down the lump in my throat. "I ached with pride, too. I was so happy when you got signed. So fucking proud when you laced your skates up during that first game. You earned every piece of that dream and I wanted that for you, even as I hated that you made it without me. That was the hardest part. Knowing I was a selfish bastard. That I'd spent years resenting you and mom and Anna for being able to live your lives while I seemed stuck, but also because it felt like I couldn't be scared or in pain or angry because I had to be strong for everyone else. I can't even look at Mom sometimes without remembering her sobbing right outside the door to my hospital room."

My heart is pounding beneath my sternum, slamming into my organs like a battering ram trying to escape. Sweat drips down my forehead and my lungs burn. I haven't felt this out of breath since my last long run during peak marathon training. Maybe not even then. Maybe I haven't felt this since sprint drills with my brother. The ones where we ignored everyone else on the team and almost killed ourselves trying to beat each other. It didn't even matter who had won those races.

"I'm sorry," I say again. "I was selfish. I'm still being selfish by staying away. I know that. My head wants to fix things, Vic. I swear it does. I just don't know how."

My brother says nothing, and I pull the phone away from my ear to check that the call hasn't dropped. Between the two of us, Vic has always been more of the rambler and I'm the listener. Vic was the one who always knew what to say and when to say it. Now the silence is stretching out into eternity, ringing between us.

I'd messed everything up. This was why I stayed away so long. The problem with years of guilt and blame is that they fester when left for too long. In theory, the therapist in me would have told anyone else that it was never too late to let go of the anger and guilt. It doesn't mean that everything will go back to the way things were before everything went wrong, but there was always value in airing heavy emotions. In practice? Well, in practice, it's always easier to give advice than to take it. That's why I have a therapist of my own. We've spent years addressing why I cut my family off, why I shut them out. I just never felt much motivation to change the status quo. Not until recently.

"If you're a selfish bastard, then I'm a selfish bastard." Vic sounds winded. Strangled. Like his vocal chords aren't working properly. It reminds me of the morning after the first pro game we'd seen together. We'd screamed our nine-year-old hearts out until our throats were toast. It had taken close to two weeks for our voices to return to normal.

"You aren't." I say. It's not selfish to go after what he always wanted. It's not like he chose to leave me behind. I know that.

"I'm serious, E," Vic says. "I knew you were sick. I knew what your diagnosis had cost you. But after the first surgery, when the doctors were optimistic about the future, I still spent hours pissed off that everyone was too worried about how much you ate or pissed to remember that I even existed. I couldn't talk about Juniors or my average points per game, because that would upset the person I was supposed to share it with. Anna was away at school and mom was posted outside your room, and I was left bumming rides to practice and games. I was forging signatures so I could miss school and travel. My life was headed where I'd always wanted it to go, and the only thing people wanted to talk about was you."

Funny.

The only thing I hadn't wanted to talk about that first year was cancer, and my twin hadn't been able to escape it.

"So, I'm sorry," Vic sighs and I know he's pulling his hand through his unruly hair even across a cell phone connection and multiple states. "Because every single fucking day I ached for everything you'd lost and I worried about your future and I wished that for just two minutes you could stop hogging all the motherfucking attention."

That shocks a laugh right out of me. "I'm sorry for being a fucking inconvenience. What with the chemo and the carving out chunks of my bone and replacing them with slices of metal." There's no heat in my words, and I laugh again. "I suppose I should have been more considerate."

"Exactly," Vic says. "At last you see it from my point of view. I'm clearly the victim here."

"Right. A victim with a multi-million-dollar contract with a team that is in good-standing as we get closer to the playoffs. I don't feel sorry for you."

"Of course not," Vic scoffs. "Because I'm being ridiculous. And yet not at all. I'd have assumed you'd be the first to tell me that all feelings are valid no matter how illogical they seem. We should have talked about this years ago. Or at least in person."

"I think fear of doing this in person is what led to years passing," I say, scrubbing a hand across my jaw.

"Or resignation to the status quo."

"Or that." We both laugh.

I feel antsy in my skin. Energized. Like I could get off this call and run a solid ten miles and then maybe do another round of weight training at the gym. The building's equipment is state-of-the-art, and I make use of the facilities often, but not this late at night and not twice in a day. I'd kept a strict workout regime since leaving hockey behind; it was part of my original rehab, but it was also one of the few things that felt normal. I should do a google search, find some gyms in Quarry Creek. For the next time I visit. None of the homes I've bookmarked has a gym, but I could make one.

My brother has one too. One he rarely touches since he tends to work out with his teammates. One he'd give me access to if I just ask.

"Back to more serious matters," Vic says, as if we haven't just ripped open old, badly healed scars. "I had a reason for calling."

"Not moving," I say again. "My job is here." As if I don't still have that flagged email sitting in my inbox, asking me to toss my hat in the ring for the director position at Grace Hospital. As if I haven't looked over my client list to see if I could step away, to match them with other practitioners, to continue working with them remotely. As if I haven't drafted a response and trashed it at least twice a day since the email first pinged into place.

"Then it probably won't bother you to know that I saw your Quinn out on a date."

I bobble the phone, letting it clatter to the floor. When I bend to pick it up, there's a crack running through the middle of the screen. Miraculously, the call hasn't dropped, so I slide it back to my ear, trying to avoid slicing open my skin on any sharp edges.

"A date," I repeat, and I know it's not true. I know that because Quinn and I are Quinn and I, and she told me she was meeting a coworker for drinks. And I trust her. I trust her. I fucking trust her. But it still feels like the edges of my ribcage cinch in around my heart and lungs, squeezing until I can barely gasp in air.

Quinn.

My Quinn.

Copper curls rioting around her heart-shaped face. Strong shoulders and bouncy tits, soft stomach and wide hips. Smiling at some lucky bastard who doesn't know half the things that make her special, make her unique, make her everything. Quinn with a book stashed on her person, just waiting for the time when she can pull it out, not a care in the world. Quinn's bow-shaped lips curving into a soft pout as she presses them to someone else's. Fuck.

It's not a date, I remind myself.

"Yeah, some big blonde guy down at that little coffee shop off Pine. They split some fancy cake thing and--"

I can't hear more past the thundering rush in my ears.

It's not a date, but someday it might be. Someday it will be because whatever we've decided, just the two of us, for us, right now, can't last forever. Because eventually everyone wants the long-distance to end, the random visits to become a permanent stay. She'll want more than what we've agreed to, no matter how much she might love me. Hell, I want more already, but I'm pretty sure I'll never walk away from her. I'm pretty sure I can't.

Quinn Cooper is the first person I think about every morning. She's the one I want to talk to at the end of a long day. She's the one I think of when something makes me laugh, or rage. She's the one. I'm done kidding myself. Life doesn't just hand us what we want whenever we want it. Waiting for the right time to start a life with the only woman I've ever loved is ludicrous. Especially when I know better than most that we have to create our own opportunities. I know better than most that things can change, we can lose, in an instant.

"—turns out it wasn't a date after all. He's a colleague with a wonderful husband named Terrance."

Vic is still chattering away when I tune him back in.

"What?" I ask.

"Not a date," my brother repeats and I knew it, never doubted it, but relief still turns my limbs soggy, heavy. "I promise that your redhead didn't spot me herself, but I asked Jen about him. Music teacher at the same school. They sometimes coordinate lessons. Kind of cute that they debrief with coffee each week."

"Should I be concerned that you have Jen's number?" I ask because I've been meaning to for a while now. The last thing I need is for my twin to put moves on my Quinn's roommate. That would be an extra complication we don't need.

"Nah, she got my number from Quinn and asked me to talk to her class for career day or something like that. Do they do career day for kindergarteners?"

"I don't think career day is a thing that young," I say.

"Well, it was something. I wore my gear. Took some pictures. Told them how much I have to practice, when I started skating, that kind of stuff." His voice is subdued again, and I don't like it.

"I bet you made their year." I tell him, thinking of Graham at that very first game.

"Don't worry," Vic says, "I won't mess with your girl's girl, but aren't you glad she called me a few weeks ago? And aren't you glad I uncovered the not-date-date?"

"If you knew it wasn't a date, then why say it was a date?" I ask.

My heart is still out of whack, puttering along a little too fast and dropping beats at random. I need a sedative, an aspirin, a defibrillator. I'm pretty sure my building has at least one in the lobby.

"To help you pull your head out of your ass so that you'd admit that you were jealous. Jealous because you're head over heels in love with Quinn and you need to move here to claim your lady for your own."

Melodramatic, but not wrong, because if Vic is right about one thing, it's that I'm in love with Quinn Cooper. He just doesn't know that I already have done something about it. Jealousy isn't goosing me into action. My twin is wrong about that, but it is helping me in another way.

"Vic," I say into the phone, cutting off my brother's rant about true love and soulmates. "I think I'm going to need some help."

23
QUINN

The knock on my door is the first surprising thing about Saturday. The man standing at my door is the second. My heart gives two wild thumps in my chest at the sight of sandy blonde hair and wide shoulders, but the smile is all wrong. It's a little too wide and open for the man I love. The twinkle in the brown-green hazel of his eyes is just a touch off.

"Victor Varg." I open the door wider and gesture Erik's twin into my living room. "How can I help you?"

"Quinn Cooper, just the woman I've been dying to see." Vic toes off his boots before walking across the room to my small brick fireplace. He peruses the photos framed on the mantel, a large finger running over each smiling face as though he wants to commit them to memory. "You don't have any of my brother."

"I haven't known him that long." I say, trying not to sound dejected. We don't take photos when we're together. We talk. Or lose our clothes.

"He's known you long enough." Vic plops down onto the couch and stretches his arms along the back. "He has a picture of you with some super large fluffy orange thing. It's framed and everything. Don't worry, he keeps it in the living room, so I doubt he's using it for inappropriate reasons." Vic winks.

"Tessie." I say, "my cat." I'd sent him that selfie weeks ago. Before his second trip here. Before my dad's surgery.

"He lives alone though," Vic says as if I haven't spoken, "So it might not matter where he keeps the photo. He could still get freaky with it. The frame is a bit of a fancy touch, though."

I try not to roll my eyes at Vic, but it's a near miss.

"He told you about a photo of me?"

"Nah babe. I saw it at his apartment." He grins for a moment, then drops his chin to his chest and shakes his head. "Don't tell Erik I said that. He has a mean right cross."

"I shouldn't tell him I know about the picture?"

"The 'babe' babe."

Right.

"I doubt he'd hit you over that," I say.

Vic must have visited Erik during their game in Chicago. They'd played the night before, rounding out a week on the road. The team must have flown straight home after the final buzzer if Vic's here on my couch. That shouldn't surprise me. Of course, they had to come home fast. They have a home game tomorrow. A red-eye flight means that they can get in some practice before facing off against Toronto, and the team doesn't need to shell out for a hotel room, but the guys must be beat. Vic yawns, proving my point, and tries to cover it with a strangled cough.

"He's extremely possessive of you. He warned me off your roommate."

"I'm going to warn you off my roommate." I glare at him, but there's no heat to it.

"I think I'm offended," Vic says with a smile. "Jen loves me."

"Yeah, like people love puppies until they chew up their furniture and shit in their shoes."

"People love puppies because they're adorable." He said with mock outrage.

"Why is your brother warning you off my friends?" I ask.

Vic's grin is bright as he turns it on me, and I know—I just know—that I've walked right into a trap.

"Because," he draws the word out like a ringleader in a circus trying to drum up the crowd's excitement for what's coming next. "He doesn't want me to do something stupid and fuck things up for the two of you."

That's a sweet thought, but Jen and I don't interfere in each other's love lives. I'm pretty sure she's not into the Arctic forward, but I've been wrong before. Either way, I wouldn't let it affect our friendship or our living situation. If Vic hurts her, I'll hurt him, but that won't change anything. I tell Vic the same, but when I threaten him with bodily harm, he throws his head back and cackles.

"Quinn, my darling, dense, almost-sister. He's not worried about me messing up you and Jen. He's worried I'll mess up things for you and him. That if I do something awful, which I take offense to by the way, that it could cause an issue for you and Erik."

"That's fucking dumb." The words are out of my mouth before I can swallow them back, and Vic raises an eyebrow as he watches me. He isn't as relaxed as he's pretending to be. I just can't figure out why. "Erik and I agreed to be something. Boyfriend-girlfriend. Long distance. I don't know exactly, but I do know I wouldn't hold him responsible for something someone else does. Jen's an adult. You're an adult. Your decisions are not my problem and I won't let go of someone I love because other people in our lives have the potential to be idiots."

"Good," Vic says and I frown at him.

"Good?"

So he wants my blessing to date Jen? It's not mine he needs, but that's okay. It's the Cheshire Cat grin that tells me I'm way off base, that I've missed something major.

"I'm going to tell you something about Erik, something he probably assumed wasn't a big deal. You need to know this one tiny piece of information and then what you choose to do with that information is up to you. Okay?"

I nodded, certain that I'm going to regret the direction this conversation is about to take. Anything I learn about Erik, I want to learn from him, but Vic's brows furrow, he's bouncing his legs on the balls of his feet, and I think he might vibrate off the couch if he doesn't get this out.

"Do you know the standard treatment plan for localized forms of osteosarcoma?"

"Chemo and surgery," I say. I'd googled everything I could about Erik's type of cancer the minute I'd recovered from the shock. I'd done the same for my dad months ago.

Vic steeples his fingers. "Limb salvage surgery involves removing the tumor and infected portion of bone and replacing it with a metal graft. Erik did almost three months of chemo before his first surgery."

"It didn't work," I say, thinking of the metal joint of Erik's prosthetic ankle. How he must have gotten his hopes up thinking he'd be back on the ice soon, only to come out of surgery down a limb.

"No, it did work." Vic turns to face me, his eyes solemn. "The thing about salvage surgery is that they never promise you'll be good-as-new. It's the hope, and it's possible for a lot of people. We all thought it might be for Erik. He was an athlete, he was in great shape, he responded well to chemo, was serious about getting back to hockey, but.... His gait was never quite right. He ended up needing a second surgery after the metal in his bone loosened and after his second surgery, he developed contractures. The muscles and tendons around his shin bone stiffened and shrank. He was in almost constant pain."

I don't understand.

"Erik is an amputee. I've seen his prosthetic."

"Right after our eighteenth birthday, a month after I went to play in Canada, Erik asked for a full amputation."

And that makes all the difference. That's what Vic is trying to tell me. It wasn't just that the disease stole the future he'd wanted. It was that he'd had to make the choice, after hoping to at least keep his leg, to have it removed. My heart stutters at the pain he must have felt in making that decision. The hurt that it came right on the heels of his twin's career taking off.

"He kept his leg the first time, because he knew it meant giving up a hockey career, but maybe it meant keeping the other parts of his life, the skating, the ice. But he lost both Quinn, and he had to convince people he wasn't crazy or that he wouldn't regret his choice. High-impact sports are out with a limb salvage," Vic says, voice low and urgent, "but skating was still an option. Erik hasn't been back on the ice since the day he limped off with his shin red and swollen."

"Until me." I swallow down the thickness in my throat. "Until you."

The silence stretches between us until I can hear each breath and the individual thumps of my heart. There is a static building in my brain, a white noise itch I want to get rid of, but I don't know how. Vic is still as stone, his eyes watching me as if he can peel back my layers and see my thoughts stamped across my internal organs. The first time he'd been back on the ice in over a decade. And he'd done it for me.

No.

He'd done it with me. The ultimate proof of his trust.

God, I love him.

His strength, his bravery, his kindness. I love every single thing about Erik Varg. Whether he's here or in Chicago, it doesn't matter because my life is better when I think of him, when I talk to him, when I can touch him. Better for having met him. To think I'd been annoyed about going to that game all those weeks ago. Had hoped I could sit and read undetected in the stands, but there he'd been to wake me up.

"That's what I thought," Vic says and there's a small smile teasing the corners of his mouth.

And I don't know what to say. There's nothing I can say. Because the man I love, the man who loves me, lives almost a thousand miles away and I miss him more every single second of every single day.

Jen peeks her head around the door, Tesseract squirming in her arms.

"Vic," she nods at the professional hockey player seated on our couch.

"Jennifer," he nods back and Jen blushes as Tessie jumps down and makes her way to her favorite heating vent. Vic pulls his phone out of his pocket and taps a few buttons on the screen. When he speaks again, his voice is back to normal—light and laughing. "On that note, I need to get going."

"Hey, I was hoping you were home. Got any plans this afternoon?" Jen asks me and I don't know what to say. Before Vic had shown up, I was going to work on lesson plans, some set design for the fifth-grade musical, and read the book I've been putting off. After Vic's visit, I'm debating researching jobs or at least weekend flights to Chicago. He's mine for right now, but how long until he finds someone local? Someone not carrying along a truckload of baggage and fear and worry? I don't want to lose him. I don't want to be away from him.

How many months until the end of the school year? Teachers are in demand everywhere. I bet I could find a job in Chicago if I put out feelers.

Would Erik want that?

Do I want that?

If my dad is stable?

Yes. Yes, I want to be there. I want to be with him. Full time. In person. Right?

The front door swings open again and I don't even look. Vic can grab whatever he left behind without me. I think my brain might shut down on me. Except it's not Vic, it's my dad. My dad and Vic. When did my house turn into Grand Central Station?

"Hey Sweetheart," Dad sweeps me into a tight hug. "Look who I found in your driveway."

I expect Vic to say something about just being here, but he doesn't.

"That's because he was leaving." Maybe it isn't fair to be upset with Vic over the morning's revelation, but I can't help it. I'd been happy just being something with Erik before ten minutes ago. Now I'm drafting a resignation letter in my head. That was not on my bingo card for this year.

"Is everything okay, Dad?" I don't remember making plans, but he seems to be in good spirits. He has his Arctic jersey on with Vic's name and number plastered across the back, his knit cap pulled down to his onetime eyebrows, and a big smile on his round face.

"Of course, I'm just here for the game."

I look at Vic, who seems unconcerned that he might be missing warmups. "Game?"

"Yesterday's game against Chicago." Dad says, making his way to the couch. "I missed it, but got it recorded."

"Dad," I say, trying for understanding and gentle, but failing. I love these people, but I need everyone to go away right now and leave me alone to job and apartment search. "If you recorded it, you'd have to watch at home. It's not saved here."

There's a moment of silence as the two men look at each other and then at Jen, who is wide-eyed and shaking her head.

"I have the game footage," Vic says at the same time my dad says, "We can stream it from one of those websites."

Vic plops down next to my dad and tosses something in my general direction. I catch it on reflex, unfurling it to find an Arctic jersey with Vic's name and number on the back.

"Did I forget you were coming over?" I ask, knowing damn well that I have forgotten nothing of the sort, but I also don't know why he's at my house to stream a game he can watch at home on his bigger television.

"His internet is down," Jen takes a seat too, "He texted me to see if he could watch here until the guys can go fix it. I said it was fine."

"Of course it's fine." I frown and check my phone. Did I miss a text?

"Quit dawdling, Cooper, and go put on that jersey. You're holding up the game," Vic says as Jen navigates the television and the opening reel for the Arctic plays through the living room.

I step into the kitchen to strip down to my tank top. Normally I'd have no issue doing that in front of Jen and my dad, but it feels wrong to take off layers in front of Vic. I pull the light blue fabric over my head, impressed to see the jersey is almost too big. This isn't how I planned to spend my Saturday, but I guess I don't mind. There are worse ways to pass a few hours than by watching hockey with people I care about. And I could use some time to not think about Erik and moving and what comes next.

I should talk to him about it, right? Before making grand plans? I pull my phone out, not to unload my thoughts on him, but because I miss him. It's been longer than normal since we last chatted. I type and delete several messages, each feeling needier than the one before. I don't want to seem lonely and desperate without him. Even if I feel lonely and desperate without him.

ON ICE

> *Quinn Cooper:*
>
> **About to watch some hockey.**
>
> **What are the odds your brother explains things as well as you do?**

There is no immediate response, so I put my phone away and head back out to join the crowd. The last seat is in the chair we never use. Tesseract is sitting on the back, tail twitching. I cuddle into my tabby as the players hit the ice. It's nice, sitting in my living room, surrounded by family… and yet I miss Erik so much that it makes my stomach clench and my heart ache.

Vic keeps up a steady stream of conversation through the first period, but it's less about the mechanics of the game and more stories about who said what on the ice. Vic, I've noticed, is a gossip. Dad eats it up, hanging on each word like a small kid seeing fireworks for the first time. It makes sense. Dad understands the rules of the game, so the extras are fun for him. Jen is alternating her attention between smiling at Vic, scrolling on her phone, and sneaking glances at me. Jen watches even less hockey than I do and she's beyond lost but being a good sport about it.

I'm trying to pay attention, I am, but I still almost fall off the chair trying to reach my phone when it buzzes.

Erik Varg:

> He's a show boater. Don't believe a word he says.

> About hockey.

> The rest he's good for.

> I miss you.

This isn't the right time for this conversation. My brain knows that. It's better to wait and talk over the phone if we can't be face-to-face. At the very minimum, it should wait until I'm not sitting in the same room as my dad and Erik's brother, pretending to watch a hockey game. That doesn't mean I can stop my fingers from typing out each careful letter any more than I can stop the smile from spreading across my face. The grin is so big I can feel the ache in my cheeks already, even as my heart threatens to stomp right out of my ribcage.

> What would you say if I looked into jobs around Chicago?

I watch three little dots show he's typing a reply for what seems like an eternity. They blink at me, then disappear. Blink, disappear. Blink and disappear until I'm ready to throw my phone through the flat screen television. The game is on an ad break, so I doubt my dad and friends would even notice. Vic's texting furiously, Jen is still scrolling, and my dad is watching a car commercial with a goofy grin under his hat. I put the phone down, determined not to look. A watched pot and all that jazz.

When it vibrates again, I practically crack the screen from the force of my grip. My pulse is out of control. My brain feels fuzzy and my stomach pitches. I'm stitched together with frayed nerves. My hands tremble as I swipe open the screen, eyes blurring as I try not to throw up.

> That won't work, Quinn.

The buzzing is louder now. There's a strange knocking sound too as I swallow again and again. My eyes itch and I need to excuse myself from the living room now, right now. I slide the phone back into my pocket because I can't respond right now. I can't think right now. Can't breathe. I knew there was a chance he would say no. Long distance was already a stretch. I don't get to be upset now because I'd changed my mind without warning.

The knocking sound is getting louder as I stand from the chair. My eyes meet Jen's. Jen, who is mouthing my name and pointing at the television screen. Vic is on his feet too, moving around the back of the couch and full speed towards the door where... someone is knocking? The sound isn't in my mind? My dad is still on the couch, still smiling, but watching my every move.

"Quinn," Jen says again. "Quinn!"

I follow my friend's waving arms—I can go cry by myself in a minute—and watch as the camera pans down the Arctic team bench at the United Center in Chicago.

Twenty men in matching jerseys and helmets are holding up an enormous banner, their gloved hands crinkling the edges of the paper where they hold it. The commentator is droning on about something unprecedented and I barely remember to read what the sign says.

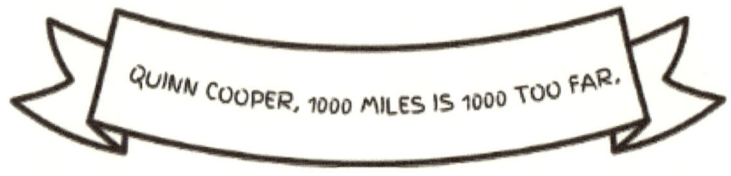

Quinn Cooper.
That's my name.
The sign is…
It's for me.

At the end of the row, a televised Vic is grinning from under his half-shield and helmet. His gloved hands aren't holding the banner, but pointing up into the stands behind the bench. The camera shifts and there is Erik. On national television. In the front row of a professional hockey game. Holding another sign.

24 ERIK

I step through Quinn's front door into absolute chaos.

Vic texted me a thumbs up right before the camera panned across the players and I hope I've timed this entrance exactly how Jen and I planned it. It was probably naïve to expect I'd open the door and walk into her waiting arms, exchange some words of love and affirmation, and then have everyone else clear the fuck out so I can spend some time alone with the woman I love. I need to explain that my condo is going on the market this weekend. That by the end of the season, we should be in the same place for good.

And then maybe I'll see about a nap. I didn't fly out directly after the game, like Vic and the team, but I took the earliest morning flight I could get a seat on and went directly to my brother's house with my disgruntled cat and most of my belongings.

Instead, Quinn takes one look at me and bursts into noisy sobs. Not the kind in romance movies, where a single delicate tear inches down the heroine's unblemished cheek.

No, these are like a ruptured dam, water cascading down her red cheeks and shaking her entire body as she gasps desperately for another breath. Her roommate stands behind her, patting her back and mouthing something I can't hear, Sean sits on the couch looking like he doesn't know if he should be pleased as punch or if he should murder me, and my brother looks two seconds from bolting out the unlocked door.

I do the only logical thing I can think of. I step forward and wrap my arms around Quinn's round shoulders and tug her into my chest.

"I hope," I say. My voice is gravel against her ear and I feel her shiver against me, "that these are happy tears, and that you're glad to see me."

She clutches at me, fingers digging into the muscles along the top of my shoulders. I'm pretty sure she's going to leave little half-moon indents in my skin and my possessive hindbrain wants those marks all over me. I lean back an inch so I can get a better look at her face, and Quinn pulls me in tighter. Her wet cheeks slip over my neck as she wipes her nose on the collar of my shirt, and I don't even care.

"You're a fucking bastard," she says, holding me even closer. "I thought you—your text. I thought you meant—"

"Woah," I cut her off, strong arming her away from me so she has to meet my eyes. "I'm an idiot Quinn." I think I hear Jen mutter "yep," but I decide to ignore that. "And okay, not my finest moment, but I meant it won't work for me because I won't be in Chicago and I'm selfish. If I'm cutting the distance between us, then I sure as fuck don't want you adding it back in. I'm not going anywhere. Good luck trying to get rid of me."

She swipes the back of her hand over her eyes, rubbing away her tears. Her gorgeous eyes are red-rimmed and swollen, her nose is red, and she's never looked more beautiful to me than she does at this moment.

"But your job," she says and I grin down at her, unable to hold back my smile for another second when I have her this close. When our future is right here.

"I'm taking the position at the hospital. All my previous clients are going to work with me remotely or transfer to new therapists." It had been disturbingly easy to send that email to the HR department and formally accept their offer. It had been harder to leave my old practice, but it had to be done. Taking what I want, putting my happiness first, is okay.

"Your apartment," she says, and I lean forward to press our foreheads together.

"It's going on the market this weekend. My realtor just sold another unit in the building and is confident it'll go fast. I can stay with Vic and my mom until I get a place of my own." That had been almost the easiest part. Vic had offered before I could even ask.

Quinn drops her voice, so I have to focus to hear her. "You'll be okay with that much togetherness? I know your relationship is healing, but—"

"It'll be okay, Quinn." I kiss the tip of her nose and pull her back into my chest, dropping my chin over her shoulder. "I moved back to fix things with them, too." I press a kiss to the skin of her neck and she presses back, aligning our bodies.

I might need to recite hockey stats.

"Your cat," she says and I laugh.

"Don't send me away, Quinn. If for no other reason than you take pity on Loki and all the TSA workers between here and O'Hare. That cat will one hundred percent ground a plane if I try to stuff him back into that tiny little bag."

Quinn tries to choke back her laugh, but it leaks out in a watery burst and my limbs thaw as my pulse kicks up at the sound.

"You can always spend your time here," Jen says, wincing when we both turn to look at her. "Sorry, eavesdropping. Shouldn't have done that. I'm just going to be going now." She marches to the front door, grabbing both her coat and Vic's arm. "Come on, Vicky, we're going to give them some privacy."

"What?" Vic looks shell-shocked. "You mean we did all the legwork and don't get to see the payoff?"

"Victor Varg," Jen put her hands on her slim hips and gives him a glare that I would hate to receive. "You walk out that front door right this instant or I will call your mother."

"That's not fair," Vic says, as Quinn's dad gets up from the couch too. Sean pecks his daughter on the cheek and claps a hand on my shoulder.

"Glad to see you two fight for what's right in front of you." He says and ambles to the door, "Come on Vic, let's go get some wings and you can tell me more about the All-Stars game and help me set my fantasy roster."

And then the door closes behind the three of them and Quinn and I are blissfully alone with only her fluffy cat and yesterday's game on the television for company.

This is it. The moment I wanted. The one that started in The Stand arena all those weeks ago when I left my seat to get a drink and was almost flattened by Quinn on the steps. This woman has stolen every fractured piece of my shielded heart and handed it back to me whole.

"I'm sorry it took me so long to get here," I cup her cheeks with my hands. "It took a lot of coordination to pull this off and I didn't want to give too much away."

Quinn laughs again, the sound sliding through me like warm chocolate.

"You weren't kidding when you said the last few weeks were busy. I just thought you meant work-busy."

That was only part of it. Once my mind was made up, things came together a lot faster than I ever expected they would. My apartment was the straightforward part, but work was a smooth transition, too. I donated and sold all my furniture—I won't need it at Vic's—and two suitcases later, my life was fully packed. Most of the time was spent waiting for the Chicago-Arctic game. Vic braved Tristan, the team's bloodhound of a social media manager, to help pull everything together.

It hit me, while I was stuffing a handful of boxes, that it shouldn't be this easy to up and leave my old life behind. I want more roots than I'd put down. I want those roots with Quinn. I want to be so entwined in her life that it will take an eternity to separate us, if it's even possible.

Or maybe it's that I pulled my head out of my ass—with my family, with Quinn—and the Universe heaved an enormous sigh of release and greased the wheels.

"I love you," I say, and slide my fingers into the riot of her hair. It's cool and silky smooth against my fingers, and I love how the curls wrap around my hands like they have a mind of their own. I tug her head back and her lips part as if in welcome. "It has been killing me to have to say that over the phone when I want to do it in person. I love you. I love you. I love you."

"I love you," Quinn says and I sip the words from her lips, drinking them down like the finest champagne. They pop and fizz in my bloodstream, making me lightheaded.

My tongue sweeps the seam of Quinn's mouth until she opens for me and I can taste her for real. We moan together; the sound caught in our kiss. I take a step back, then back again, turning until I can drop onto the couch and bring her down on top of me, her knees parting as she straddles my lap. My free hand falls to her thigh, feeling the warm softness under my fingers. I can't resist squeezing once before I trail my touch up the cotton of her leggings and cup the curve of her hip. I pull her closer, rocking her center against my erection as I plunder her mouth. My lungs burn, but I'm not ready to come up for air. Not yet. The world record for holding a breath is over twenty-four minutes. I can handle a little longer.

My fingertips play with the end of her jersey. "You're wearing my jersey." I press another kiss to the corner of her mouth, her cheek, her chin, her throat, "I want you to wear it forever."

"This is Vic's jersey, but I like the sentiment." There's a teasing lilt to her words as she looks over her shoulder like she can see the appliqued letters and numbers.

"It's mine," I say, dragging her focus back to me. "Vic's number twenty-five. I was always twenty-six."

She pulls back again, fisting the jersey as she pulls it around to get another look. She can look later. The number won't change. It's a twenty-six. Vic sent me no less than twelve photos to prove it.

"What? Why?" Quinn's panting the words as her hands cup the back of my neck.

"I'm stating an intention, Quinn Cooper. Work with me here." I bite down on the skin of her throat and she rolls her hips over mine, a strangled moan breaking free from her swollen mouth.

I tug the jersey up and Quinn helps me get it over her head, leaving her in a thin white tank top. It's one of the ones she loves to wear, with the skinny straps that leave tiny pink lines on her skin. Her nipples pebble against the fabric and I can't resist sliding one hand up her ribcage to cup the rounded weight of one breast in my palm.

"I've always found it funny that your last name means wolf, and the Arctic has a wolf for a mascot."

"Funny?" I suck one teasing point into my mouth, working my tongue around the cotton as she clutches the back of my head.

Quinn writhes in my lap. It is its own form of exquisite torture, one I want to experience every fucking day of my life.

"Not funny," she gasps. "Serendipitous. Lucky. Coincidental."

I move to the other breast. I like seeing the dark tint of the fabric where my mouth has been. The tank is almost sheer under the wet, a hint of pink showing through. It's enough to make me want to steamroll us ahead. Skip everything until we get to the part when I push inside her. To the part where we claim each other. I also want to slow down and savor this moment. Make it last for eternity.

"You don't think it's too fast?" Her nails scrape my scalp and I fist the cotton, almost ripping the tank from her body.

"Probably," I say. "But I'm done with the what-ifs."

Quinn presses her lips to mine, sucking my tongue into her mouth. Her hands move to the bottom of my shirt and she presses her fingers into my skin. My stomach jumps under her touch as she pulls the fabric up and over my head. I'm drowning in heat, my dick aching in my jeans as her mouth finds mine again. I don't even hear my shirt hit the floor.

"I want to be clear," I say, feeling like I need to get this out into the open before we move past the point of no return. Past the flash point. "I've loved you forever, Quinn Cooper. Possibly since that first day when I watched you pull out a e-book in an arena full of hockey fans while you sat directly behind the home team. You were always the right person."

She sits back on my thighs. The warm weight comforting as she listens to me bare my soul.

"Right person. Wrong time and place." She nods because she gets it. She always gets it. Gets me.

"Yeah, well, I got sick of waiting for the right time and place." I tip my forehead to hers again and close my eyes, breathing in the scent that is Quinn and sunshine and everything good in my life. "I made this the right time and place because if I didn't... well, you'd be the one to haunt me, Quinn. For the rest of my life, I'd have missed you and wondered what we could have been." I touch my mouth to hers. Not a kiss, just a brush of lips to lips. "I don't want to wonder any more, Quinn. I want to know."

She's quiet for longer than I'm comfortable with, studying me with eyes that miss nothing. Her head tips to the side, curls spinning away from her face. She's sitting here in just a tank top and a pair of old cotton leggings. Every single time I see her, she takes my breath away.

Quinn presses a soft kiss to the stubble covering my cheek and slides off my lap. I want to protest. To pull her back into place against my chest because now that I have her within reach, I don't want to let go, not even for a moment. But she slides onto the couch next to me and snuggles into my side. Her pulse slows as she twines our fingers together.

"I want to know too." She traces my thumb with her own. "Hence why I was ready to close the distance myself. I was going to look for jobs for next year, assuming my dad was doing okay. I'm choosing to be optimistic."

I'm broken apart by her faith in me. In her dad. Her courage to go after what she wants. And I was a dummy who hurt her, no matter how briefly, because I didn't think before I said something.

I wince. "I wasn't supposed to be texting you. I was under strict orders to be on radio silence."

"Orders?" She shakes her head. "I don't care. I want you to be sure that you're changing your life for you, not just me."

"Quinn, if the fact that your roommate, my brother, your father, and my mother all came together to help me surprise you doesn't prove that I have a support system here, then nothing will. I'm home for a lot of reasons, many to do with you and many to do with fixing what went wrong between me and my family. But you'd have been enough, Quinn. All on your own, you are enough."

"Of course there was some elaborate plot," she chuckles, her head resting on my shoulder. The soft weight of her makes my chest ache.

The banner had been my idea. Vic talked to Tristan and got the team's support. Sean concocted a reason to watch the game a day late, which gave me just enough time to fly back with Loki. Jen ensured Quinn avoided watching the actual match up and avoided social media where every sports network has been frothing at the mouth over "Varg's hidden twin" and the stunt we'd pulled during the Chicago game. My old game footage has been making the rounds and interview requests have been pouring in. The Arctic's PR team has been fielding it all. My mom is cat sitting. And the woman next to me is the reason we've all come together.

"I love you."

Quinn tugs me to my feet and my heart lurches ahead, a train picking up steam on a downhill track. I'm not worried about the out-of-control speed. I'm too busy enjoying the thrill of the ride. "I'm in this with you," she says as she leads me to the stairs. "You're officially my boyfriend, Erik Varg. This is exclusive."

"Yes, ma'am." I nod as she pushes me up the first step.

"Upstairs," she urges. "I love you, you love me, we're in love, but the couch belongs to Jen and she'll kill me if we defile it."

I try not to take the stairs two at a time, dragging my girlfriend along behind me. At the top of the landing, I press her up against the wall and fuse our mouths together.

A kiss. A promise. A future.

EPILOGUE — QUINN

1 year and a few months later...

The crowd is on fire tonight. Not literally, that would be tragic, but the energy is infectious as Vic's line takes the ice. They're playing Chicago, just like that first game over a year ago, but this time Erik's wearing the Arctic's baby blue instead of red. We're also in a box tonight, instead of crammed into the too-small seats, and while I'd like to say that I'm not growing used to the luxury of the private viewing area, that would be a lie. The box has seats, a bar, and space. There's even a little TV in here in case we don't want to watch the actual game below us. The seats aren't as close to the bench, but the view of the ice is better and I'm keeping better track of the puck as the guys pass it back and forth. That could also be a year's worth of watching hockey under my belt, too.

I'm still not the biggest hockey fan—don't tell Vic—but I no longer avoid the game. Between my dad and my boyfriend, it would be impossible to try. Dad still has his season ticket, and Erik bought Andrea's. Sometimes I go with one of them, but most of the time they go together. I see them from the couch at home, their heads tucked together as they discuss plays and penalties, so happy it makes my heart clench. A few times Maria went, sitting with my dad and waving every time the camera panned across them. Erik and I took pictures of the television and texted them for old times' sake.

We had too many people tonight to use regular seats, so Erik got permission to use Grace Hospital's box. That's definitely a perk of the job, and one we'll happily take advantage of on nights like tonight. I'd say it isn't every day that someone you love gets their 6-month all-clear following chemo, but it's happened for two people in this box. I may have only been around for my dad's first NED, but I am forever grateful for Erik's, too. We even got a cake to celebrate.

Erik slides his hand around the front of my waist and pulls me back into his chest. I rest my head against his shoulder and watch as the whistle blows and play stops.

"What are you thinking about?" my boyfriend asks. His words tickle the shell of my ear.

I'm thinking about Graham and that first night we sat next to each other.

I'm thinking about the color coming back into my dad's skin and the fuzz of his new hair.

I'm thinking about how I don't see Jen enough now that she's moved out and Erik's moved in, and I'm going to ask her if she wants to get lunch later this week.

ON ICE

I'm thinking about how happy Maria is to have all three of her kids in one place since Anna is in town.

I'm thinking about how exciting it is to be watching the Arctic dominate during this first playoff game, and how Vic could conceivably pull off a hat trick.

I'm thinking I'm happy. Right here. Right now.

I tell him so and I can feel Erik smile against the skin of my neck. He didn't shave tonight, and his stubble rasps against my skin. I shiver and he tightens his arms.

"I like seeing you happy." He kisses the curve where my neck and shoulder meet, and I try not to let my knees buckle.

Our friends and family are giving us a moment of privacy, but we're still surrounded by them. Now is not the time or place to lose my mind over Erik Varg. Jen is a few feet away, pointing out different players to Sofia. Anna and her wife Jo are showing my dad photos of their mountain cabin and greenhouse. They live almost entirely off-grid in the Rockies and Jo runs yoga retreats. Maria is over by the bar, sipping a bottle of water and chatting with Uncle Harvey and his wife. It's everyone all in one place, except for Vic, and he's technically in the same place, too.

It's intermission now, and the music is flowing through the arena as the seats are empty fans rushing to grab a drink, a snack, a bathroom break in the fifteen minutes between periods. The clock is counting down the minutes, and the player stats are scrolling across the screen. The Arctic is up by three heading into the third and Chicago just can't seem to find their footing in this matchup. Spirits are soaring all around us.

"I like seeing you happy, too." I cover his hand with mine and he laces our fingers together, squeezing just the right amount.

This box is full of laughter and family and hope, so different from that first game Erik and I went to. The realization leaves me almost dizzy and disoriented. My heart is pounding in my ears. A shoop-shoop-shoop sound that leaves me wondering if I should see a doctor until I recognize the opening lines of the song and see the giant pair of lips on the Jumbotron. The KISS Cam is still in full working order. It zeroes in on a young couple who look absolutely giddy as they press their mouths together.

"Think we'll get a repeat?" I say to Erik, pointing at the screen and I feel his laugh more than I hear it.

"I think we should take a family vacation." He turns to look behind us at everyone in the box. "When Vic's season is over, let's go away. You, me, your dad, Mom, Vic, Anna and Jo, even Jen and Sofia, and anyone else we want."

"A family vacation." It would be fun getting away with all the people we care about. There hasn't been a lot of travel, not with dad undergoing treatment, and while we've carved out our own moments of joy, I haven't been able to take a full breath until this most recent scan came back. Six months is a big milestone. The term "cancer-free" was used. I'd cried sloppy tears into Erik's chest and felt twenty pounds lighter once I dried my eyes. "Let's do it. Want to brave the mouse and theme parks? Chicago? Overseas?"

Erik's mouth tips up and the little creases show next to his eyes. He's beautiful always, and my heart turns over again.

"Anywhere you want Quinn." He says.

The camera moves on to another happy couple.

"I'll have to think about it. Maybe we can ask Vic and Anna or your mom where they'd like to go."

Erik steps back from me and I turn so I can keep him in my line of sight. His eyes search mine, shifting back and forth as though he's trying to read something in my face.

"I thought for sure you'd have a place already picked out." Erik says and I frown. I've never left Quarry Creek. Why would I have a vacation destination picked out? "Alaska maybe?"

Alaska.

I've always wanted to go to Alaska. When I was little, I imagined getting married surrounded by untouched nature. Actually, I imagined getting married surrounded by polar bears and penguins, but things changed as I got older. How did Erik...

"Jen may have mentioned it," he says and shoves his hands deep into the front pocket of his jeans.

Jen may have... I freeze, looking up into fathomless hazel eyes. Erik pushes a lock of hair behind my ear and his fingers caress my cheek.

"Erik." I can barely breathe, my whole body flushing hot. There's only one reason Jen would mention my onetime dream to my boyfriend. "Are you—"

He shakes his head and presses our foreheads together. "Not tonight, Quinn, not at your dad's party."

I didn't know this was happening. Didn't even know it was an option, but now I deflate a little at the knowledge that he isn't proposing. It's too soon. We've only talked about it in a hypothetical sense. We've only lived together for half a year. Erik takes my hands in his.

"How does tomorrow sound?"

Tomorrow?

"If I ask you tomorrow, will you say yes?"

Will I say yes?

"Erik."

"Tomorrow, Quinn. Tomorrow I'm going to ask you to marry me. Say yes."

And then he kisses me and as he runs his tongue along my bottom lip, I hear someone call out, "Hey, Quinn and Erik are on the KISS Cam!"

EPILOGUE — ERIK

1 day later...

I ask.
She says yes.

Vic's Book is up next.
NOT THAT KIND OF ICING – coming soon

Join Stella's **NEWSLETTER** for bonus scenes, sneak peeks of upcoming stories, and more…
If you enjoyed this story, please consider leaving a rating/review, or telling your book-loving friends.

ALSO BY STELLA STEVENSON

The Trope

Mother Knows Best

The Escalation Clause

On Ice

COMING SOON

Not That Kind of Icing

Blind Luck

Limelight

Black Witch Moth Season

ACKNOWLEDGEMENTS

I truly don't know how this book would have been written without my community of people. The initial draft opened a lot of old wounds, but editing it after my dad passed was pure torture. I am forever grateful to the support system that bolstered me and helped me put this book down on paper, word by word. As much as it hurt to do, writing it was as necessary as breathing.

To my **husband**: thank you for letting me disappear for hours to write. Thank you for painstakingly talking out different elements of your sport. For being patient when I needed you to explain icing for the millionth time. Thank you also for holding our family together when I felt like I was falling apart. I love you more than words can express.

To **Cerissa**: this book would not exist without you. From plotting to style choices, from tears and worries to raging and venting, you kept me sane when I felt like I was spiraling beyond recognition. Thank you for pushing me and hyping me. Forever your octopus.

To my **mother**: Thank you for all the times you watched the kids, all the times you helped me celebrate Dad's life, every comma you replaced and misspelling you found. I am so lucky to be your daughter.

To **Callan**: Thank you for your love and feedback. This book might have never seen the light of day without your words and support.

To **Emily**: forever my sister, forever my capital F Family. You always ask about my books, always share them with everyone you know, and I am so grateful to have you in my life.

To **Cara**: Thank you for making me smile when I felt like I had very little to smile about. Thank you for watching movies with me, telling jokes, and reminding me there's more than grief and loss and hurt.

And, as always, thank you to everyone who reads, rates, and reviews. You keep my books alive.

Thank you, Stella★

Made in United States
Troutdale, OR
04/21/2024

19347203R00202